HYDE
AND
SEEK

JOHN A. HODA

1

———

8 SEPTEMBER 1888

EDWARD HYDE

Doctor Jekyll created me when he was five years old. *Hide me,* Henry silently prayed when his mother or one of her male friends, especially the man I later murdered, would sneak into Henry's darkened room late at night. I had to endure unspeakable horrors in his stead. I learned to live with the physical pain no child was made for. If I did not please her or those men for some made-up transgression, I suffered beatings and was then starved, and locked in the dark cedar closet. The servants were none the wiser and, if they dared question Mrs. Jekyll about Henry's whereabouts, they found themselves unemployed. His father travelled often for business and any letters from him announcing a delay in coming home meant more vicious treatment.

Over time, Henry summoned me with the word *Hide,* and I eventually became *Hyde.* Later, as an adolescent, he gave me a second name, *Edward,* when he allowed me to venture outdoors with some spending money as a repayment for all I suffered.

What I knew of London society was seen and felt by Henry and, at first, I followed his routines, but eventually I ventured to other parts of town, especially along the docks on the River Thames.

Later, Henry gave me permission to explore the vices of London the way no young man from respectable London society should—whoring, fighting, petty thievery, opium and whisky. In the beginning, I ventured out for an evening, but over time I gadded about until my money ran out. After all, I was forced to live the life he could not bear, so I lived the life of a randy libertine as a reward. As he matured, he tried curtailing my adventures but, as the stronger personality, I manifested when and where I damn well pleased. He even afforded me my own home, furnishings and clothing, as my comings and goings at the Jekyll house were causing a stir.

Slowly, Henry and I began to appear differently. His protected upbringing allowed him to grow tall and strong. I developed as an animal might, sinewy strong and fleet of foot. Henry was pleasant and affable, whereas I was caustic and irascible. One had to earn my trust. I was barely literate, never having had the benefit of proper schooling. I learned to count money only after being cheated numerous times. I could play the violin in the dance halls or gin palaces, as my learning was in Henry's hands—our hands. I learned to fight like an amateur boxer or a Chinese sailor, but I never saw Henry throw a punch in anger.

In the beginning, my existence was conjured up to ensure Henry's survival. I spared him from the terror no child should experience. I had to watch from the ether as his emotionally stilted life unfolded. He suffered no great pains, thanks to me, but on the other hand, he felt no great joy or happiness; such was the bargaining of a five-year-old. Love? What did we know about love?

Now we are back in London, and I have to be careful to avoid Scotland Yard's Inspector Newcomen, who had been hot on my trail for the murder of Sir Danvers Carew. For now, I live in the shadows, biding my time.

To Henry's understanding, I am a liability, a murderer who has run amuck. After our trip to the West Indies to escape Newcomen, Henry believes he no longer needs me. Oh, the poor sot!

———

SOMETIME BETWEEN 4:45 A.M. AND 5:45 A.M.

THE WHITECHAPEL MURDERER

I place a coin in the prostitute's hand and motion to her mouth, offering to pay for a specific service. The coin quickly disappears into the folds of her dress. Her toothy smile seals the deal. If only she knew what she's bargained for.

"I've just the place," the woman says. She leads me out from under the steady yellow gas lamp lighting of Hanbury Street, through a lodging house, and then down a few steps to a rear yard. Despite her inebriated condition, there is no hesitation or confusion in her gait; she's used this spot before, I'm sure. A five-foot-tall, rough wooden fence separates this space from the adjoining property. Scraps of wood, some rotted and split, lie about the yard, their usefulness spent. Against the rear, is a similarly decrepit shed and, quite the luxury, their own privy. I wave my walking stick about to let her know that I desire privacy.

"Nobody likes surprises," she whispers in agreement, then prowls a circuit of the yard. Without the thin security of the gaslight, the night is so dark that I can barely make out her bland features, her mottled, puffy face, and the unwashed straggly hair I'd observed on the street. She is short and stout, heavier than most, and wears tired clothes and worn-out shoes.

Dawn's imminent arrival will announce another dreary day to Whitechapel. The building's occupants will come out here to relieve themselves before getting ready for work. Did I wait too long?

My few words to her out on Hanbury Street, along with my evening attire and gleaming boots – suitable for a gentleman attending a concert or other such event in the West End – undoubtedly convinced her I am her ticket to a few days of good food and safe lodging. I will indeed ensure she will never know hunger or cold again.

I am unprepared for the creak of the privy door on the other side of the fence, and I freeze. Still, I'm able to relax until she reaches for my crotch the way my mother had.

"No!" I squeak like that frightened child all those years ago.

I inhale sharply and hold my breath. I want to be sure my response to her impetuous action does not cause a stir. We wait until I silently let my breath out.

She winks and watches for my next move. The stillness of the night magnifies the moment. The sliver of moon hides behind a cloud. We stare at each other until satisfied we will not be interrupted.

I smile, then grab her by the throat, driving her backwards to the ground with such ferocity that a shoe flies off her foot, striking the crude fence with a slight thud. My hand never loses its grip as I slam her hard to the dirt. I pin her near arm with my knee, her torso with my closer knee, and her other arm with my free hand, leaving her to flail her legs about to no effect. I learned to do this after a bad experience in Cairo when a little darling mashed my face with a rock and almost escaped.

With my grip upon her throat, she can neither scream nor breathe. Over the pounding of my heart, I hear a man's heavy footsteps on the other side of the fence making his way back to the dwelling. What did the man hear?

Footsteps fade, and another door creaks as the unseen interloper returns to his lodgings. Anyone who had bothered to look over the fence would have seen a man of indeterminate height, weight, and age with a top hat and cape, straddling his evening's pleasure. But no Londoner would so boldly intrude upon his neighbour; the unwritten law of the city demands that privacy be respected above all.

My eyes never leave hers. Did that neighbour run out onto the street to find the nearest constable?

Her terror-filled stare, bucking legs and her twisting torso heighten my arousal. This moment is exquisite. There is nothing she can do. I loom over her in total control. The alcohol pouring out of her sweat is sickly sweet. She cannot blink away from my tight smile and riveting eyes. The transformation from living to dying is mine to enjoy once again. She finally succumbs to her fate and stops fighting as I hold firm my death grip. I wordlessly count each of my ten inhalations and slow exhalations. I learned to do this after being too hurried once in St. Petersburg.

Her fixed upward stare and open unwavering mouth give me the release that her lips could never have supplied. I shudder with delight. My emission soaks the extra layers of Egyptian cotton girding my crotch. Her hips stop twitching, and her legs splay open, an unwelcome invitation at this point. I loosen my grip, satisfied with my handiwork, and draw forth my blade. I lift her dress and cut off her undergarments, for which I have another use. Her skin peels open like a piece of maggot-infested fruit, but that is of less interest than her clothing.

The newspapers will report what the neighbours will find

come daylight. The inquest will determine that the manual strangulation was the means to a greater, more horrific, and silent ending. But they will be wrong. Nothing can replace my absolute domination of her body as I hover inches from her anguish-filled face in her final moments. I will relish those memories for days until they slowly fade and the urge to strike takes hold of me again.

———

HENRY JEKYLL

My shaving kit rests next to the full sink of water. On the opposite side, neatly laid out, are a cotton face cloth, gold pocket watch, black leather wallet, and a monogrammed handkerchief that I inherited from my dear departed father, *HJ,* no middle initial. Prominently displayed on the chest of drawers are the gold and onyx cufflinks he gave me on my graduation day from the Royal College of Physicians. He was so proud.

The man staring back at me in the mirror is tall, muscular and deeply tanned, with none of the worry lines or dark circles around the eyes I'd had before my life-saving trip.

Sunshine pours into my dressing room and reminds me of those long lazy days on the beaches of Jamaica. A long walk is in order for the day. Even the dark wood of my mahogany drawers and wardrobe sparkle with release from the tyranny of shuttered windows. To be home and free of that cursed Hyde lifts my soul. Everything is in order: my vitality, my affairs and my return to society. I dress with a song on my lips and will enjoy my leisure as a man of my position should. I feel like I have been released from prison, a jail of my own making, and I can be thankful for all the blessings bestowed upon me.

Mr. Poole comes into the room. He has been with me for years. Despite his grey hair and slightly stooped posture, he is always impeccably dressed and deliciously precise in his speech. "Shall I tell the cook to prepare for two?" he asks.

Since my return from my two-year sojourn in the West Indies, my younger brother has taken breakfast with me more often. Absence makes the heart grow fonder, I suppose.

All is now well. The terrible black cloud hanging over Cavendish Square, before my departure, poured out torrents of rain, cleaned the filth from the streets, drowned the vermin in the sewers, then departed on blustery winds of change, leaving behind bucolic summer days as a gift for my return.

"Yes, Poole, George Jekyll is always welcome at my table," I reply.

———

FRANCINE MURPHY

I step around the passed-out drunk snoring on the doorstep of my building. An open tin pocket flask in his slack hand catches the light, and the sun's reflection shines in the puddle below it. The smell hits me immediately. Truth be told, gin makes me violently ill. My immediate and severe reaction to it probably saved my life. Whisky is a different story, but that amber elixir was too expensive for the meagre salary my Seamus brought home. Too bad, as I have a taste for fine drink, like my father and his father before him.

After I lost my baby and my husband left me due to my thirst, I sank lower than Jonah's whale to the bottom of the ocean. I was drowning in booze and sorrow. The red curls that had drawn Seamus's eye fell strand by strand on London's streets as I descended towards a just fate.

It wasn't the Almighty, nor the Holy Spirit, nor the angels who lifted me from the depths. Where were they when I cried out in my hours of miscarrying my precious baby, who died because of my sins before drawing a single breath? Nowhere. It was Mary McCreary, with her five hungry children, who took me in and raised me up from the depths of my despair. Mary showed me how to live without the drink and to find my self-worth.

For months and through my countless tears, Mary showed me how to stand taller than I ever did when I was married. She kept me from wallowing in self-pity and told me of what was possible every day I didn't drink and focused on the future. Mrs. McCreary is a living saint and holy beyond words, even though, privately, she swears like a dock worker.

Over time, my red hair grew back thick and curly, and my hands and arms took on a strength I never had when Seamus took care of me. I stood almost as tall as he: five feet, nine inches then, and I stand taller now.

I partake not another drop of liquor, no matter how it tempts me. I realize it is a poison that will kill me if I ever entertain it again. I throw myself into work instead; I do washing, sewing, cleaning and all kinds of honest work in the factories.

But, even during my darkest hours, I never did listen to the call of the streets. The women who use their bodies as a last resort to pay for gin, keep themselves too drunk to recognize their misery. They are sick and need healing no sermonizing can ever cure.

My salvation came from one woman with gentle and strong arms stretching down to lift and hold me up as many times as I needed until I could walk by a booze house without a single glance. What Mary McCreary did for me, I vow to do for others. That has become my purpose. Help other destitute women overcome by their need to numb their pain with drink.

"Francine Murphy?"

I know the raspy voice of my landlord calling after me from across the street. That he wears a top hat and overcoat on a warm day, along with his unsteady gait as he walks towards me, tells me more about his poor health than his age. I've been avoiding him since the first of the month when my rent was due. The clip-clopping of the cart horses on the narrow cobblestone street fades from my senses as he stands in front of me, trying to catch his wet breath.

I reply, "Mr. Withers. How are you this fine day?"

His wordless answer is to reach into his coat pocket, and he hands me an official-looking document. I open it carefully and read quickly. He knows my County Cork upbringing included reading, writing and ciphering. Had I been another tenant, he might have had to read it aloud.

I close our distance, so that the neighbours cannot hear our business. He is surprised, and from the look on his face, appears to be afraid of what my temper has in store for him. He retreats a few uncertain steps, not looking where he is going. The streets don't get the proper cleaning in Whitechapel. One has to keep one's eyes on where one steps, the horse droppings being what they are. But providence is with Mr. Withers, and he remains upright, his boots unsullied.

I say, "I understand why you must do this. Good, honest work is scarce these days, sir. You are in business, and I am not your charity case. If I do as you say, and leave without a fuss, would you be kind enough to tell anyone who asks that I was a good renter who fell on hard times?"

"I will do no such thing, Mrs. Murphy. The other tenants in the building have complained about you bringing filthy drunken prostitutes into the building at all hours of the day and night. If you were not delinquent on the rent, I would have evicted you for cause."

"Mr. Withers. One of those women you refer to is completely sober, the other two have not touched a drop of the devil's drink since their arrival, and none of them have traded on their bodies while staying with me." I move in closer and poke him in the chest with the eviction notice. "The only way any of my neighbours would know about these women's past is if they were soliciting their services. So don't be standing there so indignant and righteous."

He backs up, steps in a horse dropping, straightens his concave chest and narrows his eyes. "You will vacate the premises by the end of the month."

2

8 SEPTEMBER 1888

HENRY JEKYLL

After breakfasting with my brother, I set out for a long brisk walk. I am now possessed with the energy of a man half my age. I make straight for Regent's Park. I stroll through quiet residential neighbourhoods, with the occasional cab dropping off ladies with their morning shopping. My senses are alive with the smell of late summer flowers blooming in well-tended gardens. Workmen doing street repairs tip their hats to me as I pass. Food carts brim with fresh fruits and vegetables. Red apples compete with yellow squash and leafy green spinach. The musty smell of potatoes reminds me that we didn't have a potato blight in my absence. With the noise of the metropolis well behind me, I wind my way to my favourite place in all of London since my return. There are times, I must admit, I take the first train to the seaside to watch the sunrise, to breathe the air and stare at the crashing surf. But on this day, I am called to the grassy fields, leafy trees and dusty paths of the spacious former royal hunting grounds. It provides me with a space to breathe and to reflect. I had arrived in the islands, seasick and worn out from battling Hyde. Over time, with the help of the local medicine men and witch doctors, my strength and vitality returned as Hyde was vanquished.

I find an iron bench on a slight rise in Regent's Park facing the taller buildings, smokestacks and church spires of London. The air is fresh, with an eastern wind blowing the soot and cinders out to the English Channel. Young families take their lunch on the lawns overlooking the lake. One family fashions a kite from newspaper, sticks and string. My eyes appreciate the vista, and my face bears a smile that escaped me for most of the decade before I went on my life-changing trip. The kite makes its maiden flight and the family cheers.

Now back in England, I miss my walking cane, a gift from Utterson, my dear friend and personal lawyer, for these long jaunts. Did I forget to take it this day? Had I misplaced it? No, I desperately wish forgetfulness is the reason. Sadly, the cane was used by Hyde to strike down a man a few years past, and it precipitated my downward spiral to where I was so out of my mind in despair, I fled the country. If not for my own sanity, then for my neck, as Inspector Newcomen of Scotland Yard was close to capturing poor Edward running about Soho.

He had the evidence. My cane had split in half lengthwise, one half found in the gutter near the man Edward had savagely beaten and stomped to death, the other half propped behind a door in Edward's home. An eyewitness had watched in horror as Edward brutally attacked the man. There was no question as to the perpetrator. Utterson related the story to me first, and then it was Newcomen who hounded me to produce my friend, Mr. Hyde.

The breeze to my back causes the child's kite to soar and dive. His family's glee draws me out of my gloom for the moment. The red-and-blue cloth tail flutters as the kite soars and dips. I could have remained morose over the memory, but instead, I concentrate on the young family, towheaded boys and squealing girls in braided pigtails running underneath the kite as it swoops close to the ground, inches from their outstretched hands. Other families lounge on blankets spread out for picnicking this sun-splashed summer day.

It was on the islands where I learned to take simple pleasure in watching the brown-skinned children frolicking on the beach in the clear turquoise water, jumping into the waves and laughing, and the simple pleasure of my long barefoot walks on the white sands with the gentle waves. My troubles behind me, I am becoming better at not ruminating on what happened before my hasty departure from London.

Neither Edward nor I were arrested. I often imagine what it would have been like if an arrest had been made of Hyde, and they had checked in on him at night, only to find me wearing his clothes and shaking off my blackout behind the jailer's bars in the morning. Maybe worse would have been the opposite, where the esteemed Doctor Henry Jekyll, being detained overnight, had become a dishevelled and snarling Mr. Edward Hyde by the morning. Thankfully, those days are behind me now. I am free from the shackles of living a double life, one that I control and one that I didn't.

I stand and stretch my limbs. Loping down the slope, I jump in the air between the children and flick the kite's tail as it soars along with my spirits, upwards.

Our duality was never discovered before Hyde was extinguished on the islands. Newcomen never made the connection. Hyde was never arrested, and our singular neck was never fitted for the hangman's noose.

I weave between other children running and kicking a ball. They could not have been more than four or five years of age.

I was about their age when Edward was summoned. Having no memory of those days and nights when he inhabited my body, I would come out of the trance hours or even days later, with no knowledge of what happened, wearing different clothes and with bruises and scrapes I could not explain. I awoke in the middle of the dark nights with night terrors and didn't know their origin, but I could only imagine what Hyde had saved me from.

Whatever happened to Edward was best left for him to deal with. I sensed the poor boy had seen things and was subjected to abject horrors. Later in my adolescence, I learned to mix a few elixirs from my father's medicine cabinet, and Edward returned. He enjoyed all the things a good and proper young man in England could not. A young man's lust and chance to flex his muscles were a gift to Edward for all he spared me from and, by the grace of God, I did not become syphilitic or maimed—but it now leaves me unable to form lasting relationships with my peers or affection for the young ladies in fashionable society. The trade became more pronounced as I achieved success as a physician taking over my father's immense estate. I am content to put on my public face at all times, as is good and proper for a man of my breeding and position. Hyde is my private persona. I was blissfully ignorant and probably a little jealous of his bawdy behaviour but, as time progressed, reports of his angry outbursts began to worry me. He had trampled a young child, and the family forced him to make reparations. Utterson reported Hyde being surly and agitated while they all waited for the bank to open. A check was cashed, then monies changed hands between the offending party and the offended parents.

My colleagues and associates reported sightings of my 'companion'. They assumed my reluctance with the eligible ladies and companionship with a man they never saw me with were connected, and it was something even my closest confidants would not broach in polite society. It made it easier for Edward to be spotted in the rowdy places or mixing it up with drunk sailors or ruffians without me, and I could confess true ignorance. I was glad my associates were keeping tabs on him.

As I got older, Hyde would manifest without any need for potions. During the hours he was running amuck, he was out of my control. I had no means of summoning him to return.

After killing that man, everything changed. It was only a matter of time before Hyde would be arrested. This was my dilemma, and as Hyde stole more of our time, I became desperate. Did I dare tell my closest friends and associates that, while in a blackout state, my bad 'self' committed the homicide? They had observed Hyde acting badly on previous occasions. They would not believe I was the same bad actor.

If my confession convinced them that Hyde and I were one and the same, the law was clear about crimes committed during blackouts. A man waking up from a blackout with a bloody knife in his hand, standing over his dead best friend on the floor, and having no memory how it happened would swing from the gallows just the same as if it were done with malice. Would leniency for a mental condition have spared Hyde from dancing in the air? How long would life in an insane asylum have fit his temperament? How would I have sanely fared if doomed to a lifetime of being imprisoned with those who weren't sane?

Did I consider turning myself in to Newcomen to confess it was me and not my friend? He would think I was protecting Hyde. The description of the killer was made by a witness who was familiar with my altered ego. How long would they keep me under observation until Hyde appeared? What if Edward never returned?

I stare at the white marble steps leading to my front door. I turn to scan the street with all the bustle of commerce. *How did I get here so quickly?* The walk from Regent's Park to my residence is not long, but I missed out on the smell of the gardens and the smiling faces of passers-by. I chide myself for those dark ruminations on the final stretch of my walk. My life has been split apart since childhood. Whole days and weeks are missing. No more, I promise myself.

Unfortunately, my thoughts and dreams return to those dreadful days when death by suicide seemed my only escape. Now I am back walking familiar streets, talking to acquaintances and navigating London's social scene, but the news is filled with stories about a madman.

From my top step, I hear boys hawking newspapers on the corner, titillating passersby with the gory details, some real and imagined, of the latest killing in Whitechapel. I am relieved Hyde is not darting in and out of the fog doing God knows what while the killer is loose.

3

---

11 SEPTEMBER 1888

THE WHITECHAPEL MURDERER

The train to Cheltenham is late arriving this pale morning. My collection of newspapers, tucked under my arm, waits to be enjoyed once I board. I folded the lurid tattlers inside the more respectable financial news, lest anyone take a stab at my very private and prurient interests. Reading about my exploits is new to me. My evenings' excitement, during my travels, did not find their way into any reporting. *Did the authorities even know the vile things were strangled? Did they care?* Life was cheap in the quarters where only roughnecks, criminals, drunken merchantmen or soldiers would venture after midnight. The services the women provided were easy to find for the right price, and the providers were easily replaced with those more willing and desperate as the nights deepened.

There was one night in Amsterdam, followed by the next night in Munich, where I did not know of what witnesses had seen or heard. By the time the reports were filed in either country, I was in Prague.

Now I operate in only one place. A place with constables,

17

watchmen and persons coming and going throughout the darkest hours. I take a keen interest in the reports out of Whitechapel. What the police have to say has made the game more interesting. The danger increases, along with the odds of getting caught if I don't stop, but I have my reasons.

I board the train and settle into a private compartment. The city gives way to farms, forests, and fenced-in pastures for horses, sheep and goats. Late summer, with its warm breezes and brilliant sunshine, will soon give way to the endless drizzle and fog of winter. I enjoy the ride as much as my nocturnal forays into the East End.

"Ha!" I exclaim as I read. I scan furtively about, fearing my outburst will draw attention. By all means, Mrs. Fiddymont, do identify the man seen in the tavern with marks of blood upon him. Probably some poor butcher or horse slaughterer.

Oh, how macabre this is! Neighbours in the adjoining house were charging a penny to every person wanting to peep at the spot where the creature had reposed into eternal damnation. Probably the same people who look the other way when the collection basket passes them in the pews.

Yes! I continue to read about a suspect. My good friend, 'Leather Apron.' Pin it on a Jew. I barely contain my glee. I am much taller than Leather Apron, thinner and clean shaven, save a neat moustache. I do not frequent Whitechapel, unless I am looking for my excitement. In and out.

The police, fearing a riot, tried to control the crowd of young toughs as they set about fighting anyone who crossed them or who was unfortunately caught on the street during their rampage against the Jews. Ah, the police used men under-cover to break up the fights. I would need to be more vigilant, lest some drunk in a vestibule was actually sober and fast on the whistle.

I dive further into the papers. What's this? A medical student plucked out his own eyeballs. That is so unfortunate. What would cause a man with such a promising future to do such a thing?

The next newspaper's front-page article, about my work in the backyard of Hanbury Street, would have been sensational and ghoulish if it was not almost completely accurate. The discovery of the body was made within minutes of my departure. Throat cut from ear to ear. The front of her body ripped open from groin to breastbone. The body was disembowelled, with entrails flung round the creature's neck. My handiwork. All done to point to one person. I had spotted the wretch staggering from the Three Bells public house about the same time as the last witness observed her around five o'clock. They found my coins in her dress. What a price to pay for two farthings.

Turning to a different paper, I catch up on one of my previous exploits on Buck's Row. I will make sure to remember the Scotland Yard inspectors' names and that of Detective-Sergeant Enright, should they ever come knocking on my door. A watchman along the railway nearby stated he heard nothing. I know why. When I passed the watchman, he was sleeping on a cart of what appeared to be unclaimed freight. The dozing man was near a lamppost. I strolled by in the shadows. It seems some of the clothing from the corpse could not be accounted for, according to the coroner, who questioned the police at length. Of course, not all the garments are accounted for. I know why.

So engrossing is my reading, I am surprised when the conductor calls my stop. Do I keep this dreadful rubbish or discard it? I memorize what I need to know. I do not require a scrapbook for my exquisite forbidden release. Reading about my work does stir up urges, but they are not appropriate for a proper man about to court a fine lady.

I step out of the car and follow business travellers to a bin where they discard their morning papers. My salacious tattlers follow suit.

The cab is waiting for me. I nod to the driver. It is a quick trip to my destination. An exquisitely manicured lawn, separated by a smooth drive, leads to a circular driveway. The white marble fountain and surrounding seasonal flowers complete the design, fronting the impressive three-storey manor house built of the best quarried stone.

There, the elderly butler greets me with a surly shuffle down the massive hall. "Lady Jane is waiting for you in the stables, sir." The butler takes me to a changing room, where my riding boots, britches and tailored ruffled shirt await me. A quick change, and I am off.

Birdsong softens as I approach two saddled horses held by a sullen stable boy. Lady Jane is already on her mount.

"Can you talk to your father?" I say. "Perhaps he can do something about getting the trains to run on time." I mount my usual black horse. It tolerates me more than the other nags in the stable. I take the reins, and we are off.

"No hello for me, darling?" she says as we make our way along the fence line leading to trails in the forest behind the estate. Her black-and-red riding cap accentuates her delicate features and untanned face. Blonde hair peeks out from the cap. Riding gloves cover her soft hands cradling the reins. Her steed needs no coaxing. She is but a whisper of weight on its back, and the horse knows the way.

"You need to talk to your butler about proper manners. I travel all this distance by rail and made my way straight to your heart, Jane, and he acted like it is my fault."

She laughs. "He acts that way with all my suitors. You did nothing wrong."

A flash of jealousy rises in my chest but stops at my throat, lest I say anything to give her the satisfaction of getting a rise out of me. I know I am one of many men to fill her dance card during the London Season. I am content to dine with her and attend music recitals as part of larger groups. I am more travelled than her other suitors, and my stories about Africa and the

Orient enthral her. But some stories can never be shared, truth be told.

"Darling, I am returning to the city this Friday for a Shakespeare play and then to Jesmond's birthday gala Saturday night. A group of us plan to attend both. Would you care to join us?"

I enjoy this time alone with Lady Jane, but in London, I am part of group activities with her entourage. There are numerous friends and acquaintances climbing or descending the social ladder, not to mention a phalanx of suitors always hovering about. I am older than all of them, but I use my worldly experience gained from my travels to my advantage. Where a few boys can talk about travels abroad, most are snooty schoolboys sniffing around the hems of her Parisian dresses. I am bored with their witty repartee, but when the opportunities arise, I take centre stage and recall my travels painting vivid word pictures of the Nile, the catacombs of Rome and riding Moroccan camels. "Of course, it would be my pleasure." I return her smile.

As we ride deeper into the estate's forest trails, I fill my lungs with the clean, pure air and rid my mind of the putrid smells of Whitechapel. It is only the two of us in this vast preserve. No ragamuffin children darting about. No drivers whipping cart horses to move faster. No wailing babies held against a clothed breast while their mothers dump wash water onto the streets to mix with God knows what.

"After the season, do you plan to stay in town or repair here?" I ask. She enjoys the swirl of non-stop activity catering to the well-heeled in the London social scene, but it is a season with rules, and it will be ending soon.

"Father wishes I return here. He says the city is no place for a girl to remain until the holiday. Why do you enquire?"

"I agree with him, and I thought he might want to invite me on his fox hunts. I would be most happy to oblige him if it meant I could gaze at you by dinner candlelight next to a warm fire."

Her Mona Lisa smile tells me more than her silence.

Movement in the glades, deer jumping and fowl taking flight, offer pleasant interruptions. The cool shade from majestic hardwoods canopying the trails is soft and pleasant on my face.

She breaks the silence to ask me to tell her stories of exotic places, and I regale her with a few embellishments. Lady Jane wants to travel, and I am more than happy to accompany her if the dowry is right. My financial circumstances are fixed until I can inherit. Then there is the matter of physical attraction. I would not be the first man to take a wife for appearance's sake, but my predilections are harder to explain than any other errant husband if I am caught.

My thoughts drift back to my most recent conquest. The terror in her eyes. Her legs flailing and fingernails scratching the dirt to find anything to strike me with. The writhing of her hips until her breath expired. Those memories mix with the rhythm of the powerful animal beneath, now under my control, stirring my loins.

Noticing my far-off stare and smile, Jane asks, "What are you thinking?"

"Of steaming down the Nile past the greatest wonders of the world, and how they pale compared to you, Jane."

4

---

11 SEPTEMBER 1888

FRANCINE MURPHY

"How do you know me?" Doctor Jekyll asks.

The carpet below my feet is plush. The upholstered brown leather seat on which I perch across the ancient black walnut desk from him is soft and comfortable. Portraits of stern men, I suspect his lineage, scowl down from golden gilt-edged frames, their opinions about me already formed.

On the desktop between us rests a smooth brown stone not larger than a deck of cards. A paperweight of personal significance, I assume. The white teacup of fine porcelain holds my hot tea. I doubt the meeting will last long enough for it to cool in my hand.

"Doctor Jekyll, I was given a letter of introduction from the sexton at St Giles in the Fields."

His dark eyes scrunch in confusion. From a side credenza, he removes a satchel of unopened letters.

He shuffles through them quickly. Many of the letters have exotic postmarks.

"Anderson. Michael Anderson?"

I nod. I don't know what Anderson wrote, but it was a letter of introduction from a man who told me how grateful he was for what I had done. Me, Francine Murphy, a woman who miscarried a child, drank herself out of a marriage, and who has no formal training, no connections in London society, and no business sitting before this wealthy man, asking for a large sum of money. Anderson believes in me and what I have done. That will have to do.

From his desk drawer, Doctor Jekyll removes a dagger. Quite the letter opener. It cuts with barely a sound, and the letter flutters open. He reads quickly and looks at me quizzically. He returns to his reading. He places the letter on the table between us and begins flipping the stone in his hand. I observe a new appreciation of his visitor. I blow lightly onto my tea and peek over the rim. His coal-black eyes study me. I hold the saucer and cup so ladylike that Mary McCreary would be proud of me.

"Is this true?" he asks.

I nod again.

He stands to his full height and walks to the bank of windows facing his garden. He rubs his tanned face and stares at nothing in particular.

Older? Yes. Attractive? In a hurt animal sort of way.

Without facing me, he says, "Mrs. Murphy. What you did for Anderson's sister is astonishing. He had lost her to the streets where she sold her body for a drink. No matter how many times he pled with her, she would not listen to him. The church would not accept her for social services. They said she was too far gone, a lost cause. Her sins were too great. But somehow, you turned her around. Anderson is not a man of many words. For him to write me in this fashion tells me a miracle occurred."

"Doctor Jekyll—" I start.

Backlit now, his expression is unreadable as he halves the distance between us. He towers over me.

He says softly, "Mrs. Murphy, I may return to my practice someday, but I am still on my sabbatical as we speak. I am not sure I deserve the title of doctor any longer."

I set my cup down and fix a gaze on his firm chin. Now is the time, if ever, to broach the subject of the meeting.

"Louise is my assistant now," I say. "We rescue one woman at a time. We want to give them their own room with a lock and key, clean new clothes, and a purpose, for as long as it takes. The space I am looking at needs work and I have operating expenses. My rent…" I stop before I get emotional. I refuse to be a sob story. "I am not looking for a handout."

"But why me, Mrs. Murphy?" The question is good and I don't know how to be delicate in answering it. Asking for money is difficult for me. Since I was tossed out of my home by Seamus, I have relied on the charity of Mary McCreary and a few others. It energizes me to become as self-sufficient as possible.

"Louise suggested I speak with her brother, and her brother thought of you. The amount of your tithe at St Giles would more than cover everything needed to help more women like her."

His sharp inhale and stiffening back are not good signs. Did I play the only card I held too soon? Did I play it poorly? I already regret my choice of words and sip too quickly, the hot tea burning my lips and tongue.

He returns to his seat without looking at me. The large desk now appears to be a barrier between us. The letters return to the satchel, and the satchel returns to the credenza. He quickly lifts the dagger and slides it safely back in the drawer. He flips the stone from hand to hand without making eye contact. I take a more cautious sip and vow that I will not leave until I finish it.

I say to him, "Since your return from your travels, you have not been back to St Giles. Only your brother fills your family's pew on Sundays. Mr. Anderson was told by the wardens you did not renew your pledge. He felt I should approach you about this opportunity to do something worthwhile outside of the church, for desperate women the church has turned its back on." I have no choice but to see how he reacts to my knowledge of his pledge or lack thereof.

He steeples his fingers on the table and looks over my head. Not a good sign.

"I am a private person, Mrs. Murphy. My affairs are strictly my business. My relationship with the church is complicated. My life has changed drastically in the past few years. Anderson was remiss in not having spoken with me first." He sets the stone on the letter. He wants to say more but thankfully stifles that urge.

I set my cup and saucer down to make my point. "He tried. He asked your brother repeatedly if I could meet with you and was rebuffed each time. I could only secure an appointment through your servant, who took a liking to me." I offer a weak smile.

His deep breath in, followed by a slow exhale, signals that our meeting is ending. "And why is that my concern?" He arches an eyebrow and cocks his head. He sits back in his chair folding his arms.

I retrieve my teacup and take the last gulp of tea. It is still too hot and burns my throat. Tears come to my eyes. I stand.

"My relationship with the church is complicated too," I tell him. "Where is their charity for the most desperate women in Whitechapel? The Catholics are the same way, just so you know. We have a lot in common, you and me. I'm sorry this all came to you as a surprise. There are things in my life I do not want to be public knowledge, either. I will say nothing to anybody about this. I do appreciate your seeing me today and thank you for the tea."

He stands and looks lost for words. The portraits are

speaking for him to remain silent. He clenches the stone in his right hand.

"I will see myself to the door," I add. I am dizzy as I stagger down the hall and pull on the massive front door to escape my embarrassment. The bright sunshine blinds me at once and adds to my disorientation.

What was I thinking, blurting out he wasn't giving his church their due? Why didn't I just yell from the rooftops he is not square with his maker? I'm a total stranger, and I tell him I can use the money he's not giving to his church? *You really stepped in it this time, Francine Murphy. The money was there, and all you had to do was let him come up with the idea of how he could help you without mentioning the tithe.* What am I going to do now?

I do not know which way to turn. I arrived from a different direction than where I'm going next. One thing for sure, there is more to Doctor Jekyll than meets the eye.

———

HENRY JEKYLL

I am amazed by the woman who just walked out of my study. Even though our business was concluded, I could have stared into her green eyes and listened to her soft brogue the rest of the morning. She brought a total stranger back from the abyss. She returned Louise Anderson to wholeness. She did this in Whitechapel, a festering cesspool of human degradation and pestilence. What training did she possess? What is her process? At first, I assumed she wanted me to formulate a remedy to ease the pains of alcohol withdrawal, but when she connected me to my church and my not fulfilling my tithe, she touched a raw nerve. My privacy was under assault. I was blindsided. I am still a gentleman of good standing in society. I did not make my true intentions with the church known to anyone.

For years, I juggled my complicated relationship with Hyde. We lived a double life. For her to speak about my finances and lack of charity so plainly placed my senses on full alert.

Yet, she struck a different nerve with her parting words. None of my prayers nor almsgiving have vanquished Hyde. According to Anderson, the church gave up on his sister, a lost sheep, yet this remarkable woman did not. She banished the demons of drink.

Why didn't George say anything? Why didn't Anderson introduce her to me himself? Although I realize he would have jeopardized his position in the church by suggesting I take my charity elsewhere.

My head is spinning, but there is another feeling bubbling up below the surface of my consciousness. It starts with a strange warmth that fills my belly. I touch her teacup. It is still warm. Is it a longing to touch the hand that held the cup moments earlier?

5

12 SEPTEMBER 1888

FRANCINE MURPHY

A stunning portrait of Alexandra, the Princess of Wales, stares down on the jurymen around the table in the library of the Working Lads Institute. The white-plaster ceilings are high, and the space is well lit by natural light. Maybe the princess could impart some wisdom on them. They need it. The coroner, Mr. Wynne Baxter, with thick black eyebrows and even thicker black moustache, casts a worried expression. He has appropriated this space, this beautifully furnished library with sturdy tables and rows of books adorning the walls, for yet another inquest into a murder. My uncomfortable seat along the back wall has become sadly too familiar.

Louise and I knew Emma Turner and Polly from the streets, but it was Annie Chapman we had worried about the most. Repeatedly, we tried talking to her at the dosshouse where she flopped. The other ladies there said that she was denied a bed hours before she returned to the street on the morning she was killed.

Here at the Working Lads Institute, a place where the young

men sleep and recreate after working thirteen hours a day, six days a week, we hear testimony that, for a lack of four pence, Annie was put out on the street.

It is not lost on me that only men have been charged with gathering facts about a murdered woman while seated comfortably around a long wooden table in an impressive edifice built for boys only.

Sitting there at the inquest, it is difficult not to stand up and lecture the coroner about the obvious facts. Not a sound was heard when any of the women were killed. They were all splayed out the same way, with the butchering becoming more vicious. Three brutal killings of girls on the weekends, inside a month, with all the murders occurring within a walking distance of each other. I know those rutted roads by heart. Yet, different police constables and inspectors speak at each inquest. I have attended the last two, but I don't see the police connecting the deaths as part of a pattern. A sick and twisted man is preying on the most vulnerable women in the most ravaged part of the city.

If these slayings occurred in the West End near the concert halls or museums, the inquests would have been filled to overflowing with reporters from all over the known world.

"Just wash down the blood and get about your daily business," Louise says as if she is reading my mind.

"One less temptress to corrupt a gentleman and relieve him of his hard-earned wages," I reply while scanning the portraits of the royals and other prominent members of society adorning the freshly painted walls. I nudge Louise to show where my eyes have settled. "Nobody forces them to travel to Whitechapel in search of their secret fantasies."

"Where there are no buyers, there are no sellers," Louise says.

"It's the first rule of business," I agree. "There is a reason prostitution is called the world's oldest profession." In all the late nights into the wee hours of the morning, I search for women clinging onto the lowest rung of society. I observe this brisk business in Whitechapel of selling one's flesh for money to buy gin. Louise confided in me that the first time was the worst and, as she became better at selling her body, she drank more to numb the pain of who she had become. It became a vicious circle until the day she turned to me rather than kill herself.

More residents testify to hearing no sounds. Annie was killed not ten feet from a bedroom on a summer's night.

The next witness called, a Mrs. Durrell, testifies about seeing a man and woman outside of 29 Hanbury Street where Annie was killed. She fixes the time at 5:30 a.m. Under further questioning at the morgue, she identifies Annie as the woman she saw. What about the man? What did he look like? She can only describe the voice as that of a foreigner, a man with shabby genteel clothes and a deerstalker cap. The inquisitors are so fixed on establishing the time of death; they fail to ask the obvious next question of the police. Of all the witnesses on the streets that night, could they describe a man walking about wearing a deerstalker cap?

We can't help but make a minor disturbance as we depart the library. I hold my breath so as not to utter some words Mary McCreary taught me in those rare profane outbursts.

Out on the street, I fill my lungs with the foul heavy air, a mix of factory and mill exhaust, and exclaim, "They will never find who is responsible!"

6

12 SEPTEMBER 1888

HENRY JEKYLL

The cab drops me in front of the Gladstone Club on Pall Mall for a night of dining and cards. Both George and I are members of good standing, thanks in part to an endowment left by my dear father, whose import-export business has provided for our comfortable existence since his passing twenty years earlier. The day is still warm and will be until the summer sun sets. A slight breeze keeps the air moving towards the river and thankfully not coming from it. The River Thames is the lifeblood of the largest city in Western civilization, but it acts more like the intestines, absorbing good and bad alike and spitting out that which is foul and rotting.

The two-storey Neoclassical eggshell-white building serves as a meeting place for prominent London gentlemen from all political persuasions and occupations. The broad admission process is unique and makes for pleasant conversation and camaraderie.

I snatch a newspaper from a boy heralding the latest murder in Whitechapel and make my way to the library. I am early, in part to read the latest news from that area. Mrs. Murphy has made quite an impression on me, and I want to learn more about the tragic events there since my return to England in late July.

The gas-lit chandeliers and southern-facing windows provide more than enough lighting for those of us spread around the reading tables in front of the stacks. I wonder if she knows this Chapman woman. What about the others? Ghastly news. I don't recall reading or hearing about this many terrible happenings in one location during my entire lifetime.

As I make my way to the club's dining room, I have no appetite, such are the gruesome descriptions provided by my newspaper and others strewn about the tables. I stagger to the dining room, lost in thought.

"Brother, why the long face?"

George is nattily dressed in a maroon felted vest under a freshly pressed black dress coat. His starched shirt with gold-plated cufflinks completes the picture of stately wealth.

I sink into the chair and order my favourite rum drink. "The morbid business in Whitechapel."

"Yes, terrible business," Sutton says, then burps. "Terrible." The toothpicks on his bread plate tell me the number of martinis he's already consumed. Olives are his appetizer of sorts. He is between our ages and comes from the Suttons of Sussex, who made their fortune in sugar. Rarely rising before the noon hour, Sutton lounges at the club all day and, if asked, goes with any person wanting to sample the nightly events in the West End—topper and tails worn daily, just in case. He's a wonderful fellow to gad about town with.

"What are you talking about?" George asks.

"Come now, you must be spending all your time with your church friends," says Albert Blackwell. Old money, Canadian lumber. He is closer to me in age. He winters with his entire clan in Provence. His tailors are Italian, whose slim cut of clothes work well on his short and thin frame, and he wears Egyptian cotton shirts and summer suits during the season.

Sanders hands me my drink. I sip and approve. I took a liking to rum when I visited the islands, but here at home, I dilute it greatly. He takes our orders. We always ask for the same cuts of meat and potatoes—a fish or fowl order would raise eyebrows—but he writes them down just the same. My memories of my days in the islands and the cuisine based on fish, rice, fruits and beans remain, but old habits die hard and I am filling up my clothes again. The weight is coming back, regardless of how far or fast I walk about town every day.

Samuel Sutton says, "Well past midnight, some lunatic sliced up a lady of the evening, it is rumoured."

"And?" George asks.

"Sad business, really," Sutton says as Sanders hands him another martini.

Sutton's expression after taking a liberal drink is the opposite of sad, I think.

"Were any of them accompanied by a man?" George persists.

"No," I say.

"And what were they doing out there after midnight without a chaperone?"

"Looking to earn enough money to sleep in a dosshouse." I know where my holier-than-thou brother is going with his questions. I often tell him he should have trained as a lawyer or a vicar.

He slams his tea on the table. "Well, I suppose that's an answer." He shakes his head at me.

"Not everyone is blessed with a constitution to abstain from all spirits, brother. Gin has taken over their minds and bodies." I know that feeling from some other peculiar out-of-body experiences. I understand that helplessness. I possess firsthand knowledge of not being in control of my entire countenance.

Sutton and Blackwell have been treated to many a Jekyll brother argument at this very table.

"So not only were they selling their bodies, but they were doing so to buy their drinks instead of their lodging." George smirks in victory.

Sutton interjects, "That's what's being testified to at the inquests."

Blackwell says, "After their drinking possessed them, some of their men would not take them back."

"Those women reaped what they sowed," George concludes as he rearranges his cutlery.

"What if they can be redeemed? What if they can be led away from gin and returned to goodness?" I ask. I know now it is not impossible. I do not know how, but only who can do it.

Blackwell has been listening carefully. "There would be fewer opportunities for evil men to prey on these ladies."

A silence falls over the table as the entrees arrive. Excellent timing.

"When were you going to tell me about Louise Anderson?" I stare at George, not ready to grant him the victory after only one round.

"Who?"

"The sexton's sister. Louise Anderson."

George is feigning ignorance, while with the other two, it is genuine.

"I learned recently our church sexton wanted to connect me with the woman who did just that, Albert." Using a breadstick as a pointer, I explain, "Louise Anderson had succumbed to the gin demons and had sunk to the lowest depths of despair. She was returned to normalcy and is a whole person now."

"How?" Sutton asks with more than a passing interest.

"Another woman rescued her from the streets, took her in, and restored her to sanity." I take a bite, chew and swallow. "Does that help your memory, brother?"

"Oh, yes. You see, fellows, my dear Henry's shadow no longer graces the narthex of St. Giles in the Fields, and that spirited man, Anderson, yipped something or other in my ear to pass on to Henry. Of course, if my brother would accompany me to worship, I would not have to be pressed into service as a messenger boy." My younger brother learned early how to fight with words when his fists would flail harmlessly on my chest.

"I am sure it is one way to deflect your own failure to pass on an important message to me while ignoring the miracle Anderson told you about."

Blackwell is first to react. "That is remarkable. I've only heard about recovery in expensive sanitoriums when some poor wretch was so far gone."

Sutton stares at his empty glass and for once isn't looking about for Sanders.

"I know," I say. "There can be salvation for even those the churches have given up on." I choose not to hear a weak rebuttal from my younger sibling, and I stand. "All this talk reminds me to wash my hands before I dine."

Why has this argument with George caused me to lurch from the table on unsteady legs until I am halfway to the washroom? Without mentioning Francine Murphy to any of them, I realize what she did for Anderson's sister is miraculous. In ten minutes at my bank, I can make her dreams a reality at very little personal cost. I think about meeting Anderson before church on Sunday to arrange another meeting between myself and the green-eyed red-haired woman who has filled my waking thoughts since our first encounter.

Standing at the urinal, I no longer fret about the stiff-necked sermonizing of my brother. Suddenly, hands on my back propel me forward, my face smacking the wall as I gasp for breath. My bare member feels the cool, smooth and wet surface of the porcelain enclosure. My face flushes red with righteous anger. The voice is guttural, and I recognize its owner by the question spit in my ear. "Where's Hyde?"

I spot my door to freedom blocked by a burly, tight-lipped police constable in a dark blue wool serge uniform. He leans his sizeable bulk against the wooden door and stares at me.

No club member would be allowed in to aid me or later testify to this detestable treatment. My arms are pinned, with my hands helplessly hanging to both sides of my privates.

Before I can take it back, something possesses me to say, "With your wife, Inspector Newcomen."

He sweeps my feet from under me, and I crash to the floor, my shoulder erupting in pain. I look up to see a truncheon about to split my head. Newcomen's blunt instrument brushes my ear. The tile floor shatters under the impact. I tuck myself back in my trousers and try to focus on his face.

He pulls me up to a seated position. "Next time, I won't miss on purpose," he snarls. "Where's Hyde?"

"I went away and do not know his whereabouts." I don't care to know what spiritual realm Hyde is inhabiting. All I know is I have been myself night and day since the fateful night when he was vanquished. Ever since Hyde was banished to the ether, the sunrise is brighter, the air is sweeter, and I am my master.

"You walked away from all your possessions, your house, and you failed to mention your destination to your butler or your brother. You departed in such a hurry that you made no arrangements for any of your affairs. You met up with Hyde and fled London."

It is my turn to take the upper hand. I am staring back at a normally clean-shaven man who is not now. His eyes, usually clear, are bloodshot, perhaps from lack of sleep. His furiously dancing eyebrows and clenching jaw try to work out an impossible puzzle.

"You know that how? A ship's manifest? Informants in the

villages I visited. Strange happenings involving a man fitting Hyde's description?"

I manually examine my shoulder and determine nothing is broken. An ugly bruise will appear in the morning.

I continue, "I severed any dealings with Hyde the minute I learned of his murderous behaviour. I wanted nothing to do with him. I wanted him out of my life. Can you expect Hyde to remain in his usual environs when he is wanted for murder? Good riddance to him. I hope never to be reacquainted with him again."

"Henry, we are waiting for you," Sutton calls from the other side of the door held shut by the constable, who is looking at Newcomen.

"Be only a moment. I slipped and fell on some water and am trying to make myself presentable," I say, as I stare up at the man holding his nasty weapon over my head. Will there be a truce?

The Scotland Yard inspector leans close to my ear. "I think your friend is back in town and that you know where he is." He pushes my head back down to the slick tiles. The hair on the back of my head soaks up liquid from the floor in a room where drunk and errant gentlemen relieve themselves. I make a mental note to attend the next club meeting and urge the building care-takers to pay more attention when they wash the bathroom floors.

"Have a nice dinner, Doctor Jekyll," Newcomen says before leaving.

7

---

13 SEPTEMBER 1888

FRANCINE MURPHY

"I know no one in government, I have no friends in high places, and I lack the funds to pay my rent," I say to Mary McCreary. I often think I add to her long, greying hair framing a weathered face with eyes my colour. She is the only store owner on Commercial Street who accepts credit for regular customers. A practice held over from her recently passed husband.

Her flat is three rooms of organized bedlam. Her oldest children help the younger get ready while she makes breakfast. I take the tea kettle from the cast-iron coal stove and pour out the first cups of tea for the day. I smell the small container of cream, make a face, and decide to drink my tea straight.

While today's biscuits, hot out of the oven, cool on the table under the expectant eyes of the youngest, we sit down to talk about my ideas.

Mary splits the biscuits, then I apply jam to them. The children reach out for them with polite 'thank you' until just three biscuits are left.

I am about ten years senior to Mary's oldest. I wonder, and not for the first time, if Mary has lost one of hers the way I lost my baby. It might explain her taking a liking to me.

"We know the church will not support your plan, dear," she says.

"At least not directly," I say. "Louise's brother suggested talking to the flower guilds or the altar guilds. They have money for lilies and candles. Maybe they can make a onetime gift to the mission."

"What about that rich doctor who stopped giving his tithe?" Mary passes me more biscuits, and I slather on jam and pass them around.

"Doctor Jekyll? He passed. I think my knowing he stopped tithing was embarrassing to him, and he was put off by my direct approach."

Mary nods without judgment. "If the women on the guilds can't or won't loosen their purse strings for you, might you ask them for a referral and see if the gracious ladies will give you a reference?"

"That will take some time, I am sure."

"Anything worth doing is worth doing right, Francine."

She should know. I look around the table at Mary's brood and wonder where she found the patience, time and time again, to bring me back from hell.

"That makes sense, Mary. I can talk discreetly with women who have influenced the men in their churches to part with some funds. They'd know who would be immediately receptive to my plea and who would give me a polite no." The more I think about it, the more I like the idea. "But I learned from my meeting with Doctor Jekyll not to ask them directly to siphon funds from existing earmarks, but to put forth my problem and see if they can find a solution."

She smiles. "So, you will ask the women to point you to the

men who would listen to your problem, and you will allow them to give you their solution?"

I nod. I have learned from my lesson with Doctor Jekyll. I have vowed not to repeat that mistake.

She laughs. Her green eyes twinkle. "You'll make a smart wife someday, Francine Murphy."

The children are fed. They all do their part at cleaning the flat. Another long day in Whitechapel is about to begin. Mary's optimism is infectious. We decide to split the last biscuit.

———

FRANCINE MURPHY

"Get out, or I will have you arrested for trespassing on private property, you damned socialist."

The noise from the factory floor below intrudes on our meeting as the sheepish secretary, who thought I had a good idea, now thinks better as she holds the massive oak office door open for me. The fumes rising from the workstations are phosphorus. Matchstick making is mostly a woman's job in Bow, a short walk from Whitechapel. A terrible strike over the working conditions here earlier this summer did not help the general foreman's attitude. He is tall, rail-thin, and has the temper, strawberry hair, and accent of a Scotsman.

"Call them if you must, but there is no need to curse me or label me a socialist," I tell him. "I am making a wise business proposition to you, Mr. MacGregor. Tell me why you do not think I make a valid point."

I stand my ground, fists on hips, and my fiery eyes don't leave his. Other strong-willed reformers stood on this very carpet as recently as June, and I am sure he didn't take a liking to those females either. His eyebrows furrow with indecision and then he fixes a thoughtful gaze above my head. He comes around from behind his paper-strewn desk to address me now from a close distance.

"Women walk away from their employ here daily for no given reason. Some for piecework at home, others for a better life. Some take ill, while others meet misfortune in their personal lives, like the drinking you are talking about. For every woman who leaves an empty spot at a table, there are ten more willing and able to take over. Good wages are scarce for women who are desperate to find work. It's that simple, Mrs. Murphy. I see no reason to reach out to those hopelessly drowning in gin when I need not look beyond our gates every morning."

I learn another valuable lesson here. Unless the women possess irreplaceable skills, they are less important than the machines they work on or the resources they change into gold for their employers.

"Thank you for granting me this time without an appointment. I appreciate your thoughtful answer. I better understand your position here and what you face to keep the company profitable. Should you ever feel the need to have me assist a woman who has fallen to the ravages of gin, I would not hesitate to do so."

"Thank you, Mrs. Murphy, but I hope never to call upon your services."

The iron stairs from the overseer's office, with its banks of smudged windows, coil down to the shop floor. I feel a hundred pairs of eyes on my back as I make my way through the workstations towards the entrance. The scent of fresh wood mixed with the pungent odour from the cauldrons of bubbling phosphorus fills my nostrils. I promise myself to never work in this hellhole.

Finally, I escape to the outside, where I welcome the stench of the alley between the factory's grey stone structures. Out on the street, I take in the bright sunlight and smoke-scented air as if I am on holiday in Youghal in my beloved County Cork.

I know what it is like to work in a factory. Dark, dingy, dirty, stale air. Sweat and body odour of the workers toiling away long hours. Standing on my feet eighteen hours a day with foremen docking my pay for even so much as talking. I could not relieve the boredom of the soul-crushing repetitive tasks. It is a hard life and one difficult to escape.

I keep north of the River Thames and head to the fashionable neighbourhoods where there is money. Old money or new money, it doesn't matter. It is made on the backs of the poor and working class, either here or around the British Empire. The bustle of the factories and mills fade as I walk through Victoria Park and the bathing pond where children splash and frolic. The green grass is manicured, and seasonal flowers add a gaiety to the vast expanse. Memories of swimming in the ponds near my village hold me close to those happy times before my family moved to London in search of reliable wages. Village life and farming are difficult even during good times. Stories from my elders of the Great Hunger are deeply ingrained in all of their grandchildren.

Exiting the other side of the park, I encounter residential streets. Servants to the upper class maintain the properties. Nannies chase children. Gardeners care for the colourful plantings. Butlers, livery drivers and cooks haul in the provisions for dinner, a complete system of servitude to swaddle the upper class. These jobs are prized, and loyalty to the family is paramount. Dogs and cats are pets and not used to chase down rats. Horses' coats are brushed and kept shiny. No one lounges in doorways or alcoves. The streets are swept of droppings regularly in the night, and the gas lamps are kept in excellent repair. After midnight, women walking on these streets would come home from a later performance of the arts and would not be confused with streetwalkers.

I travel towards the nearest church and meet with the sexton on duty. In quick order, I learn the names of the women running the flower and altar guilds. He doesn't know the exact street address of either, but he describes their nearby homes.

I find the three-storey freestanding Georgian home with a chest-high hedge easily enough.

In excitement, I take the sandstone steps two at a time. I ring the bell, and the door is opened by a nicely dressed older man.

"Mrs. Mercer, please." I smile.

"Whom shall I say is calling?" comes the unsmiling reply.

His polished shoes are older but kept in immaculate condition. The creases in his trouser legs are from a fresh pressing. A black belt keeps a slight paunch in check. The cuffs of his white shirt are not frayed. A good sign. He is well taken care of by the Mercers of South Hackney.

"Francine Murphy. Sexton Browning at St. John of Jerusalem suggested I talk with her about the flower guild."

My face is scrubbed, my light brown dress and shoes are clean, and I wear a matching hat over my washed long red hair.

He frowns a practiced frown and stands ramrod straight. We listen to the grandfather clock tick stridently.

"It can't wait until Sunday, I am afraid," I add.

I am admitted to a hallway longer and wider than my flat.

An older silver-haired woman wearing a green tea gown with long sleeves comes into the adjoining parlour from a different room and sits on a high-back black leather couch. The butler escorts me there. After introductions, the woman points to a chair across from a low glass table. "Miss Murphy, would you care for some tea?"

"Yes, please."

Mrs. Mercer nods to a maid. "How do you know Sexton Browning?"

"Sexton Anderson at St. Giles in the Fields," I lie.

"I see," she says, but she really doesn't. This is small talk until the tea is served.

"When will your man start the autumn plantings?" I spied a

shovel and wheelbarrow at the far corner of the home's founda-tion before mounting the steps. The mounding had begun in earnest. The lady of the manor handles her gardens, and she lights up in delight. I learn more about crocuses, dahlias, gladi-olas and begonias during my tea and scones than I could ever have imagined.

Eventually, Mrs. Mercer says, "But you didn't come to talk to me about flowers, did you, Francine?"

A sharp woman, careful in words and actions, not to be beguiled by my lilting brogue and soft smile.

"Actually, yes, I did, but for an excellent reason." I set my tea next to a half-eaten scone. "From the altar, you see and hear what's going on in the church before and after the services. You know who is making an Easter and Christmas memorial, and you know exactly what each family wants for baptisms, weddings and funerals. You know how your church really works better than the vestrymen." I see Mrs. Mercer's reaction. I am sure none of the men in her life have given her credit for any of what I've just praised her for.

"I am going to appeal your sensibilities. I am going to tell you things you will find very disturbing, and then I will ask you for your help in pointing me in the right direction. May I impose on a few more minutes of your time?"

"You may proceed." She sets her cup down now.

"The men in your church, in my church, and St. Giles would react in horror and scold me for making any proposal, but the women will listen, Mrs. Mercer. I come to you from Whitechapel, where those horrible murders of women are happening. They are prostitutes. They sell their bodies to buy food and lodging, but mostly to buy their gin. They are almost unreachable, but they were not always that way. Some were married and bore children. Others were someone's sister or daughter, and they led a normal life. They could have been the woman who served us our tea or will make your dinner tonight.

They wore good clean clothes and took care of their personal hygiene until they lost respect for themselves and sank lower than Jonah in the whale's belly. Those are the women I am a talking about, Mrs. Mercer. But I don't see them as the church does. I see them as whole. Restored. I help them become whole again. I bring them back from the living dead. I have done this successfully more than once. I did so with Mr. Anderson's sister Louise."

I take a sip of my tea and chew on the rest of my scone while Mrs. Mercer chews on all that I've revealed to her.

"Are you looking for money?" she asks bluntly.

"Yes, but not from you, Mrs. Mercer. I am good at what I do, but I am not good at asking for funding. I need to talk to a strong woman, one who is a leader and not a follower, one who knows that the unthinkable does happen to good upstanding women, because she has seen it happen to women who were completely and utterly devastated by the loss of their husbands. The women in your church help other women get through those terrible times. You have seen countless women survive and thrive in their widowhood, thanks to the support of churchwomen. It is not from handouts from the vicar or the vestry. The support comes from other women. Am I right, Mrs. Mercer?"

"You are."

"A drunken man can be redeemed, but a drunken woman who sells her body cannot be, according to our churches. How can the women of the church help the lost sheep, the black one at that, that even the Good Shepherd has given up on?"

"How many women have you helped?"

"Three, including Louise Anderson."

She stares at me while the grandfather clock ticks the seconds away. Shade from passing clouds drifts across the parlour rug. I've made my pitch and have to wait for Mrs. Mercer to make the next move.

"My husband plays poker on the last Wednesday night of the month. I hold a women's Bible study that night starting at seven p.m. Could you convince a few of those women to join us?"

"I can."

We stand and embrace.

I take the Cambridge Heath Road back to Whitechapel. Block by block, the composition of the neighbourhood changes for the worse. The late afternoon sun leaves one side of the street in shade while I stroll on the optimistic, sunny side. My indirect approach with female church leaders may lead to funding from benefactors heretofore unreachable. Mary McCreary and I may have stumbled on the indirect path to my funding. I wonder if I had to do it over again how I might have approached Doctor Jekyll. He was a good listener and truly believed what Mr. Anderson told him. There was a softness behind his stern rebuff I couldn't quite place my finger on. I linger on our meeting for the last part of my walk home and how intrigued I am by the private man with a complicated church relationship.

I enter my apartment to find the women sitting around the table. Their heads remain down. I can't wait to tell them the good news. "I met…" Tear-streaked faces greet me.

Louise says, "I've received word my brother did not wake up this morning." She sobbed. "He was worried sick about me all the time I was on the street. He never recovered his health. It is my fault he is dead."

Her guilt adding to her sadness made me quickly forget my excitement.

8

---

5 FEBRUARY 1853

THE WHITECHAPEL MURDERER

I woke up sweating and sat up in my bed. I couldn't breathe. My nightshirt was bunched around my neck. I fitfully wrestled it down. My dreams were vivid and dark. In my nightmare, a dark and heavy object pressed down on me. Terrified, I gasped for my nanny. "Betty!" I cried out, but I heard no answer. Gulps of air did not help me settle.

No answer. The moonlight shone into my bedroom. Vague shapes became more recognizable.

"Betty!" I screamed. No sound of approaching feet or a comforting voice to be heard. I jumped out of bed and ran to her room. I pulled open the door into darkness. The curtains were drawn, and I felt around her bed. "Betty!" I said again. The bed was empty. I scurried down the hall, opening doors, and saw no servants where they were supposed to be. Was I still dreaming? I wondered. I sprinted to the centre stairway and saw the flickering light of the sitting room's fireplace below. Down the stairs and around the corner I went.

On the rug, in front of the fireplace, I saw the shape of two people. They appeared to be wrestling. I walked over to them, hypnotized by

51

their movements and sounds. They were not wearing clothes, and the man on top glistened with sweat. The light of the fire illuminated short dark hair. The person on the bottom was face up with their legs splayed to either side of the other's thrusting hips as if urging the contest to continue. A voice came from the other side of the man's head. The sounds were nothing I had ever heard before, like the person on the bottom was mewing.

Who were they, and what were they doing in our home? I stood transfixed and could not utter a word. Where were the servants? Why did they let this happen? Now the man was making noises, grunting like a pig, a disgusting sound, and finally there was silence. He rolled off the other person and my eyes widened in recognition. "Mother!"

She was up in a flash, gathering clothes in her arms. "You dirty little boy. How long were you standing there?"

The man turned quickly away to shield his face, but I'd had a good look at him. What had he done to my mother?

"You filthy creature. Sneaking around. Who told you that you could leave your bedroom before morning?"

I was too stunned to say anything. My nightmare was replaced with something I could not comprehend. Covering her nakedness with parts of her dress, she flew at me and turned me around. She ran me towards the stairs faster than the legs of any six-year-old could match.

On the staircase, she jerked my arm up each time she took a step. I thought she was going to pull it out of me as I dangled in the air with my toes scraping along the carpeted stairs. "Mother, stop. You're hurting me," I pleaded.

"Shut your mouth or I will really hurt you." She dragged me down the hallway towards her rooms and then to the empty room next to theirs, one she used as a sitting room. She flung open the closet door and swung me into the racks of clothes. I sat on the floor, feeling the searing pain in my arm. I looked at her face. I had never seen her that angry. "If you make one sound, I will take a horse whip to you. Do you understand me, you dirty little boy?"

My arm ached. I sat in the corner with my knees drawn up under my nightshirt and cried. In the darkness, I acquired a few of her clothes and wrapped them around me to keep warm. I even put my feet in a pair of her shoes. The hours passed slowly in silence, and I must have fallen asleep.

She suddenly opened the door and placed a bucket in the room. I was blinded by the sunlight behind her. "Do your business in that. If I hear a word from you, I will whip you. Do you understand?" She slammed the door and locked me in total darkness again, save for a sliver of light under the door. The heavy smell of the closet closed in on me. It was as if the nightmare had become real, with the darkness pressing in. I lay down on the wooden floor towards the light and wedged my face against the door where the cold air seeped in. The day turned to evening, then the evening into night. I lost track of time. The following morning before daylight, she opened the door and motioned me to walk towards her. The room was lit by a single candle flickering on a chest of drawers.

On the cold floor of the sitting room, I stood before her. "Lift your shirt," she said. I did as she commanded. "Higher," she barked.

I lifted it up almost over my head when I felt her hand grab my boyhood. I wanted to step back, but she held me with a vice-like grip. "Drop your shirt." I did and was staring at large clothing shears.

"If you ever say a word about what you saw, I will cut it off." She held the shears up against my cheek, the cold metal pressing it in. "Not a word."

"Yes, Mother," I whimpered.

She let go of me, then opened and closed the shears for effect.

"Go to your room without making a sound. The servants will be here shortly, and they will prepare breakfast. Are you hungry?"

I nodded.

"Not a word." She flicked the shears open and closed again.

———

14 SEPTEMBER 1888

THE WHITECHAPEL MURDERER

That morning, thirty-five years ago, I ate porridge with raisins. The servants, back from their holiday, did not suspect a thing. My mother chatted with the cook about what to prepare for the day my father returned from his business trip. I took a second helping and smiled at Betty. Never was I so happy to see her. I'd survived the brutality of my promiscuous mother. It was not until over a half-dozen years later that she forced me to keep other secrets, when, on my thirteenth birthday, she and her boyfriend snuck into my bedroom and robbed me of my virginity. They took from me any shred of decency with the things they did to me until I went away to school.

At boarding school, when the other boys talked about their adventures and fantasies, I thought it strange. I disconnected from any feelings when they talked about infatuation, love and all their awkward fumbling at dances.

I received a message one day from my father, that my mother was hospitalized. She never returned from the hospital. I was rushed home for her funeral service. It was later that night that I got drunk for the first time, returned to the graveyard after midnight, climbed the iron fence and pissed all over the pretty flowers on her grave.

I found no pleasure in pleasuring myself or courting the pretty ladies as I grew into manhood. The stirrings began on my first trips across the Channel with the fellows to the Continent. As the nights got later and the drinking freer, I would roam the streets looking to redress my grievances by finding a woman of the night and exacting my revenge on my filthy whore mother.

The memory of that first night in Brussels never fails to stir me. I was drunk and surly. My mates and I went out on the streets in search of prostitutes. One by one, we paired off with the ladies of the evening until I was by myself. She approached me from the shadows. Older and weary. A crooked smile with missing teeth. Freckles, or smudges of dirt on her cheeks, I couldn't be sure. Her clothes were tattered and smelled of being slept in.

"Looking for a little fun, are we?" she asked in French.

Little did she know what my idea of fun would be. "Yes," I replied in English.

"Follow me," she said as I trailed behind her from the bustle of the street to the quiet and darkness, down an alley to a patch of wet grass behind an empty horse stall. She set the price, and I handed her the coins.

She spread her cloak on the ground in a practiced motion, hitched up her dress, lowered her knickers and spread her hairy legs. I kneeled between them, undid my belt and stopped.

She smiled at me and rubbed my flanks with the inside of her thighs encouraging me to get on with it.

I smiled too and lurched for her throat with both hands. The memory of what followed was exquisite. Her face was replaced by my dead mother's as I squeezed the life out of her while warding off the blows from her fists until she could not move anymore.

I RETURN FROM THE MEMORY, back in my bachelor's apartment, staring into the fireplace and the smouldering embers. I know I must venture out this coming weekend to secure my release. It is time again.

9

15 SEPTEMBER 1888

HENRY JEKYLL

I can't see more than one hundred feet from my bedroom window because of the dense fog. Anderson's funeral is set for ten a.m. I hope to see Francine Murphy there. Will the fog lift to a sunny warm late summer's day?

I breakfast alone. My brother, recently elected to the vestry, will meet me at the church, as he has a vestry breakfast meeting there. I have made a generous donation to the flower fund for arrangements both at the church and at the gravesite, on our behalf. A nervousness comes upon me. A trepidation, really. I have attended enough funerals of persons with whom I had little or no acquaintance. Now another tragic death, which might have been nothing more than a death notice in the newspapers had it not been for one particular person connected to the decedent. Is it the feeling of going back into church? The blue hymnal and red Book of Common Prayer do nothing special for me. The preacher and congregants hold no sway over my decision to return there today. As I dress in proper mourning attire, I am excited about the prospect of seeing that remarkable woman again, not fearful. So, what is it, this feeling warning me? I instruct Poole to schedule dinner, as I will not engage in any frivolity at my club come evening.

I step outside into the morning's dense white blanket of moist air, which increases my sense of foreboding.

A cab pulls up immediately in front of my home, and I say to the driver, "St. Giles in the Fields."

The cab is larger than the usual two-seater, but this morning's weather probably keeps the smaller coaches in their stables. The black window curtains conceal the interior, not that I can really see inside on this dreary morning.

I open the door and find my seat facing forward. I am surprised to see the cab occupied. Two burly constables in heavy wool serge coats stare at me.

"Inspector Newcomen would like to have a chat with you at Scotland Yard," the larger of the two says. Both tap truncheons in their palms. How did they know I would hail a cab?

Remembering my last encounter, I understand why I felt edgy when I dressed. I am not prone to premonitions and did not fully understand the sense of foreboding. Since my return to London, I am happy and carefree. Can I get word to my personal lawyer and friend, Utterson, before the questioning starts?

Scotland Yard is near to the river. As I step out of the cab, one constable waits for me, while the other brings up the rear. I am relieved to see that we are in fact in front of the building and not standing near a deserted warehouse. No clamouring or bustle can be heard past either end of the block, so thick is the soup-like shroud upon us. We march into the building past several uniformed men and into a warren of offices to a plain room with a wooden table and two chairs bolted to the floor. Strong hands on my shoulders thrust me into the empty room and I am told to wait.

No windows. No artwork. A wall-mounted gas lamp bathes

the room in a dull yellow light. I have no chance to get a message to my attorney. The room is only ten by ten feet, with a mustard-coloured plaster lathe and wide-plank wooden floors. I remain standing on the opposite side of the table, unsure of the greeting I shall receive from the inspector. I hear footsteps of protesting prisoners and their escorts, shared laughter of men with a common purpose, and their snippets of conversations about a street robbery or a petty theft.

After an hour of standing about, I slump into a chair. I think about the eulogies probably being offered for a man of selfless service to the church, where he now rests in repose. Would the remembrances be about his acts or how he was a good family man and friend? Achievements are fleeting but love of family will be remembered by each generation he touched.

With no extended family to speak of and only my brother, who would come to my funeral? Who would throw flowers on my coffin?

I can still make it to the interment if the questioning is quick. What will be the scene at the gravesite? I have no way of knowing if the weather has improved. I imagine Anderson's immediate family and friends, none of whom I know by sight, save one. The priest and the miserable altar boys, other well-wishers wanting to be seen, and Francine Murphy. The family will invite attendees back to the house, where the hospitality committee will have fine food warm and ready on good chinaware. The church ladies will clean up and send gatherers home with a parcel for their dinner. I will feel out of place at the reception, but I only need a minute to reschedule another meeting with Murphy. I might even converse with Anderson's sister, Louise. I remain hopeful she has stayed sober through her loss.

Three hours pass before Inspector Newcomen enters the room with the larger of the two constables, a man of immense size and scowling countenance. He remains stationed by the door.

Newcomen sits across from me. He wears a grey dress coat, white shirt, black tie, grey trousers and black shoes with dirt crusting on the heels—not much different from my mourning attire. I study his thick black hair, menacing moustache, and otherwise clean-shaven face. The last time I saw him, I was more preoccupied with the blunt object he nearly crushed my skull with. Whatever possessed me to say something about his wife?

He is as tall as I am but more broad-shouldered. I suspect some sort of repeated hard labour is in his past before joining the Metropolitan police. He places his closed pocket notebook on the table next to his blunt-nosed pencil. His folded hands are twice the size of mine, and I withdraw mine to my lap.

"Any luck with finding Mr. Hyde?" he asks quietly. No apology is offered for his lateness. The lamp hisses. The constable clears his throat, and Newcomen remains perfectly still. This man of violent action sits passively across from me, trying to read my expression, as if we are playing high-stakes poker.

"I have not seen nor heard from him since my return to London," I say.

He reaches for his notebook, opens a fresh page and tamps his pencil on it the way one would press tobacco into a pipe.

"The girls who were butchered in Whitechapel—could that be his handiwork?" he asks.

"No," I blurt out. We are not playing cards, but this is a high-stakes game—my neck in a noose swinging from gallows cross-beam if I don't play mine right.

"Why are you so quick to answer?"

I know that since my return I have been in my right mind. When I fall asleep each night, I wake up the next morning with no strange clothes on my body. I have no unexplained scrapes, cuts or bruises. I have no lapses of memory for any period, but that cannot be my admission to him.

"From what I read in the newspapers," I say, "the killer displays a certain knowledge of anatomy and possesses some surgical skill. I know Hyde to possess neither."

The pencil shifts in his meaty hand to the top of the blank page as if to record my next statement.

"What is your friend's occupation, Doctor Jekyll?"

A practiced answer leaves my lips. "He dabbled in the markets and went broke. I assisted him with his finances while he lived in London to help him get back on his feet."

"Where did you first meet him?"

I draw a blank as we have never met. I think of another down-on-his-luck fellow I befriended and blurt out, "A Soho pawnshop where I visit occasionally to shop for violins."

"Go on."

"He was pawning his father's watch, and I was taken by his sad tale. We left the shop together, and I saw in him an invest-ment worth chancing on. It's not the first investment to not work out for me I'm afraid."

"When was this, Doctor Jekyll?"

I think. When was the first time I lied about Hyde being an associate of mine?

"I don't rightly know, but my bookkeeper would." All my expenditures for my alter ego are kept in a dusty ledger back in Cavendish Square. Newcomen scribbles down my answers. He takes his time. He's in no hurry. I am reminded Newcomen never formally interviewed me before I rushed off to the West Indies. In the intervening two years plus, he must have learned more about Hyde and his peculiar relationship with his benefactor.

A frown and a twirl of his pencil follow my response. The constable shifts his sizeable bulk from one enormous foot to the other.

"Where is he from?"

"I cannot tell you. I never asked. He was well travelled and lived in many places." I feel comfortable with this lie as well. That answer is ready on my lips from my previous discussions with my cohorts about my peculiar friend when they pressed me.

"What about his daily activities, routines, where he churched, dined, other associates, women?" Newcomen persists.

"He is a private person, we only discussed business ventures to invest in." I feel the heat of deceit spreading across my chest and into my throat.

"What kind of investments?"

This is an easier question to proffer an explanation. I recall for him the numerous investments pitched to me over the years at the club. Most were small capital infusions and done as favours for club members to show my goodwill. A few panned out rather nicely. I don't tell Newcomen about those as they can be traced to other living shareholders. I blather on and he scribbles for close to thirty minutes.

He shrugs his massive shoulders and rotates his neck. Newcomen would rather swing his truncheon at me than write what I'm saying. He looks at me from his notepad and says, "Can you describe him to me?"

I've often wondered that question myself and I quizzed my friends and associates repeatedly about Hyde's physical appearance. I learned early on that we are quite different in appearance and would not be mistaken for each other. Utterson had shown me the sketch drawn by a police artist after the witness saw Hyde beating Sir Danvers Carew to death.

From that composite of the sketch and what I was told, I slowly detail for him a fabrication close enough to be true. Doctor Jekyll, a practiced liar. The words roll effortlessly off my tongue.

He sets the pencil down, steeples his fingers and leans in. I am not sure if a volcano is about to erupt.

"Doctor Jekyll, you provided food, lodging and financial support, yet you don't know where he came from or of his daily activities. This man is your friend?" He looks up at the constable, who is shaking his head at my lies, and adds, "What I find remarkable is persons who have seen Edward Hyde have never seen you in his company."

I let his statement hang in the air. Spending much time with lawyers in my acquaintance and business dealings, I know no question has been asked.

I uncross my feet and recross them. I place my hands on the table palms down and shrug.

"Your response, Doctor?" His eyes never leave mine.

"I do not believe Mr. Hyde is in London. I have not seen nor heard from him since I departed on my trip over two years ago. I do not think he has anything to do with those grisly deaths. I do not think I can be of any more help, Inspector."

He reaches for the notebook and places it in his inside coat pocket and his pencil in a side pocket.

"I understand," he says. "You are free to go."

Unsure about this feigned friendliness, I stand and make my way to the door, now opened by the constable. He has kept me in this barren, poorly lit room for the entire morning, made no threats, asked only a few probing questions, then allowed me to depart. It doesn't feel right.

"One last thing, though," he says, looking up at me. "You have the skills and knowledge to butcher those girls. Do you not, Doctor Jekyll?"

"Along with other doctors, barbers, taxidermists and horse slaughterers," I reply.

"Yes, that's true, but none of the others have a mysterious friend who is a known killer."

Dumbfounded by his reply, I am at a loss for words. What does one have to do with the other?

The constable walks me a different way out of the building, and I find myself at the rear entrance. The air is still heavy, but the fog has lifted. A thick cloud cover blankets London. The foul air is as sweet as any breeze I inhaled on the islands. It is the breath of freedom. Free from Hyde, and free from my tormentor, Inspector Newcomen.

I hail an empty cab and give the driver directions to the cemetery. My thoughts volley between the excitement of seeing Francine Murphy again and the ominous observations made by the inspector. A lightness in my heart with the memory of her face battles the heaviness in my chest from the queer interrogation.

The trip from Scotland Yard to the gravesite feels longer because of these competing thoughts and feelings. I direct the driver to the only activity along the serpentine paths deep in the graveyard. We pull up, and I get out. Workmen with shovels are filling in the Anderson grave. The lovely flowers and card I provided are thrown upside down on a nearby cart. Are any of them salvageable? I gather several with unbroken stems. A nice table setting, maybe.

10

—

15 SEPTEMBER 1888

FRANCINE MURPHY

Anderson's home is small for the neighbourhood, but it is befitting a man of his stature as the Sexton of St Giles in the Fields. It is tidy and well-kept, with everything in perfect working order. I'd never met his widow until today when I offer her my condolences. The widow gives me a grieving smile and tells me that her husband talked often of the miracle. She squeezes Louise's hand in hers while she speaks. "He was so proud of never giving up on his sister and went to his grave with no regrets."

I am sure he would have liked to live another twenty years, but I will not argue with a widow on the day she buries her husband. I scan his grieving family and consider his grandchildren, who will never bounce on his knee again. They are not old enough to comprehend all that is going on, but the smell of food, especially the cakes and pies, tells them it is a special day. I imagine one or two would be as old as my Patrick, had I carried him to birth. I try not to dwell on those thoughts and reply,

65

"Part of Louise's return to wholeness was because of his unwavering faith in her."

Louise stays by her sister-in-law's side to receive the mourners who came back from the cemetery. I learn the names of Anderson's children and their spouses and his two brothers and their wives.

The receiving line soon ends, and the church women go to work handing out plates of food and serving tea or coffee. Snatches of conversations I overhear centre around the dreadful happenings in Whitechapel. I slice my meat and fork my food without comment. I am more than aware of each of the murdered women, and I knew the last victim personally. Annie Chapman was not ready to give up her life on the street, and because of that, she gave up her life to a butcher. There is a whispered sense of relief the slayings are confined to that section of town. These people feel safe and unaffected by the killings of prostitutes, thinking that nothing like that could ever happen here. I don't offer my address from where I will soon be evicted. My only connection to this parish lies in a freshly dug grave.

Louise points out a well-dressed man about my height and weight. He has a calm manner. He is part of the contingent of vestrymen who offer their promises of help. "That's Doctor Jekyll's brother. He's the one who was supposed to relay the message of your meeting."

I try to guess from his features his intent in not passing on Anderson's request. He moves about the room with a lightness of step. I assume he is playing the role of a church steward making the rounds, a sombre duty at this gathering of the flock.

"Whatever his reasons, I cannot dwell on the past. I must continue my search for funding, or our mission will be suspended in two weeks."

Louise receives her plate from a church lady and says, "I have more news. My sister-in-law just offered for me to stay here with her. My brother's savings and a small offering from the church will allow her to stay in this house. The church will find me work as a servant with one of the families, and that will help defray our expenses."

"This is good news, Louise. You have a safe place to live, food and the promise of employment."

"I can't be running around the streets of Whitechapel with you, Francine, I'm afraid," she adds.

The implication is clear. She is expected to return to a life of normalcy and help care for her brother's widow. My time with my friend has run out. I will miss her greatly. We made a good team once she could walk by her previous haunts without stepping inside. I rely on her to be with the others when I've errands to address. But I feel happy for Louise. The unexpected death of her brother has opened a door for her out of Whitechapel.

"Who knows? You might find a suitable donor in this church family who can assist the mission," I say.

"Always looking at the positive side of things, dear. You know I owe my life to you; I will do what I can when I can. I am forever indebted to you."

"I only offered you my hand on your journey out of hell," I say.

"You did more than that."

"Can you still go with me next Wednesday night to see Mrs. Mercer in South Hackney?"

"Come by for dinner and we will go afterwards," she says.

"That's a plan."

During our conversation, our plates are removed. Unencumbered, we both stand and hug, lingering in the embrace. She was the first woman I helped in the way Mary McCreary helped me. Louise helped me show other women what was possible when they decided they'd had it with selling their bodies for gin.

I do not refuse the piece of cake wrapped up for me as I say my last goodbyes. Louise is in a good place now. She no longer needs me and is ready to move on with her life.

I depart the Anderson household and find the clouds are slowly breaking up, with the sun trying to peek through from the west. The walk does me good after hours of sitting with mourners. How many of them would venture to Whitechapel on foot? Other than Louise, none of them would offer to accompany me at night as I make my rounds. Maybe Louise could loosen their purse strings or convince a wealthy patron to make a onetime gift to the mission. Once Louise becomes comfortable in her new environs, will she still remember me? Those memories include living in a hellscape and doing unspeakable things to pay for her drink. She will make good on her promise, I am sure, but after that, there will be no telling how committed to the mission she will remain.

I trudge up the stairs to my flat and immediately sense things are not right. The door is ajar. I call, "Hello?" Hearing no reply, a sense of foreboding comes over me. The women who stayed with Louise and me during their reentry to wholeness are gone. I should have insisted they accompany me to the day of mourning. Items from my dressing table are scattered about. The comb my mother used on my hair before bed every night when I was a wee child is missing. Their beds are unmade, and their belongings are gone. I check the rest of the floors of the lodging house and do not hear or see anything suspicious. I return to my room and pry up the loose board where I keep my most precious belongings from my life in Ireland and my marriage to Seamus. I touch both wooden boxes and fasten the board back in place. I am smart enough to remember what a person will do to get their next sip, and I am glad they never saw me reach into my special hiding place. My memories of my mother will never leave me, but the comb can never be replaced. Maybe they haven't sold it yet? On the other hand, I realize soon I will not have a place for them to rest and recover. I debate whether to keep searching for women in need of my help or postpone the mission until I have reliable lodgings.

I fear the worst for the women. I know their haunts and it will not take me long to find them in one of their gin palaces. I realize constant monitoring, like I did with Louise, is necessary. A woman finally released from the shackles of alcohol needs to be present at all times in the rooms occupied by those still hearing the sirens' calls. Lesson learned.

My meagre savings are still intact. I sit at the table by the stove and pick at the moist slice of cake while I wait for my decision to come to me. There is no shortage of women in need in Whitechapel.

As dusk settles, I change out of my best clothes and take on the mantle of Francine Murphy; the woman searching out women of the night who are broken. That is my mission. I have no choice but to keep moving forward.

11

16 SEPTEMBER 1888

THE WHITECHAPEL MURDERER

What church tolls midnight?

Somewhere in the distance, the last toll bounces off the clouds like a solo clap of thunder and echoes back down, making it difficult to determine from which steeple it came. For many residents of Whitechapel, Sunday is their only day of rest. Some honour the Sabbath; others, like those out and about on this cool, wet night, would probably opt to sleep off their hangovers.

Raucous laughter drowns out the piano, fiddle and tambourine music in the pub across the street from where I stand under a broken street lamp. I wait to see how other men move about. It is late enough for a curious man about town to be wanting to sample the forbidden fruits. I walk slowly on Commercial Street and take in the music and laughter from the other gin palaces.

Before entering an alley or a side road, I pretend to tie my bootlace. I watch for constables and night watchmen making their rounds. I make a mental note of open windows where someone could scan an intersection. I pay attention to any man with a consort, strolling into the darkness. I wait for their business to conclude before focusing on the women. I will pick one soon and follow her while she plies her trade. The ones who enter the public houses and gin palaces between trips into darkened alcoves or other discreet places are the best choices. The more drunk and tired they are, the easier it will be to surprise them with their demise at my hand.

By two a.m. the traffic on the major thoroughfares lightens. A woman with long red hair talks to two other women. Are they comparing notes on their night's prizes? I have seen this woman before, I realize. Her hair is the giveaway. She walks without staggering and talks without slurring. Her accent is Irish, her tone friendly. The other ladies alternate between shrill cackling laughter and whispered responses. She holds the hand of one, but the other woman pulls it away; then the two other ladies stagger down the street towards several Russian sailors making their way to the pubs. The redhead walks into the alley away from the light and safety of the street. Who is she looking for?

So focused on the woman, I fail to spot the constable approaching the corner while making his rounds.

Before the constable reproaches me, I say, "Where might I hail a cab? I'm lost and need to find my way home. It's well past my bedtime." My practiced and precise wording works.

"Your best bet is going to the train station." The constable points the way. "The return train from Dover will arrive in twenty minutes. You will find a cab there. Be careful and stay out of the shadows. Gangs of thieves prey on the drunks at this hour."

"I don't imbibe. Thank you for your kind service, Constable." I smile and walk towards the train station. The constable's only view is of my profile, with my hat pulled low and my coat lapels turned high. Do I risk making a move tonight? The police are on the lookout for a man wearing a deerstalker hat.

My fashionable West End attire looks nothing like the previous descriptions. I make a show of making haste and click my walking stick on the cobblestones. Witnesses could later tell the police a well-dressed man left Whitechapel in a cab.

No witnesses would be questioned two miles away, where I hail another cab back to the Tower of London.

I skirt the wider streets and enter Whitechapel from the alleys. It is four a.m. before I locate a gin palace to place under surveillance. Just then, a woman staggers out and makes her proposal to a passer-by. The indignant man shoves her away.

She teeters on one foot from the push and from how much she has had to drink. "And the horse you rode in on!" She slurs at the man, then spits at his back. She makes her hands busy straightening her dress.

I warily circle her on the street and approach her from the darkness. Black hair, parted in the middle, hangs limply to her shoulders. An unfocused smile and practiced line greet me as she sizes me up. Her long grey coat appears tattered at the sleeves but otherwise is clean. Her legs are bowed, and her shoes are worn down on the outside edges. She could be ten years younger or older than me, depending how long she has worked the streets. A hard life makes a person's age difficult to guess.

I hold shiny coins between my thumb and forefinger and rub them enticingly. "Somewhere where we won't be disturbed," I say. She reaches for the coins, and I pull my hand back. "Not here."

She tries to entwine her arm with mine, but I tell her, "Lead the way."

She walks unsteadily along the street away from the gin palace until she finds a narrow opening between warehouses. Before I follow, I look back up and down the street and see no one paying attention to me. I scan the windows across the street. Satisfied that my return to Whitechapel has gone unnoticed, I trail her in near darkness to the rear of the property.

In the darkness, she turns to face me. The thick air is still. Clouds obscure the stars. A shed with a cart tilted on its axle will be the only witness.

"Your first time?" she asks.

I shake my head. I know the number of times I have strangled prostitutes, but I don't think she would appreciate knowing that number.

"You just seem nervous," she adds.

Does my anticipation show? One woman, one city was my routine until I returned to London with its police, watchmen and reporters. Every time I fulfill my desires now carries more risk, but it also adds to the thrill. It makes my release more intense and vivid.

I walk with her to behind a slight rise next to the cart shed and turn to face her. I hold out the coins, and just as she reaches for them, I drop my walking cane, freeing my dominant hand. She leans towards me as I pull the coins back to my shoulder. This is when I make them off balance.

At that moment, an animal shrieks from an opening between the brick buildings. "Damn cat!" a man's voice roars. The noisy warning gives me a start. I pull my coins back from her grasp. She rocks back on her well-worn heels and turns as three other people enter our space. I watch over her shoulder as a woman leads two men in rough clothing into the rear of the property.

"So, who's first, boys?" the leader says to the duo following her.

I pick up my cane, tap the woman on the arm, smile at her and give her one coin. I slink around the far end of the property to an opening in the dilapidated wooden plank fence and disappear into the night.

12

16 SEPTEMBER 1888

HENRY JEKYLL

I leap out of bed. "No!" I scream as I look in the mirror.

It can't be.

Hyde was vanquished, but here I stand, fully clothed, with no idea where my body has been. I last remember using my toilet around two a.m. My breathing is ragged; my temples throb. Wide-eyed with bewilderment, I don't know what could have resurrected Hyde. I never wake up with my shoes on, but today I do, and the dried mud speaks of nocturnal travels for which I have no memory. "God help me!" I cry.

What if the police encountered Hyde on the streets last night? What if they mistook him for the killer roaming Whitechapel?

I look at myself. One shirt cuff is held by a cufflink, the other flaps over my hand. My tie is loose, but my belt is too snug around the waist. I move my limbs painlessly and without restriction, unlike after the times Hyde went out for his nasty excitement. Nothing hurts, except for my head.

I slump into my chair and hang my head. I want to cry. He is back. He is back in London when he should have been nothing more than dark oily smoke reaching the stars on that beach by the witch doctor's hut in the West Indies. Had I been foolish to believe he was really gone? All this summer, I was so convinced the demon he had become had been driven from my body and spirit; I had felt a release and lightness, like an untethered balloon soaring upwards. Every day was a blessing, whether it rained, or the sun shone. A darkness falls upon me now in my warm, dry and bright bedroom. What am I to do?

A knock precedes Poole's entrance. "Is there anything the matter, Doctor Jekyll?"

"No, Poole, I will be downstairs in a few minutes for breakfast. Please prepare lavender tea." I go to my bed and search for the missing cuff link. It is not in the covers, on the floor, or anywhere in plain sight. It had been given to me by my father, and Hyde losing it troubles me.

I change out of the clothes I have no memory of putting on, then take a rag to my boots and wipe away the caked mud from between each heel and the sole, along with the deposits around the edges. The act of cleaning up after Hyde is gruesomely familiar, yet oddly calming.

My primary task for the day, regardless of learning that my nocturnal persona has returned, is to visit St. Giles and introduce myself to Anderson's widow hoping she can pass a message on to Francine Murphy. I decide, drawing upon a well of hope, that my nightmare is a singular event and will not be repeated. Thus, I change into my Sunday worship attire. As I put on my regular shoes, there comes another knock on the door.

"Sir, you have official visitors," Poole says. "Please come quickly. The police are waiting for you in the vestibule."

"Did they say what they wanted?"

"Only to know if you were home and would I fetch you. I said that you were just now awake."

His worried expression only increases with my astonishment the police would so rudely knock on my door without an appointment, and on a Sunday morning no less. Poole has seen Hyde in the past and did not approve of him then—and rightly so. Did he see Hyde here today? Are the police looking for Hyde? The clothes Hyde wore are on the floor in a heap next to the boots. Are they looking for a man wearing them?

"Send a messenger to Utterson to come here immediately. Tell the police I shall be downstairs in a moment. Do not let them wander about." Utterson, my best friend over the years, is a respected barrister. He will know what to do.

I hang up the clothes and place the boots in the rear of my wardrobe behind my other footwear. I scan the room for any other evidence of Hyde. Satisfied he used nothing else; I make my way on shaky legs to the front door. My headache worsens when I steal a glance through the windows into the bright sunlight. There must be a half-dozen of them. Certainly, too many to effect an arrest. What on earth do they want? Is their appearance in Cavendish Square coincidental with the re-emergence of the monster within me?

I steel myself for the worst upon spotting Inspector Newcomen amongst the group. "You're a tad early for breakfast. You should have told me you were bringing friends," I say.

"Doctor Jekyll, we have a search warrant for your surgery. Please take us there immediately."

"On whose authority?" I stand my ground on reflex. I have no initial thought of why my surgery is of interest; Hyde has never borrowed my professional tools before.

The inspector opens the document and gestures to the bottom. "Magistrate Harrell, signed this morning." He turns it around to permit me to confirm its authority, though he declines me the privilege of holding it myself. I imagine an elderly man in his bathrobe and slippers surrounded by this group, his wife alarmed by the intrusion on a day of worship.

Utterson would know if search warrants can be served on Sundays. I wish he were here now, but that will take time even with a fast cab.

"What are you searching for? I may save you some time." I do not move to allow them to pass me.

"The search relates to the murder of Annie Chapman on Hanbury Street in Whitechapel last weekend. It is all here in the warrant. Now if you would, please lead us to your surgery."

Newcomen's attitude is insistent but polite, unlike his detestable recent behaviour towards me. It is an act. If called to testify, the other officers and my butler will have nothing to report but his professional and polite demeanour. But there is something else about him. I sense a fait accompli about to take place. His half-dozen men gather inside my door. A warrant signed on a Sunday morning shortly after dawn. What does he hope to find? A dread falls upon me. It is the return of Hyde, I am almost certain. As I consider this, crows call to each other from nearby rooftops.

Poole hands me my tea. He says, "The message is being delivered with haste."

I take a couple of sips and hand the cup and saucer back to him. "Gentlemen, this way."

I force my legs to neither quiver nor buckle as I walk the hallways. I have trod these floorboards a thousand times both in daylight and in the dead of night. I slow as I approach the door to my surgery, then ratchet the door open and take in the space where, in happier times, I plied my profession. I have only visited this room a few times since my return to inventory the formulary, but the housecleaner mops the floors and dusts more often than my few visits. Nothing appears amiss.

Yet, in walking the length of the room, I notice the absence of any bloody clothing mentioned in the warrant, and the absence of my surgical instruments: scalpels, knives and saws used for the most delicate surgery and the most severe amputations. Only dust outlines in their accustomed positions. The room is musty, and to my first glance, appears free of any intrusion. I stand next to the window facing my courtyard and watch Newcomen's men spread out. I open the unlatched window to let in whatever fresh air London's fetid atmosphere will provide.

They methodically open drawers and cabinets and dump the contents on the floor to paw through. They tap for loose floorboards and remove all the wall hangings. I watch them closely, my heart thundering in my chest.

"What is this?" a constable asks, holding up an item.

"A surgical implement not on your list, I would expect. Please put it back where you found it." I am not about to explain how my thoracic rib spreader is used to keep the chest cavity open during surgery.

Utterson arrives and harangues Newcomen over the timing of the warrant. He tells the inspector in no uncertain terms that all appointments with me are to be handled through his offices. Newcomen reiterates tiresomely that police affairs are not subject to the demands of barristers. Over the next hour and Utterson's protestations, they continue to tear the room apart. Our eyes leave none of them, lest something strange and new be brought into the surgery.

"How did your anonymous tipster have such intimate knowledge of my client's surgery?" Utterson asks Newcomen. I ponder that question as well. Besides Poole, George and the cleaner, who else could describe the interior of my professional working place?

"I don't have to answer to you," Newcomen snarls, his patience having now grown thin during his men's fruitless search for evidence of my guilt.

"Why would someone make such a wild assertion that my client cleaved open that woman and then brought the evidence back to his own surgery?" Utterson asks.

"Because since his return to London, your client or his friend has gone on a killing spree."

"Edward Hyde killed a man with a walking stick in anger. How does that equate to the killing of a whore in Whitechapel?" Utterson shoots back.

My barrister confessed to me before I departed for the West Indies that it had been he who connected Hyde to the murder. We both knew the stick in question was a present from Utterson to me, but we both had conveniently forgotten to tell Newcomen that minor fact.

"Perhaps it was not Hyde who killed these women," Newcomen volleys back.

"No blood-stained knives, no shreds of women's clothes. I am afraid your anonymous source sent you on a fool's errand, Inspector," Utterson says.

Newcomen looks to the helpless stares of his constables and growls back, "Or they were removed before we could execute the warrant."

"How many people knew you were coming here this morning?" Utterson asks. "Are you saying your men or the magistrate tipped off the good doctor?"

Newcomen's face reddens, and he clenches his mighty fists like a boxer about to deliver a knockout blow.

Utterson doesn't let up. "Did your informant know you were coming this morning at dawn?" He shakes his head and wags a finger at the policeman. "My client was woken from his slumber by you and your men, he had no prior warning."

I tingle. A feeling comes over me unlike any fever. It emanates from my gut and spreads to my limbs and scalp. I sit down, and Utterson looks over at me. This would be a terrible time for Hyde to manifest.

"Are you all right?" he inquires.

"I believe so. All of this is quite distressing." I previously relayed to him the tale of Newcomen's attack on me at the gentlemen's club and the odd set of questions posed to me at Scotland Yard. A question of my own bubbles out of my mouth before I contain it. "Where were you, Inspector Newcomen, when you had me sequestered in Scotland Yard for three hours before your arrival to interview me?"

All the eyes in the room turn to Newcomen as the search halts.

He opens his mouth, looks at Utterson, shuts it and sneers at me. He makes no eye contact with any of the constables now milling about in the flotsam and jetsam left in their wake. He whirls around in a tight circle and says, "We are done here."

He storms out of the surgery, and the uniformed officers follow like ducklings, leaving Utterson and I alone. We breathe a collective sigh of relief.

"Thank you for coming," I say.

"You should let me ask the questions," Utterson says.

"You are probably correct, but we didn't receive an answer, did we?"

"I don't want to ask him that question in the future," Utterson says. The meaning and warning are clear. If Utterson and Newcomen are to square off again, it will be at the time of my arrest.

We walk about the space and take in the carnage. No amount of cleaning can ever make up for the violation of this space. All the contents of all the enclosures are strewn about. I realize something on the edge of my consciousness, something I will not divulge even to my most trusted friend and legal counsellor.

"Newcomen was sure he would find something here," I say. "His personality changed from polite and solicitous to his true, thuggish self when he didn't find what he came to retrieve."

"And you think he planted evidence?" Utterson asks.

"The coroner in that woman's inquest questioned the police

about missing garments. There were no reasonable explanations given," I say.

"It would not be the first time an overzealous policeman acted in such a manner."

"The police are under terrible pressure to solve these women's murders," I reply.

"Might explain his behaviour towards you, my good man."

I nod as we make our way out of the surgery.

"Do you think the press will get wind of this?" I ask.

"Only if Newcomen walked you in irons out the front door with the evidence in his other hand," he replies. "Or if you wish to publicize the matter yourself. Newcomen's behaviour might cause no small social stir."

I have one more piece of business regarding this matter and need Utterson to be on his way before I pursue it. "Say a prayer of thanksgiving at St. Giles," I reply. I pat him on the back and see him off in his cab. My meeting with the widow Anderson will have to wait for another Sunday.

I scan the square. No police, and no Utterson in sight. The bright sun shines favourably upon me now. I stride quickly round the outside of my home and enter the courtyard from a gated walkway. I lope over to the garden bed below the window where I stood during the search.

In the garden below the window are two boot prints. Someone shimmied out the window and dropped in the soft soil there. The latch on the inside was not caught when I came into the room to air it out. On closer inspection of the outside sill, I spot my missing cufflink glinting in the sunlight. It now makes sense. The dirty boots and the cufflink are clues Hyde left for me. Whatever Newcomen planted in the surgery was removed by Hyde before dawn. I turn to observe the birds flitting about. The flowers reach their petals to the sky, and I relax in the peaceful tranquility of the garden. I allow the calm of this space to envelope me, much like my days on the beach in the islands. I was fooled by Hyde. He allowed me to think I was rid of him, but he appeared like all those times when I was a child crying out for him. He saved me once again. The wretched murderer is my protector once again.

Slowly, a thought crystallizes. Then another and another. I turn them more into a series of questions. What if Newcomen really received an anonymous tip? Who then possesses such intimate knowledge of my surgery? I shake. My legs weaken, and I find myself collapsing on a bench facing a centre circle of bright yellow and orange flowers. Could it be that the murderer planted the clothing near my surgical instruments to make it look like I killed that poor woman? And how did Hyde know to remove them overnight?

13

16 SEPTEMBER 1888

HENRY JEKYLL

"What were the thieves looking for?" George asks as he enters my surgery. He is nattily dressed in a tan summer suit with matching top hat, having changed from his sombre church clothes. We aren't scheduled for lunch, and I wonder why he is here staring at the dismal scene. I am busy putting back the things the constables removed. I do not have an assistant in my practice, and should the need ever arise for me to return to it, I want to be sure where everything is. Where did my surgical instruments disappear to? Do I want to replace them? Would I be happier just making remedies for the women Francine Murphy rescued from the streets? I feel some decisions are made for you. When some doors close, others open.

"My freedom. Scotland Yard is hell-bent on making me into their suspect for all the murders in Whitechapel." I continue putting the twenty years of my profession back in order. My brother is still smarting from the verbal lashing I gave him at the club and he doesn't move a finger to help me.

The sooner the room returns to its previous condition, the

sooner I can go on with my life. The locksmith will be summoned on Monday, and extra locks will be installed on the window and doors, lest I have a repeat of what occurred overnight. "They came here before breakfast looking for evidence of the most recent killing."

"Did they find it?"

"If they had, I would not be standing here chatting with you, younger brother."

"Does this have to do with your friend, Mr. Hyde?" he asks.

The tingling rises again in my chest and restricts my throat. I swallow twice and cough before answering. "The inspector who served the warrant is the same one who accosted me at our club. He thinks so, but Utterson said it best when he told the inspector loudly that the angry man with a stick didn't make him a repeat killer of women."

"Your friend Hyde will be the death of you, I'm afraid," George says. "How is it you never introduced us?"

My brother has heard stories of my friend, Edward Hyde, from our colleagues and associates. I am sure he knows about the murder accusations. What he asks is an impossible feat. I will never discuss my peculiar friend with him or the actual truth about Edward Hyde. I hold this one secret between us, and I have never told a single person how Hyde and I are the same. I came close once by writing a letter to Utterson to keep in his confidence, but I burned it before fleeing the city.

For all the trouble Hyde caused me before my trip to the West Indies, he made up for it last night. But I am vexed by his return. How can I be both exultant and worried that my old friend picked last night to return?

"I took pity on him and tried to help him out, but after that unfortunate event, I severed all ties with him," I answer. "Truth be told, I never was with him in public, nor felt the need to introduce him to you or our associates."

"Strange that I never met him," George persists.

"You and he are from different worlds." How could I ever explain to George how Edward came to be? Could George understand his brother has a dark side, one capable of violent rage and impassioned murder?

I look about at the progress I have made putting everything except the sharps back where they belong. The sharps are nowhere to be found.

"Well, it looks like you have this under control. I am happy for you, brother. Nothing untoward happened here today. Is your cook preparing dinner tonight?"

"Sunday evening is always roast beef," I say. "Six o'clock, sharp."

He floats out of the room to have tea with other church members and make scheduled social visits, as is his custom on Sunday afternoons. George is a creature of habit. He understands his place in society—protected in his favoured position—suffers those who would rail against the status quo, and sees things as black or white, friend or foe, good or bad, with little room for argument. He would despise Hyde, and I pray that no chance meeting between them will happen. It would not fare well for one of the Jekyll brothers.

14

16 SEPTEMBER 1888

HENRY JEKYLL

Hyde did not stay where he was banished, I am sure. There is no mistaking his presence. He has come back to help me, to save my neck. I cannot sit back and wait for the killer to plant evidence again in my home. I don't know how to hunt down a killer, but I know someone who can. Someone more cunning and daring than I. Someone who knows how to travel the darkened streets and alleyways of London without drawing attention to himself. Someone who knows how to handle himself in a street fight. Someone accustomed to the bawdy behaviour in the gin palaces and pubs. I know that person well. I may not be able to answer the questions about Newcomen's integrity, but I can do something about a madman running about Whitechapel.

Before I retire for bed, I lay out Hyde's clothes for his night's travels. Everything is black, of course, and I set out his favourite boots. I sheath the dagger from my desk and also provide him with a flask of water. I count out money, and I place it in his coat pockets. However, he hunts the repeat murderer; I do not care. I do not want to dangle from the hangman's noose. By removing the scalpels and knives, I am sure Hyde disposed of the bloody pieces of clothing from that unfortunate woman as well. The gravity of the failed search warrant weighs like a stone upon my chest, but as the day wears on, I come to respect that my other half's sense of survival is greater than I ever imagined. Newcomen left empty-handed thanks to Hyde, whom Newcomen so desperately wants to arrest.

In the morning, or whenever Hyde allows me use of my body again, I will visit Anderson's widow and find out how to contact Francine Murphy. She knows Whitechapel, and the women targeted by the killer. This will become my quest. Hyde knows all my thoughts, and anything I learn will be helpful to him. By assisting Francine with her mission, I will gather information to assist Hyde in tracking down the man tearing apart prostitutes after midnight.

Are we taking chances by having a murder suspect roam the streets at night? Absolutely, but I trust his survival instincts, the ones that kept me alive and sane all those years ago. He will serve us better. I welcome Hyde back into my life the way I did when I was a child. He will know what to do.

I start my bedtime routine with no sleeping potions. Hyde needs to be alert in the hunt. He could easily leave my bedclothes on as he slips into the outerwear I provided him.

I extinguish the light, slip into bed and stare at the ceiling. Will this work? What can go wrong? Am I asking too much? Sleep will not come easy.

———

17 SEPTEMBER 1888

EDWARD HYDE

Poor Henry! Did he think he could get rid of me so easily? If it wasn't for me biding my time to re-emerge, we would have an appointment with the gallows. While Henry slept, I remained vigilant and thwarted the scheme of making the good doctor a suspected murderer.

Yes, I am a killer. That much is true. Rude, disagreeable, short-tempered and unpleasant are what I have heard Henry's friends call me. Carew recognized me before I killed him. And yes, doing so on a public street in view of witnesses was not the best way to exact my revenge, but I was never known to have good impulse control. Henry created me so he could survive his childhood. He has no memory of the abuse, torment and starvation. When he became a young man, he allowed me to savour all the pleasures that London society forbade. I suffered the pain for him to enjoy all that my senses could take in. Which of us dominated? Why me, of course! He could barely contain my indomitable spirit, as he became more a shell of himself. He is the weaker one. I didn't make up the rules—he did. All that mumbo jumbo in the West Indies? Keeping us locked in our cabin our entire trip across the Atlantic? Bollocks! The only way he could have killed me was by ending his own life. Poor Henry thought he could have it both ways.

So here I am, walking streets I would never visit for any reason, looking for an unknown killer with special tastes and skills, attempting to prevent that beast from placing us at further risk.

I duck into a deep and wide alcove across from a pub. I'm hidden from the street lamps in the darkness. From the brisk business I observe, one would never know some of the festive drinkers have to work in the morning. My thirst for gin was never slaked, and the temptation to empty the flask Henry gave me and fill it to overflowing with that wonderful drink is great. Only a handful of people know me by sight, and probably none of them frequent this part of London. But I can never be too careful. To the best of my knowledge, only a few sketches of me exist from the time I killed that bastard Carew. I am sure Newcomen carries one in his pocket.

Yes, Henry and I are of one mind. Then I correct myself. We have never been of one mind; he created the separation. We are of one purpose again. We will survive and end the threat to our existence. I will find the killer and put an end to this madness. A killer hunting down a killer. I killed Carew, and I would do it again if I could. I would do it a thousand times until I was sure his soul was burning in hell.

The pile of newspapers rustles next to me. There is no wind to speak of. Probably rats. A woman's voice thick with drink echoes from across the street. Her lewd invitation to the man entering the public house is met with derision. She looks in all directions, and, seeing no prospects, enters the pub again. A few seconds later, she is tossed through the door like a bag of cats. Miraculously, she lands on her feet and staggers away, probably in search of a source of money to buy more gin. Pathetic creature. These are the women the killer preys on. I overheard conversations about the man from the public house where no one knows my face. I sat at the end of the bar in semi-darkness furthest away from the doors an hour earlier, nursing a beer, listening.

From the rubbish, emits a whimper. Not a cat, but a dog. I move closer and light a match. I cannot see anything. I hear it again and move the papers aside, and with the last of the flame, I spot it huddled in the corner. A terrier, the kind they use in coal mines and factories to root out rats. I light another match and clear away the debris and rags it is tucked into. Emaciated and covered with sores, black fur hanging on in splotches, its eyes pleading with me in the flame. It is not frothing from the mouth but appears near death. The match goes out before it burns my fingers. Those desperate eyes. What am I supposed to do? I cannot call attention to its plight. Like many things in this part of the city, it has been abandoned and left to its own devices. By the look of things, this dog will die soon. It is not my problem. Let it die. It looks too far gone.

It whimpers again. I want to ignore it, but I can't. It wants me, Edward Hyde, of all people, to help it. My life is difficult, but it did have its moments until I killed Carew.

To say that I am pleasantly helpful is absurd, but something about the hurt animal strikes my core. It was abandoned and left to die. It has done nothing to deserve this fate.

I remove the flask and pour some water into my hand and offer it to the dog. It struggles to move its head but laps the water from my hand greedily. I pour. It drinks. I repeat the process until I empty the flask and the dog stands on shaky legs. It is a boy and reminds me of the dog Henry had as a pet. A dog I could never touch.

I stand, walk into the street lit by a nearby gas lamp, and spot two youths walking in my direction. I raise my hand. They walk warily towards me and stop at a safe distance.

"My religion forbids me from entering a public house. Fetch me a meat pie and a bowl of soup. This is for payment." I fish out coins from my pocket. "And this is for you when you bring it to me." I hold out another coin in the palm of my hand.

The shorter and braver one takes the money from me and tears across the street while the other waits. He looks at me and sizes me up.

"I am a long way from my house and stopped here to rest," I say.

The other boy replies, "Not the best part of town, sir."

"I noticed I was taking a shortcut but got lost." I shrug. I stand under the flickering lights, a wanted man, buying food for a starving dog. When did I care about anything else but myself?

The boy returns with more meat than I can eat, and a steaming bowl of a creamy potato soup. "Here is your change," he says.

"Keep it," I reply.

"Thanks." His eyes widen.

"Here is your reward," I say, "but before you leave me, please bring me a cup of water."

Off he goes again.

The other looks at my food.

"Would you like my bread?" I ask.

He nods.

"We won't say anything to your friend."

He rips off a piece, devours it and stuffs the rest in his pocket.

"Here you are, sir." The other boy returns and holds the cup of water like it is a chalice of wine.

I set down the bowl of soup at my feet and take the cup. "Thank you for your kind service."

They jabber to each other once they are out of earshot.

When did Edward Hyde ever commit a kind act? I return to the alcove and the waiting dog. I set the meat pie down below his snout and he looks at me for permission first. Someone has trained him.

I nod and watch him eat the whole meat pie. By then, the soup is cool enough. A short while later, his tongue swabs the bowl clean. I place the cup of water by the rags and papers and fashion a bed.

"I will come back tomorrow," I promise him. He seems to understand and goes back to his makeshift bed. Before curling up, he licks my hand. I don't mind. It is a kindness returned. I can't remember receiving such appreciation in my entire existence. I rise and know then that Henry the good doctor will help us. I scan the boarded-up windows of the building and the bolted door. I pull an official-looking notice from the letter box and stuff it in my pocket.

———

HENRY Jekyll

I AWAKE with a headache in Edward's clothes, but my boots are set next to the wardrobe this time. I stand up and stretch. Nothing is broken. I gaze in the mirror. I am not bleeding. It is always a good sign after Hyde inhabits my physical being. Next to my wash basin is a piece of paper. It is a foreclosure notice of a property address I do not recognize. Next to it is a cup, bowl, my empty flask, a roll of surgical gauze and a jar of ointment. A pig's ear rests next to my father's cufflinks. A pig's ear?

I remain in these clothes, put on my boots, gather the items in my medical bag, refill the flask, then scoop up my wallet and run down the stairs, past Poole in the hallway. "Not sure when I will be back!" I shout over my shoulder.

I hail a cab at the corner. I forgot my umbrella in my haste on this rainy day, but it does not matter. I am a man on a mission. I have clues to sort out.

"Can you take me there?" I breathlessly ask the cabbie.

"Whitechapel, I suppose. Are you sure?"

"Let's not be tardy," I say.

We move briskly at first and then get bogged down in congestion traversing the old walled City of London before entering Whitechapel, following a steady stream of horse carts and cabs.

He stops abruptly and yells to me, "Here you are. It looks boarded up."

"Thank you. This is fine." I jump down, pay him and off he

goes. Seems he wants to get back to the West End before something bad happens to him in this downtrodden part of town.

"What are we doing here, Edward?" I ask under my breath. I enter the alcove and stare at the building, then turn to face a pub waking up across the street. I whirl around again at the sound of a yelp. From the shadows, a black dog approaches me out of a nest of rags. It is in terrible condition but is wagging its tail. Around its neck is my tie. Thank you, Edward.

I sit cross-legged in the dirty entrance and clean the receptive creature to the best of my ability. I bandage what I can. I give him the pig's ear and refill the cup of water from my flask, all the while realizing that Edward communicated with me. This is a test.

I smile at the terrier, and I swear he smiles back at me.

From the street, I hear, "Doctor Jekyll?"

I look up at a woman holding an umbrella over her head. At first, I don't recognize her until I see her flaming red hair. Francine Murphy cocks her head, a puzzled look on her face.

15

17 SEPTEMBER 1888

HENRY JEKYLL

"A childhood friend of mine told me about this dog," I stammer. "It reminded him of the dog I had when I was young. He said it needed my help." So far, I am being mostly truthful with her. This is a second chance to make things better with her, and I don't want to make her suspicious of my motives by starting off with a string of lies.

"You have friends who come to Whitechapel, Doctor Jekyll?" Her wary eyes search my face while the dog chews happily on his treat in my lap. I instinctively stroke the top of his head, and he makes joyful noises.

"The banker," I say. "The banker who is foreclosing on this business location is my friend and he told me about the building and the dog." A suitable lie she won't be able to check, and one that causes no harm to her. Her umbrella has seen better days, but it keeps her dark green coat, brown dress and brown shoes dry. Her questioning eyes and slight smile tell me she is having trouble believing me.

"The building? What use would you have for a building like this? Especially in Whitechapel?"

"You are right. I came to tend to the dog. The building is his idea. He knows I am always looking for solid investments."

"The dog likes you," she says.

"He needs more care, but I have done what I can today." I unfold my legs and motion her to come out of the rain. "I hoped we could continue our conversation. I could not attend Anderson's funeral or grave yesterday and could not get a message to you. This is most fortunate."

"What is there to talk about? You made yourself very clear."

"I have had time to think about your proposal. You caught me by surprise, and when you said something about my personal business, I became defensive." I wrap the remaining gauze around one hand and then unwind it to wrap it around my other.

"I thought about it too, afterwards, and I may have overstepped your boundaries," she says.

Even on a gloomy day, and wearing Hyde's outfit in a dirty entrance to a shuttered building, this conversation is exactly what I need.

"Tell me of your progress, Mrs. Murphy."

"Call me Francine," she says. Her smiling eyes arrest me.

My heart leaps and I smile. "Francine. Call me Henry. Doctor is too formal."

"Even if your hands are swathed in bandages and you smell of soothing balms?"

"My call to Whitechapel allows us to meet again. So, how are you faring with your mission?"

"Since we talked last, Doc—Henry—I've been evicted, robbed, Louise has moved to assist the widow Anderson, and our two charges have gone back to the street. I do have an appointment with the leader of a women's Bible study in South Hackney, however."

"What can she do for you?" I ask.

"Mary McCreary and I—Mary is the woman who helped me —thought that women with positions in the church may help, outside of the church's strict rules on supporting unsanctioned projects."

"Maybe someone like Henry Jekyll, who has the funds and who questions what a church is supposed to be about?"

"Exactly," she blurts. She looks away when she realizes she has put me on the spot.

"What are we to do about this little dog?" I ask. Lucky he was here to help us change the subject. Lucky would be a good name for him. Damn Lucky would be more appropriate, but Lucky sounds like an excellent compromise.

Without hesitation, she bends down and offers her hand. He stops chewing and sniffs it, then wags his tail. She pets his head, and he offers her his belly.

"He didn't do that for me," I say.

"I would take him if I wasn't being put out on the street," she says. "Maybe thieves would stay away if they heard a dog barking."

I bend down to them and pet him on the head. Being close to her, with our hands a few inches apart, creates an awkward intimacy I am unaccustomed to. We remain in our separate thoughts. I am not sure what she or the dog is thinking, but he looks like he is in heaven on earth. I know what I am thinking. Help the dog, and help Francine help me. Selfish, yes, but not in a bad way.

"How much would it take to reverse the eviction?" I ask.

She stands up and smooths her dress. "I couldn't ask you to do that, Doctor Jekyll." A formality returns to her manner as she blushes.

"You didn't. The dog needs a home. You can use a dog for protection." I look in her eyes, and she holds mine for a beat before looking away.

"I can't accept your charity."

I put everything back in my bag, including the dog's bowl and cup from which he had eaten and drunk. I pick him up and stand out in the rain to hail a cab. I don't look at her. At last, one arrives. Lucky and I turn back to face her. "We can go to my bank, then find your landlord, and afterwards, we can have lunch and talk about your proposal, Mrs. Murphy."

16

23 SEPTEMBER 1888

At midnight, a hansom cab enters Cavendish Square with a man getting out at the corner, while another scrambles in. The new man darts into a doorway but doesn't open the door or light up the entranceway. I take to the roof of Henry's home and watch the same events happen in the rear alley. One man gets out, and another exits a neighbour's horse stalls and jumps into the cab.

This tactic is to be expected. Newcomen is not one to give up trying to arrest Henry or me. I see an immediate benefit to Henry in that if the killer strikes tonight, the watchers will report that Henry never left his abode. There is no news of strange deaths from the previous night. It seems the killer prefers hunting on the Sabbath.

I climb out of the side second-floor window, reach over to the drainpipe and slowly lower myself down. As soon as my boots touch the ground, I realize I do not have a suitable plan for returning. Poole sleeps on this side of the house and will hear the breakage of glass. I have all night to ponder my

101

dilemma. I set off behind the hedges and skirt along the neigh-bours' properties until I reach the far end of the square.

The moon is nearly full and darts between scattered clouds. I remain on the darker sides of the streets leading into Whitechapel. I carry a parcel under my arm. My box is wrapped in paper and secured with twine.

A constable stops me, sizing me up. "It's rather late to be out, sir."

I lift the package up for him to observe. "I am taking reme-dies to my sick family." A fake sneeze in his direction and a heavy cough keeps our conversation short as he backs away from me.

I also carry a pig's ear in my pocket and will leave it outside the red-haired woman's door. Henry met with her twice more, and the dog is recovering nicely. She knows the potential victims and how to approach them. I know how to stay in the shadows while watching them. Since finding this woman again, Henry seems happier than I have seen him in a long time.

In my other pocket, I keep his letter opener for my true purpose of finding the killer and putting an end to his madness. I smile at the thought of being London's unlikeliest detective. I must observe the killer in the act, lest I mistakenly gut a man out on the town searching for his illicit pleasure.

Following a drunken woman and her companion to what might become her final resting place holds little prospect for success. Henry learned on the warmer nights, like this, that several hundred women earn their lodging and drink money this way.

I enter the seediest pubs in Whitechapel, where a heady draft of beer costs more than a generous pour of gin. I watch the women who leave with a man. If she returns without her companion, I make note of her. If she comes back a second time, the call of the drink is greater than the call to find a bed in a dosshouse for the night. I need to keep a keen eye out from the darkest recesses near the drinking establishments.

As the morning wears on, I learn the different alleys and cut throughs, monitoring the four pubs within a rectangle of streets. Henry had left a crude map for me to study. The matches resting on top of it reminded me to destroy it when I was through. X marks the spot of the three murders. All of them occurred within the rectangle of pubs. One pub is across the street from the alcove where I discovered the dog. I stop to rest in the dark.

At that precise moment, a woman lurches into my observation post and vomits on my boots.

"You stupid whore," I say, startling her. She shoots me a fearful look while wiping her mouth with her sleeve. She trips and falls on her backside, then quickly scrambles to her feet and runs towards the pub. When it is safe, I retrace the steps of my route and clean my boots and trouser legs with a discarded newspaper. I don't need her to report my description to the constables as the man who assaulted her. I must learn how to control my tongue. I curse myself. If the killer chooses her tonight, there is not a chance in hell I will follow them into the dark.

I decide then to walk to Henry's friend's flat. It gives me time and distance from the alcove. I find it a short distance outside of the killing zone and discover the front door ajar. I walk up to her rooms and place my gift on the floor outside. The dog smells me or hears me and barks. I hastily retreat down the hall, bounding down the steps and out onto the street.

I run headlong into three ruffians.

"What do we have here?" the largest says.

Another shoves me backwards into the third. "You need to be more careful, mate."

I hold the package in one hand, while my other reaches for the dagger. The man in front of me grabs my arm, now cradling the remedies, and punches me viciously in the kidney. My legs buckle, and I see stars with pain. He pulls the parcel from my weakened grasp.

"Take it. It's all that I have," I gasp. Now it is my time to be sick. It is not the first time I've thrown up one of Henry's dinners. I do so and spray it around me in a circle. They retreat a few steps and give me an opening to flee. If they come for me, I will slice them open like a codfish on a slab.

"What's going on here?" a man's voice yells out of a window from across the street. The toughs look away from me, and I stagger from their trap. I limp at first and painfully take running steps. They continue in the direction they were walking and drop my collection of remedies on the street. I stop and wait at a safe distance until they hastily disappear around a corner. I go back and retrieve my package before heading back towards Henry's home. I swerve like I'm drunk from the pain. I take the most direct route back to Henry's home, making sure I am not being followed. I am sure Henry will wonder why his kidney is badly bruised. In my state, I can't think of a way to communicate how my errand of kindness was met with a single punch that nearly toppled me. Add thugs to the list of people I have to be wary of. I promise myself to spend some daylight hours walking about the killing zone in disguise.

I approach Cavendish Square from the far end of the block. A ladder is needed to reach the window. Each house along Henry's side of the square has a tool shed for the gardeners, but not a ladder is to be found. Henry's nearest neighbour's shed contains a wrought-iron trellis. It is tall enough for me to gain purchase to the second-floor windowsill. I drag it with my remaining strength and lean it against the house. It will be daylight soon. The climb is strenuous, and I balance the toes of my boots on the top arch. My hands are six inches below the window. Do I clamber back down and try a different approach? Instead, I crouch on my toes, the muscles around my kidney in knots, and I cry out in pain, then launch myself upward. First my hands enter the open window, and then my forearms, and finally my elbows come down inside the room. I grunt as I bring my head, shoulders and torso through the window. My legs dangle in the air outside until I can drag myself all the way in.

I hobble through the upstairs hallway to Henry's bed. It is so inviting. Poole will help him with his boots in the morning.

17

23 SEPTEMBER 1888

HENRY JEKYLL

Why is the steamship pitching so badly? The seasickness is worse with my eyes closed. Why can't I open them to make it stop? Coming back to England should be better than the storms we had on the way to the West Indies. One saving grace is that I don't have Hyde to contend with. By my own orders, Colonel Lester from the club kept Hyde and I locked in the cabin until we docked in Jamaica. He watched over me on the voyage. His plan was to take his pension and retire there. He told me one night at the club about those plans, that he was about to leave London. Hyde was out of control and was a wanted man. We were in danger. I could book passage at the last minute on the same boat as Lester.

There were times I swear Hyde wanted to squeeze out of the portal and fall into the ocean. Whether it was seasickness or the potions the witch doctor made me drink, it was not always paradise in paradise.

Why can't I open my eyes? The bile is reaching up into my throat. I am going to vomit.

I sit up in bed, and whatever is in my stomach comes up on my bedsheets. I am in my bedroom in my home and not on the vessel. Then I feel excruciating pain emanating from my left kidney. I fall out of bed fully clothed. I cannot stand up from the dizziness. I crawl to the mirror. I tilt it with my toe and shed my coat and shirts. The ugly purple-and-green bruise extends from my buttocks to my armpit. Is my kidney permanently damaged? Am I bleeding internally? I do my best to self-examine, although I am probably my own worst patient. What would I tell an examining physician? My other self was in Whitechapel last night, so I don't know how this injury occurred. I could say I drank myself into a blackout and don't know how it happened, or that I got into a fight.

This is not the first time Hyde has received injuries and left me guessing. When I was a child, I didn't want to know. He protected me.

I slowly rise to my knees. The room does not stop swirling. I pant like a work animal.

After several minutes, I can stand. I lean on the wash basin and splash water on my face. I try sipping some from a glass. The water burns on the way down my ravaged throat. This is not the first time I have thrown up in the last twelve hours, I surmise.

The throbbing in my kidney is incessant. I slowly strip off my shirt, but for my trousers, I use the dagger to slice them off. I am naked save for my gentleman's boots. I need Poole to assist me taking them off.

On cue, there is a knock on my door. I throw on my bathrobe. I cough and speak with a quiet rasp, "Come in."

Poole looks at me, puzzled. Certainly, he knows I am aware of the order of dressing oneself.

"I've changed my mind about the boots, Poole. Can you help me take them off?"

He does so with difficulty. I keep the bile down and don't let on to my injuries. After placing my boots in the wardrobe's bottom, he says, "Your brother has arrived for breakfast."

"Tell him I will be downstairs momentarily. Just tea and toast with jam for me."

"I understand," he says.

I look at myself in the mirror again and shake my head at the ugly mark I didn't really attempt to hide from Poole.

What have we got ourselves into this time, Edward?

18

26 SEPTEMBER 1888

FRANCINE MURPHY

"Did you know a Doctor Jekyll or his brother, George, when you attended St. Giles in the Fields?"

Lizzy Stride's grey eyes have trouble focusing. Her shoulder length dark brown hair frames a pale face. She is taller than me by a few inches. This is not the first time we talk in Lizzy's favourite alley around the corner from a public house she regularly frequents. The soot and neglect on the factory walls on either side speak of better times long past. She, too, is a long way from her days at St. Giles. She was married to Mr. Stride at the time and managed a coffee shop they owned. In the last eight years, her relationship with the drink won out. Her long black jacket hangs listlessly over her black skirt.

"Hmmm?" She thinks aloud. "Can't say I do."

Mrs. Stride sways, and I take hold of her elbow. The soft, hazy light from the street lamps makes her look sickly. She peers toward the public house. Whatever she made on her transaction with the man who walked out of the alley a few minutes ago, she now wants to spend on gin. The chances of her meeting another gentleman afterwards on a weeknight is slim, and no dosshouse will accept her without payment. It will not be the first night she sleeps in an alcove or backyard. Sadly, women with no money for a dosshouse will gather in horse stalls and make the best of the straw to keep themselves warm. But even then, the women who sell their bodies for their drink are shunned by the sober women, just one rung up on hell's ladder, leaving the worst of the worst to fend for themselves.

I don't let go of her arm. "Save your money, Lizzy. I have a warm bed and a room with a lock on it for you. You just need to tell me you've had enough of all this."

She stares back down the alley where she allowed the man to use her body. The indecision is clear this time. She brushes the gentle persuasions off with less anger than in the past.

I never push. Lizzy knows Louise Anderson from the street and agreed that it was a miracle, but it is unnecessary for her.

Lizzy thinks she is doing just fine. "I have a man and a place to go, thank you very much."

She is not ready to leave the drink. As long as she has that lifeline, she doesn't think she needs to stop drinking. "Then let me walk you home. There is a monster lurking about Whitechapel at this hour of the morning, carving girls up like pigs at the slaughterhouse."

Lizzy pulls away from my steadying grip and bumps into me as she passes. The call of the siren song is too great. She's not motivated to leave her personal hell.

"I am not ready to go home, thank you very much," she says over her shoulder.

I watch Lizzy zigzag to the street and her destination. She is not being obstinate, nor prideful. The alcohol has a hold on her, that's all. I know that firsthand. Mary McCreary walked me out of my personal hell on earth. I also know I can't have a drop of the devil's drink, or I will spiral down again into the abyss. Subconsciously, most of these women know gin will eventually kill them, but the fear of what they will feel about themselves in sobriety is worse. First, they consider everything they lost and then they think about what they have to do to survive. Some steal, others trade on their bodies. Some men use them roughly. Black eyes and bruises are not unusual. Broken limbs and scarring are part of life on the streets. It's no wonder they throw themselves under carriages, in front of trains or into the Thames. In my time working with them, I understand violence done to them by others or by themselves is a daily occurrence. I listen carefully to the stories of who has died or was hospitalized each night I go out. I use those stories to help those at their most hopeless time. But can I keep them from falling one last time. There is something else now to talk to them about. This madman is butchering the most vulnerable. As the women go out every night, they judge whether they are stronger or weaker than the others. They know this from the last time they bathed or slept in a bed. From the holes in their shoes and the tattered clothes they wear. Lizzy knows the score and is ignoring the warning signs.

Once, a few months ago, Lizzy confided in me she birthed a stillborn and that it took some of the life out of her. In sharing confidences, I told her I had miscarried, and it was one thing that caused me to drink more. I wonder, if either baby had lived, would we be on the streets tonight? I doubt my life would have gone the way it did. With a baby in the house, I may have thought more of the baby's welfare than my thirst. I know countless women on the street who lost their families to the lure of gin. Everyone has their story, and I am not one to judge. Only they will know when they are ready to walk away from life on the streets.

I continue further into the darkness of the alley. Maybe I should heed my advice. The killer will not care if I'm drunk or sober at this hour.

The evening is not cold, and I am properly dressed, but a

shiver runs through me. Thanks to Henry, I have a home to return to. His money and his lawyer helped Mr. Withers rescind the eviction notice. The good doctor paid my arrears and an advance through to next year. I signed a promissory note for the exact amount with my benefactor as part of their deal. I will pay him back.

Withers was ecstatic with the windfall and agreed to change the locks with the promise I would control the only keys.

I also have a companion waiting for me at home. The kind that wags its tail regardless of what time it is. The name Lucky has stuck, and he responds to it. He's still thin, but his fur is growing back. He is getting healthier every day. Henry will not confirm or deny he was the one who left a present for Lucky on my doorstep a few nights ago. He said he might have been sleepwalking and laughed. It was the first time I have heard him laugh.

There is a deep hurt inside that man. He protects his privacy. I learned that the hard way the first time we met. Since the day I found him caring for an abandoned dog in a part of town he'd never visited before, I don't question his interest in Lucky, my mission, or me. He shows a genuine interest in my work on his visits to change the dog's dressings after applying more ointments. I know very little of him, but I am not reticent in telling him how I can convince those, almost too far gone, to try again one more time. He shows an interest in me as well. It feels different from the way other men approach me. He genuinely cares for my welfare and makes no demands on me other than to accept his loan in the spirit it was offered.

I come out on the next street in time to see several British sailors stop under a street lamp. They are deciding where to go next when one spots me.

"Hullo there, missy." He is shorter than me, thin-waisted, with wide shoulders and a wide smile. His blue serge uniform top accentuates his muscular build. His mates and drink give him the courage to approach me. The others take notice and encircle me.

This is only my second trip out after midnight without Louise since Mr. Anderson died. Immediately, I realize they mistake me for a lady of the evening. I need to think of something fast.

———

EDWARD HYDE

From the darkness of the alley, I hear Mrs. Murphy's conversation with the woman she calls Lizzy. I determine to follow this Lizzy until daylight. The killer will find her an easy mark. This will give me a chance to find the best spots to hide as she staggers about Whitechapel.

As a wanted man, I have to be careful not to attract too much attention. I should have rested until the weekend when he normally strikes, but I need to become familiar with the area if I am going to keep my eyes on the worse of the worst. My kidney still aches, and the muscles surrounding it tighten as the hours wear on. Henry provided me with a ladder after the gardener found the trellis leaning against the house with the second-floor window wide open. I had stopped Henry's watch at straight up twelve and left it on the inside windowsill facing the mansion on Cavendish Square where the police lurk overnight. I left a chisel on the second-floor window pointing at the neighbour's horse stall. He did not retire the next two nights until after midnight, so I know he got my message. He is now aware of Newcomen's boys monitoring his doorways.

My plan is simple. Mrs. Murphy knows the women by name and by sight. She knows their habits, where they take the men to service them, and how late they will stay out to ply their trade. She does not stray outside the rectangle where the deaths occurred.

Follow Mrs. Murphy to the women she is trying to help. Memorize their faces and mannerisms to spot them on the nights she is not searching for them and watch them leave their regular public houses or gin palaces. I am learning the times and routes of the constables on foot patrol. Watchmen rarely stray from their rounds as they try to stay warm and dry. Their primary function is to keep out thieves and loungers from the properties they are paid to protect. They will occasionally meet with the men in uniform on their appointed rounds and share warm tea and biscuits to relieve the boredom.

"Take your hands off me, you limey bastard!" Mrs. Murphy yells. She is surrounded by British sailors. I snake along in the shadows and acquire a suitable piece of wood as I make my way to the intersection. The dagger is too permanent.

She pushes one forcefully into the middle of the street and follows him. The others stand frozen, staring slack-jawed at this mad Irishwoman. "I will be at your ship tomorrow to report your disrespectful behaviour to your captain. How dare you suggest I go anywhere with you to do those sinful acts? I am doing God's work here. Be off with you now." She whirls to focus her anger at the one nearest to her. He backs away. "Don't you get any ideas either, mister." He trips backwards over his own feet and falls on the street. He will have some explaining to do if he returns to his ship smelling like horse droppings.

I duck deeper into the shadows and hide the piece of wood behind me, just in case, but it looks like Mrs. Murphy is on the offensive and she vents her anger at the sailor nearest to her.

"Leave now or I will report you all!" she shouts. Once more she locates the first offender and loosens a stone from the street. She takes one step forward and flings it like she is skipping flat stones on the pond, and it strikes the sailor in the groin.

He drops to the ground, writhing in pain, while the others retreat whence they came. "I'm sorry, miss. I didn't know. I promise never to talk like that again." He holds an arm above his head, shielding himself from another attack.

Mrs. Murphy says, "Be off with you now, before I lose my temper."

He finally staggers to his feet and limps toward his mates, who are laughing at him.

I smile. Henry's friend has some spirit in her. She makes me look like a choirboy.

19

27 SEPTEMBER 1888

HENRY JEKYLL

Poole's hearing is not what it used to be. The house is so large, I cannot expect him to hear someone entering from the furthest side away from his room. Since the intrusion into my home by someone wishing to plant evidence of a murder, I have been out of my dwelling only to meet Francine Murphy. Tonight, however, I have made plans to go to the club for dinner and cards with my brother and friends. I meet my newly hired watchman at my front door and take him to my surgery. I set him up with food and drink and tell him I will return by ten. It is a good idea to not leave my premises unattended, if Newcomen or the killer want me to swing from a noose for the Whitechapel murders.

I walk to Gladstone's gentlemen's club, past the undercover constable lounging in the entranceway across from my front door. I pretend not to notice him. The evening sun illuminates the usually darkened space, and he hides deeper in a corner to avoid my eyes. The weather lends itself to a brisk walk, and I need to exercise after a few days of recuperating from the badly bruised kidney.

Newcomen's men watch my comings and goings and know when I am not home. What better time to slip in after dark to do his bidding. I cannot take the chance of a repeat of the previous Sunday morning's surprise.

By establishing a visible daily routine, less suspicion will arise about Edward's nocturnal forays through the second-floor window on the side of the house. I did not let on to anyone about knowing of the men watching my home from their fixed posts. They will establish my alibi on the night the killer strikes. Every day, I hope he has stopped or has been arrested, but I have to act cautiously in lieu of knowing the truth.

Today's newspapers carry the coroner's summation of the facts surrounding the murder from almost three weeks earlier. Timelines, the police version, and witness statements all concluded that a vicious murder by an unknown suspect took place. The police have no actual suspects. Each murder points to different men and different theories.

Francine rails about how each coroner's inquest dealt with the facts of only the death under investigation. She points out that all the murders occurred near each other, each involving a woman selling her body for gin after dark, with each murder becoming more heinous. She flatly states that it is the work of one man who is not related to each of the women: maybe one, but not all. I point out that the police, to my knowledge, have never been presented with such a ghoulish set of circumstances these six weeks since the first killing. I agree with her when she says the coroner does not want to accept that each case might bear the others. I nod in agreement more than once that the inquests have to take in the totality of circumstance, not just the death in question. She tells me she is a familiar face at the inquests and has attended most of them. She can see the patterns and wonders if the inspectors testifying at each inquest compare notes with the inspectors working the other cases.

I tell her about my run-ins with Inspector Newcomen, but I could not do so without telling her about my 'associate' Mr. Hyde.

I have planned with Utterson that, should I be arrested or die, Francine will receive all the contents of one account I have set aside just for her. I want her mission to succeed with or without me. I have not told her about the account for my own personal reasons.

Being mostly open about the police fascination with Mr. Hyde and myself makes it easier for her to talk plainly about her thoughts on the murders. She tells me of how the constables walking about overnight have a set pattern concentrated on protecting property. Their dealings with the women run the spectrum from harassment to demanding sexual favours. The dead women had often complained of rough handling and false arrests. All the women believed that making a complaint to a superior officer would fall on deaf ears. Who would a magistrate believe, a prostitute or a policeman? In their time on the street, they learned to avoid the police and distrust the men in uniform. Nothing has changed in these relationships since the first murder was reported. When a class of victim is so obvious, they are still treated with disdain by all except the pub owners, dosshouse managers, and the flocks of men who come to Whitechapel every night of the week seeking their companionship.

Those streets differ from those surrounding my home. I walk to my club on well-kept pavements lined with fine mansions and the best shops and services catering to the wealthy. Couples or families on a stroll wear fine clothes and chat amiably with their neighbours. Pleasantries and greetings are the norm as the leisure class make the most of an unseasonably warm and dry autumn evening. There are plenty of hansom cabs to take one anywhere in the city. But as night falls in the rougher parts of town, the cabbies disappear.

I enter the building by the front door and enquire if my dinner companions have arrived. I also ask if there are any policemen about. As a member of good standing, I do not have to say much, other than I don't want to be disturbed under any circumstances. I also make arrangements for a runner to be dispatched to Utterson should the need arise. I feel violated by Newcomen. I have never felt the need to feel protected from others in my home or my club before. What is surprising is the need to be protected from the police. I need to thank Edward, and a maniac on the loose, for that. The former is my creation—the latter is not.

After greeting my dinner companions, the conversation turns to the recent events at my home. I groan inwardly.

"George was just telling us about your adventures with the police," Sutton says.

"You almost met two of them the other night when they had me barricaded in the bathroom the last time we dined here," I say.

His eyes widen. "That's why the door wouldn't budge."

"They think my former associate is responsible for the Whitechapel murders," I say.

"Never liked the man, the few times I saw him about town. Rough-hewn and vulgar. I dared not say a word to him lest I felt the wrath of his anger," Blackwell says.

"So, you've told me."

"George said they suspect you of the killings," Sutton says between sips of his martini. The man holds his liquor well, although I wouldn't want his liver.

I gave my brother a shake of my head. "Me, and every other surgeon, barber, horse slaughterer and lunatic in London." I motion to Sanders for my usual. "When they didn't find what they were looking for, they left in a huff. I am not sure they are done with me. The inspector looking for Hyde is a determined man and thinks he can kill two birds with one stone, so to speak."

"What were they looking for?" Sutton asks. He is nosier than the others. He has very little conflict in his pampered life and feeds off scandal, news of dalliances and business intrigue more than the olives in his martinis.

Sanders hands me my drink. I taste it and approve. "The last victim's bloody clothes and the instruments used to cut her up."

George smirks. "Can either of you imagine Henry butchering a prostitute and bringing home a souvenir of the event?" My brother is in a rare mood. He's itching for a fight, and I am tired.

Blackwell says, "That's preposterous. But what about your missing instruments?"

I shrug off his comment. "I was away for two years. I did not inventory my surgery upon my return. I was not sure I would return to my practice. How many people had access to my house while I was away?"

We all drink on that statement. George must have told them about the missing tools of my trade, but I don't recall discussing what was missing with my brother that morning. I could blame it on the headache worsening as I cleaned the surgery, putting everything away. Newcomen never commented to either Utterson or me about them being missing, either.

"True, you did leave in an awful hurry and never planned with me or your man about how to care for the house and your belongings," George says. "Anyone could have got their hands on them and sold them for a nice sum."

I know the truth—that the missing blades were in the surgery upon my return from the West Indies and Hyde disposed of them with only minutes to spare that morning. I glance about at the others busy with their drinks, but George looks directly at me for an answer.

"Someday I may discuss those events with you, younger brother, but for the time being, suffice to say, I have returned for good. I am happy to be back in London."

I see our food is about to be served. I set down my drink and unfurl my napkin, tucking it into my shirt. I want to change the subject and enjoy the excellent food and good fellowship.

"Sanders, may we have another round of drinks?" Sutton asks.

Blackwell points his fork at George's plate. "Your meat is bloodier than usual."

George keeps his eyes on me, most likely silently cursing my rebuff. "So it is."

Blackwell says, "Henry, for your sake, I hope that your associate Hyde is gone from London. This inspector seems hell-bent on making your life miserable."

"Well said, my friend. I cannot change the fact Hyde killed Carew in a mad rage, but for Newcomen to connect me to the goings-on in Whitechapel is still a mystery to me," I reply.

Sutton is too busy with his food to comment. I can tell George is trying to fashion a remark to upset me and I change the subject. "Remember when we would argue about politics? I miss those days." I stab my steak and savour the taste. I smile and make eye contact with the others. "I missed good meat when I was on the islands. Some tastes die hard."

George nods and cuts into his.

"Hear, hear," Sutton offers a toast.

2O

---

27 SEPTEMBER 1888

EDWARD HYDE

The church bells of Whitechapel announce it is midnight. I watch the busiest pub for any of the women Francine Murphy is trying to assist. Foot traffic is still brisk, but carriages and work carts are almost nonexistent. One of the latter blocks my view of the entrance.

The cart horse falters—maybe because of the load, the time of night, or its age. I am not sure. It falls to its back haunches. It is an older grey mare with a tangled and matted mane.

"Get up!" the driver yells. "Get up, I say!" He yanks on the reins, pulling the bit back at an awful angle. "Move, you worthless nag."

The miserable creature is exhausted. From my spot in the shadows, I watch as the driver draws a whip from behind the seat. He strides to the front of the animal and waves the whip. The horse offers one of its flanks for the beating.

A constable could be just around the corner. Newcomen could be out tonight for all I know. Dare I show my face?

He draws back the whip and places a savage blow on her left

rear leg. I cannot see the flesh, but from experience know that an abuser always strikes the most sensitive spots. The horse turns her head away.

"Get up." He draws the whip back again and brings it forward. Until I pull his legs out from under him in the middle of the road. I am on his back and press his cheek into the day's build-up of manure, with my blade against his other cheek. "Strike the animal again, and I will hamstring you." I move the blade to the back of his right leg and prick him. He flinches. His bowler hat lies on the ground in front of his head. The smell of alcohol on his breath wafts up from his whiskered face. He is older than me and is no match.

"Maybe I should take the whip to you? Would you like that?" I allow him to shake his head. "Let her rest. Fetch her water and feed. I will be nearby where you can't see me. The horse will finish her work tonight when she is able, and you will retire her safely. I will know if you sell her to the slaughterhouse. Have I made myself clear?"

At that moment, the horse turns her gaze to me. Until I helped the starving dog, animals feared me. I see an equine sense of hopelessness in the way she was prepared to take her beating. I know that feeling all too well. I know what it feels like to be a wounded and defenceless animal with no one to come to my aid. We are kindred spirits in this moment under the flickering streetlights. I have risked being found out by the authorities for this poor creature nearing the end of her life.

I prick the driver's other leg with my dagger for emphasis. No other persons approach us during our brief encounter. I retreat to my shadowy lair before he can look backwards. He does as I have instructed, bringing no one forward to search for me. I am correct. The horse needed a breather and some water. She slowly munches on the hay, probably aware that I am still nearby. She finally stands on stronger legs and resumes her work. The driver scans about for me but does not use the whip again on this street.

It was the right thing for me to do. I have helped a starving dog, watched out for Mrs. Murphy, and now I have helped a horse, all the while knowing I am wanted for a vicious beating in which I murdered a man.

These trips into Whitechapel to find and stop a killer become more dangerous when I take these chances. Also, people are taking better precautions. Women are walking in pairs, and men accompany their daughters and wives on their travels to and from honest work. The police have increased their presence. I can't take back my outraged encounter with Carew, let alone explain why I slayed him, to anyone, not even Henry. But I realize it has placed us in mortal danger, and if I had to do it all over again, I would wait until there were no witnesses. Carew deserved to die, but my impulsive behaviour placed us in this predicament. Would Newcomen ever care about the activities of a well-respected doctor in the fashionable part of town, had I not struck down that evil bastard Carew?

This type of reflection is new to me. Helping vulnerable animals is unheard of for me. Caring about somebody who Henry cared for is completely out of character for me.

Even though Henry no longer needed me as he reached adulthood, he allowed me to surface when the situations he was unprepared for arose. By not suffering the physical abuse, closeting, and starvation, he had no coping skills for the other unpleasantries facing a well-to-do, well-heeled gentleman. He also summoned me to live out all the vices tempting a wealthy Londoner. What was my upbringing? A horrid childhood, no education and an adult life of pernicious proclivities. I doubt anyone else in my boots would have acted differently when I encountered Carew on the street. Little does that help Henry with Newcomen. He has no memory whatsoever of Sir Danvers Carew, and Utterson could not offer any defence on our part without me risking showering a flood of repressed remembrances back on Henry's psyche. That flood, like many floods, could drown him, coming at him like a torrent of filthy debris-strewn water from a broken dam.

I know the sting of the whip and would not let the driver strike the mare again. And that faithful dog, abandoned and starving, reminded me of the hollowness in my stomach I had endured for Henry's sake.

Henry's feelings for Mrs. Murphy and her reactions to him are things I have not seen in our shared time on this earth. This business of finding the killer and ending his reign of terror carries a greater significance than I think Henry, or I, can imagine, but part of that equation is my return to the physical realm and the risk of my actions killing us. I have to be more careful.

My purpose is to remain in the shadows and wait for the wolf to stalk one of Mrs. Murphy's lost black sheep.

21

28 SEPTEMBER 1888

FRANCINE MURPHY

"This is my first visit to this home since my return," Henry says.

I watch as he struggles with the lock. The door is massive and scarred. The entranceway serves overnight loungers by the pungent smell of it. There are no windows fronting the street. This residence in Soho, seedy even by Whitechapel standards, is a half-hour walk west on the northern side of the Thames, from the women I assist.

Finally, the lock budges, and we are met by an even greater stench matched by the gloom of an unlit foyer.

"Wait here," he says.

I hear his footsteps fade as he makes his way inside. The area around the building bustles with shops, horse carts and foot traffic. Children run about the narrow streets, darting from house to house. Midmorning drizzle has given way to low clouds, and there is no sign of the sun on this humid afternoon.

He comes back, shaking his head. "The back door has been

forced open. All the furnishings have been stolen or destroyed. I shudder to think who has occupied it these last couple of years. I am sorry to have wasted your time." He closes and locks the door. "I am afraid this won't meet your immediate needs for your mission."

He hails the next cab, and we make our way back to Whitechapel. "This is too far to walk for me to minister effectively to them," I say. "I meet them at their lowest point, at a time of morning when a cab is not to be found anywhere in Whitechapel, except by the train station. Do you remember the building where I met you that morning when you were bandaging Lucky?"

"Yes."

"That would make a fine central location to take them."

He nods. I can tell he is preoccupied with other thoughts.

"Who lived there?" I ask.

"Where?" he says distractedly.

"The house we just visited."

His internal debate shows in the way his head bobs from left to right a few times. I am afraid I may have overstepped my bounds again as I watch him debate how to answer me.

"It was the associate of mine, Mr. Hyde. He was having a difficult time and needed a place to stay. He disappeared when I departed for my two-year trip to the West Indies. I shouldn't have been surprised at the conditions we found." He pauses. "You are right, it is too far from where you operate. Since I own it, I thought it might do in a pinch. I am sorry."

I change the subject. "The time needed to help each woman depends on how deeply the gin has taken over them. Once they are rid of that very physical straitjacket, we have to find out what drove them to those depths of despair."

"And?"

"Returning to husbands and children may not be possible.

Lost employment is another bridge that gin burned behind them as well. Only rebuilding their confidence to move forward is possible. They become a new person. Now, in Louise's situation, she could foster a better relationship with her brother's widow only after months of resisting the bottle. A new Louise emerged from the ashes of her previous life."

"How did your meeting go Wednesday night?" he asks.

I shudder at the memory and debate how much to tell him. "Mrs. Mercer's Bible study group treated Louise like a laboratory specimen. Once a prostitute, always a prostitute. None of them has lost anyone to gin, so they did not know the struggle involved to climb out of a personal hell. None of them has faced any of the adversity she has. After we left, Louise told me she needed to take a bath to remove the slimy film from the looks they cast upon her."

Henry shakes his head. "Money can hide many problems. Many of the men at my club would start suffering from the shakes and tremors immediately if they were cut off from their drink. They talk about mothers and aunts who drink secretly or who are medicated for non-existent maladies. They have maids and butlers to coddle them from their waking until they pass out at night."

"It is not just a curse of the working class," I say. "The upper class can hide better behind their well-maintained facades. The prim and proper church women would be sympathetic to the problems of one of their own, severe alcoholism and prostitution notwithstanding. Charity for a woman like Louise before she turned her life around is not in their make-up, I'm afraid."

I realize I have tested out Mary McCreary's idea and learned a valuable lesson. "Someone in their life needs to go to hell and come back before they can appreciate the journey of a loved one, as Michael Anderson did with his sister before he died." Anderson finding someone like Doctor Jekyll is exactly what I needed. And here I am, seated in a hansom next to a benefactor who is considering making my mission a reality. But I feel there is more to this meeting with Henry Jekyll, for both of us.

We walk upstairs to my flat to check on Lucky.

———

HENRY JEKYLL

I find this woman utterly amazing. The fierceness of her devotion to her cause is stunning. She paints the pictures of the destitution from prostitution fueled by alcoholism with bold strokes of red and black. There are no shortcuts out of hell for these women selling their bodies to pay for their drink. To listen to Francine talk about the struggles they had, her setbacks with the women, and finding funding for her project, it all leaves me feeling shallow and vain in my usual selfish preoccupations. Since my return to London, I have the need for Newcomen and the killer of the prostitutes to be neutralized. Is it terrible that, when I departed the islands, I wanted to tend to my health and wealth, and nightly carefree chatter at the club? No Newcomen and no killer running amuck will give Hyde little reason to manifest himself, and I can be worry-free again.

But something new is stirring my feelings as never before. I can pursue a relationship with this intriguing woman. Thoughts of her captivate my waking hours, and a few randy dreams I dare say.

I feel I made a poor decision, not telling her more about Hyde. Any relationship, whether business, personal or romantic, is based upon trust. But to tell her about how Edward was created in my childhood is not possible, especially now he has resurfaced. During my adult years, I had many opportunities to tell my closest friends about this improbability, that two personalities could inhabit one body, but I resisted. The doctors and scientists would want to put me under their microscope and dissect me like a frog, and any thought of offering my friends those explanations evaporated like mist on the Thames when Hyde killed that man. I was not a murderer, but in the eyes of the law, my hands were on the walking stick that beat that man to death. There is much I don't know about my early years, and none from that fateful night. Would a jury be sympathetic to me, when it was Hyde who understood my past and killed that man? I go around and around on that question. If I sit down with Utterson, will he understand why no one has ever seen me in Hyde's company, or how Hyde could so easily obtain my walking stick? The more I thought about Hyde committing murder, the more desperate for a solution I became. I even contemplated ending this misery by committing death by suicide.

By chance, I learned of my club member's travel to the West Indies at the same time the medical journals published stories about the unscientific and unsubstantiated success of some witch doctors renowned for banishing spirits, and even Lucifer himself, from those afflicted by possession. The native spiritualists lived on the islands where he was looking to retire. That is when it seemed my stars aligned, and for the first time, I felt hopeful.

The rigorous course of treatments, unheard of by my esteemed medical professors, vanquished Hyde, but he reappeared when my survival was at stake.

As we ride to Whitechapel from Soho, I am certain that telling Francine any of this would drive her from my life.

Hyde and I are on our own mission, and whereas he cannot be seen with Francine and learn firsthand about the women she is looking to snatch from the depths of Hades, I can. Do I enjoy my time with Francine Murphy under the pretence of funding her mission? Do I probe her about her work so that Hyde can be guided in his nocturnal forays into Whitechapel? Dare I tell her about any of these motives? Helping her with her mission serves my need to survive and stay close to this remarkable woman, who stirs feelings of an unknown origin in me. Regardless of my reasons, I am drawn to her like a moth to a flame, and I am convinced that her travels in Whitechapel will lead Hyde to the killer.

22

29 SEPTEMBER 1888

FRANCINE MURPHY

I watched Lizzy stagger down her favourite alley with two men. Each had her by an arm. One man has returned; the other has not. Maybe I can convince her to quit for the night. Use the money from the one to pay for her last drink and the other for her bed at the Flower and Dean Street dosshouse. I will not talk to Lizzy about anything else of importance until her lodging is secured. Sometimes, all I can offer is a shoulder to lean on, literally. I recall Louise finally stopped offering sex for money after I found her in the gutter, beaten and violated with no memory of the assault.

The other man finally emerges from the alley, muttering to himself as he fastens his trousers and belt. He walks toward the first.

I make my way down the darkened passage. I stop midway to the next street and glance down to my left for no reason, where I see Lizzy's legs protruding from behind a dustbin. There is no blood anywhere. Lizzy's legs are splayed open, with her undergarments tossed to the side. She is snoring. I resume breathing.

Laughter and the faint sounds of piano and pipes echo down the narrow passage. Water drips in a steady beat from a nearby rooftop with a splat on the pavement. The cooling night's dew settles on every surface top. The alley is wide enough for a horse cart. Their wheel ruts are filled with urine and manure. All of it creates a dull green, slimy shine underfoot.

Lizzy's parlour slippers are torn and barely cling to her feet. Dust and other matter are caked on her stockings, and her kneecaps are darkened from previous scarring. She is unshaven, and her pubic hair is matted with the dried fluids from her patrons. Her unwashed bodice and corset are no longer white but bear yellow and brown stains from sweat and daily use. Her long black cloth coat, fur-lined on the bottom, serves as a blanket to keep her body from touching the hard slick pavement. Lizzy's black bonnet is in reach. Her expression is slack-jawed. Lizzy has no teeth on her lower left jaw, giving her mouth a slanted opening.

I have never asked her age, but I know she has come from Sweden and still receives some help from the nearest Swedish church. Lizzy has clung stubbornly to the belief that, as long as she can return to her boyfriend's home, she is not without means. Maybe it will be different this time. How low can a woman sink before admitting she needs help? I have observed many women lose all their self-worth while deeply intoxicated, performing horrible acts to pay for alcohol addiction. It can go on for days until some violence interrupts the downward spin. Lizzy is swirling around the drain, and something has to change. Here she reposes on newspapers and discarded rags amongst the rats and mice waiting to nibble on her extremities. She sleeps unaware of the madman running about Whitechapel with a sharp knife. If I can wait for Lizzy to finish her business at this spot, so can the killer.

The clip-clop of a horse nearby lends a rhythm to the moment as it competes with Lizzy's hoarse snoring. A wilted rose bobs on her lapel with each intake of sweet air. It is believed the killer strangles his victims first before gutting them. He wouldn't even have to wake her.

"Lizzy, wake up." I shake Lizzy's left leg. "Wake up."

No response. I reach towards Lizzy's left little finger and pull it. "Lizzy."

I shake her right arm more vigorously, then drop it on the ground like a dead fish. I debate standing guard until daylight and securing the services of another woman to assist me in getting Lizzy up. Instead, I reach for the rose, and, more importantly, for the pin attaching it to Lizzy's coat. I can't leave her here, and there are no passersby at this darkest hour before the dawn. I loosen a slipper from Lizzy's foot. What choice do I have?

"Lizzy!" I bark. I violently shake the barely conscious woman's legs. "Lizzy, wake up!" I shout and try pulling her arms to move her into a seated position, holding them to keep her from falling back on her head as she collapses.

I grip the pin in my grasp. The water splatters, and Lizzy snores. I wipe the pin with my sleeve.

I whisper a prayer under my breath; then I jab the sole of Lizzy's foot.

23

29 SEPTEMBER 1888

THE WHITECHAPEL MURDERER

Gold-coloured wall sconces and chandeliers hold luminous candles which brighten an otherwise damp evening. The pale cream plaster walls contrast with the burgundy drapery and the perfectly polished hardwood floors to give the hall a regal feel. I cannot remember a charity event for which I paid a labourer's monthly wage, but it is all part of the swirl of the London Season. The tinkling of fine silver on good china serves as the background to gay conversation and occasional laughter. As is the custom of the season, a schedule of contrived social gatherings allows young women and their suitors the pretext of coming together. Appetizers from all over the British Empire roll out of the kitchen on carts.

Some appetizer plates, enough to feed a small family, sit vexingly untouched in front of many nervous young ladies,who are smart enough to realize their corsets will constrict their breathing if they eat another bite. Passing out or turning blue is not acceptable during these intense competitions for eligible suitors.

The quail and vegetables are served by spotlessly clothed attendants. Water and wine glasses never go unfilled for long.

The men wear their finest suits tailored from Italy, while the women are donned in the latest Parisian fashions. All the colours of the peacock are on display, with the males doing their best to puff out their chests and offer witty asides in a practiced banter as the young ladies titter at their ribald commentary.

I sit across the table and to Lady Jane's left. Every time she cuts her food into smaller and smaller bits or takes a delicate sip, I look into the cleavage of her pearl white bosom. I am sure the furtive glances by the other men seated across from her are also timed to her taking nourishment. I enjoy listening and ogling, while waves of excitement course through my loins as I think about my impending nocturnal adventures in Whitechapel. This is not the first time I will leave an event for those environs. I decide I can have both, the life of a gentleman of the West End and the taking of exquisite pleasure in the terror I bring to the vile creatures a short stroll away to the east. Two personages, working in harmony, producing leisure in society by day and the excitement of the hunt by night.

Lady Jane and her coterie invite a phalanx of eligible men to accompany them for an evening of chamber music after the banquet. My sturdy umbrella and sinewy arm around her waist supply her with dry comfort and assurance of safe footing to the concert. The music takes me to musing of my adventures around the world.

Daytime visits to inspect land holdings and dinner meetings with business partners gave me the pretense I needed for my nighttime excursions. The travel by ship or rail across seas and continents provided the opportunities to see the world.

Being the perfect gentleman, I walk her arm in arm to her family's town residence and bid her goodnight with a soft kiss on her hand. I will soon tell her of my intentions to marry her, but I need to get my financial affairs in order first.

In my present state, I appear a mere pauper to her family's wealth and position. I desire a few more zeroes in my bank accounts. I assure myself the right situation to increase my holdings tenfold will present itself soon.

My urges have mounted all week. With each titillating and sordid account of my actions in the newspapers, my zeal heightens. I have chuckled over breakfast many mornings as I read of the wild and varying descriptions of the Whitechapel murderer. None of the accounts come close to the actual truth. Still, I dress for a night on the town and keep the brim of my hat low and my collar high. Wind and intermittent showers keep the pedestrian traffic light in the West End, but that is not the case as I enter Whitechapel from the old walled City of London.

The public is becoming increasingly tired of the ineptitude of the police. They call for various resignations of officials failing to put an end to the horror.

My desire is fueled by the frenzy. Every overheard conversation includes some reference to the terrible business on the streets I tread. So much speculation surrounds the gruesome dissections, the details of how internal organs were staged outside of the body. The press is starved for stories as they regurgitate much of what has already been reported. A fear settles like a thick fog over the world's most populated city.

On the other hand, even the windswept rain cannot dampen the peddling of gin and flesh in Whitechapel. Both are in ample supply tonight. With three murders in such proximity to each other, all occurring after midnight, one would think a curfew would be in place. The public houses and gin palaces probably bribe their way to a hands-off approach by the elected officials. This is understandable for any of the cities of the world. There are rules for those that have, and different rules for those that have not. Yet this simple deterrence of a curfew provides a simple solution.

What infuriates me even more is the local citizenry drinking intemperately and whoring in public. Where are the church leaders of all the city's houses of worship? Why are they not shaming all those who engage in this disgusting behaviour? At least they could drive it indoors. Instead, a constable tips his cap and winks at me. The women's proposals become lewder and saucier as I walk deeper into my hunting grounds. Each watering hole where my prey drinks gives me plenty of choices. It won't be long now before gin renders a few easy to take down and feast on. I am like the lion watching from the bush, waiting for the lame wildebeest to separate from the herd.

24

29 SEPTEMBER 1888

HENRY JEKYLL

Francine and I return to her flat after a sumptuous meal and long discussion of her mission. We are greeted by Lucky, his tail wagging. After I take him to the yard to do his business, I inspect his skin. He still has a few stubborn spots for me to clean and bandage, but he is a far different animal from the one Edward found. We sit with him between us on her love seat. He is her dog now. I still earn a few licks on my hands, but those two share a special bond. The dog alerts her to persons outside her door, or tramping up or down the stairs, and because of such diligence, he earns his keep. What was a weak whimpering yelp a few weeks earlier has developed into a loud bark and menacing growl.

Francine disappears to her room to change into more suitable attire for patrolling the streets. I offered to help her in her noble efforts after she recounted the difficulty she had steering Lizzy Stride to the dosshouse before dawn. I can't help but admire her resolute purpose and singular drive to assist these women in their climb out of the pits of despair.

The newspapers report an increase of patrols in Whitechapel this weekend. It explains why Newcomen's men are no longer shadows around my residence. If they decide to follow us regardless, I will be in the company of Francine Murphy all the time. It is safer for both of us, anyway. Poole and the watchman will remain on guard, lest we experience another burglary where items are added to my surgery rather than removed.

Francine returns to the parlour, and I dare not tell her how beautiful she looks. I rise, but a terrible nausea drives me to collapse backwards in a heap. I stare at a blackened crack in the floorboard to keep my dizziness under check. Such vertigo is not entirely unfamiliar to me; I fixed my gaze on the locked door latch to my cabin for hours on the ship to the islands even during calm seas.

"What's wrong, Henry?" Francine's concern worries her lovely face.

I know what it is. Edward is telling me he will be in physical form soon. He needs the vessel we share. *Why now? Why here?* Lucky senses the impending change. He knows we are the same. Thankfully, he cannot explain this oddity to his new owner.

"Since my visit to the islands, a strange fever has erupted after I indulge in too much fine food. Go on ahead. I will catch up with you. This will pass." I slump backwards, my pulse straining at my veins, the world threatening to twirl away if I let my eyes abandon their desperate focus. I pray I won't vomit on her. I have nothing in my bag for this ailment. Once Edward emerges, I can only fight his urges for a short time.

"Are you sure?" Her concern turns to puzzlement.

Sweat forms on my brow. My lips become dry, and a wheezing cough rattles my bones. He will take me soon. I summon all my energy to smile. Who am I fooling?

"Yes, quite. I will be along. Take my umbrella. Where can I find you?" I hand the umbrella to her and avoid her gaze. I mop my forehead with my handkerchief and desperately fight the urge to pass out. Stars form behind my eyelids. Their galaxy swirls about the sparsely furnished room.

She takes the umbrella. "The Bricklayer's Arms on Settles Street. That is Lizzy's favourite public house."

"Leave me the key. I will lock up," I say weakly. It won't be long before Edward arrives. I use all my mental energy to hold the floodgates tight. If I am going to die by holding him inside, I want to look at her one last time.

She places that token of safety in my palm and stares into my eyes. "You don't look like your normal self."

"Too much rich food and intestinal upset," I croak. "It will pass. Don't be worried."

She departs, and Lucky jumps into my lap. I pass out while stroking his head.

———

FRANCINE MURPHY

The wind wants to take Henry's umbrella to France. I close it and shroud my hair under my cloak as a rain shower sweeps me towards Settles Street via the Commercial Road. There, I take up a position under an entrance archway.

Why did I agree to allow a man to help me on my rounds? Why Doctor Jekyll? Was it because he took a genuine interest in my work? I have never questioned his motives from the day we found the dog. I believe he has been forthright and honest. Henry maintains his privacy and protects it fiercely, but he is always true to his word. The flat is his as much as it is mine, as he paid the landlord through to the end of the year, but he treats my situation with respect and makes no demands on me. I am sure he is attracted to me, but he always acts with restraint as we look at buildings to house my dreams. Henry is naturally inquisitive and takes pains to understand how I bring women off the streets, and slowly allow them to build new self-respect in sobriety.

I turn from the windswept rain and shake the water off my coat.

———

THE WHITECHAPEL MURDERER

I dart into my favourite spot across from the Bricklayer's Arms and encounter a woman with her back to me, shaking her coat dry. Where have I seen that red hair before? I step lightly and quietly back into the street before she turns around. Was it here in Whitechapel or elsewhere? Would she greet me by name? I have walked these streets a total stranger to its denizens of the night. The thought of a shopkeeper or carriage driver recognizing me from the West End never occurred to me. And a woman? Impossible. But here I am, fortunate that no recognition is made, but it leaves me in a quandary. Where do I know the woman from? On my forays around Europe and the Mediterranean, I was nameless to all I encountered in the darkened streets. I scold myself for thinking that anonymity would carry over to a part of town near to where I live responsibly. I promise to keep a sharp eye out for this redhead henceforth.

———

EDWARD HYDE

Lucky licks my face. He recognizes me as his heavenly angel. Did Henry think he could keep me at bay all night? It is a good thing the foolish fop didn't throw up on our only change of clothes this wet evening.

Mrs. Murphy made her way out onto the street, and now it is time for me to do the same, lest she discover she has forgotten something and returns.

I check the doctor's kit. Nothing sharper than a pair of scissors.

"The game is afoot, my little friend."

I bid the dog farewell, make my way to the door and lock it behind me. Out on the street, my kidney twinges. A memory from my last visit to this address. The good doctor expected to help his friend tonight. Did he think to bring his favourite letter opener with him? What if he encountered the killer? What would he have done then?

I pull the baggy coat's lapels high and snug, my top hat low. The rain and wind make visibility difficult. I'll steer clear of Mrs. Murphy for now.

I walk my favourite routes to the opposite side of the killing zone. The occasional rain showers reduce the foot traffic and make it easier to move out in the open. Some layabouts huddling from the rain in doorways are probably policemen. I know the view each vantage point offers, as I have used the same darkened spots myself.

I take up a position where I can scan two pubs on Whitechapel Road catering to the rougher clientele and the women who entice them with promises of brief companionship, rain be damned. It is Saturday night, carrying over into Sunday morning, and the incipient Sabbath means this is the only night many of the residents of Whitechapel don't have to work in the morning.

———

FRANCINE MURPHY

"You need to stop bothering me, Francine Murphy. My friend and I are going to have a swell time tonight. Aren't we, dearie?"

Lizzy Stride, wearing the same clothes she slept in that morning, makes a show of cuddling and passionately kissing her remunerative beau. The man eagerly accepts the amorous advances and returns her demonstration of affection under the glow of the street lamps in front of the pub. Neither is sober, and they hold on to each other more for balance than intimacy. Lizzy has found a pair of worn shoes somewhere to protect her feet from the wet night, but already the footgear is torn at the toe.

Her untied black bonnet falls into a puddle, and I retrieve it before it becomes saturated with a watery slop of the day's deposits. I shake it dry as best I can and tap Lizzy on the shoulder. "Your favourite bonnet," I say, placing it on Lizzy's head when she turns to question the rude intrusion.

She scowls at me, but then turns out a wide crooked smile and says, "Thank you very much, my good lady. I shall be fine. Right, darling?" She returns to embracing the man, adding a hip grind to stress her point.

There are other women who I could check on this dreary night. I shall not give up on this one, but Lizzy is not ready for my help. She offered no gratitude when I walked her back to the dosshouse earlier this morning. She evinced no thankfulness when I made up the difference between what she had in her pockets and what the house lady demanded. Indeed, Lizzy had passed out asleep in her clothes by the time I'd settled her debt.

Lizzy makes a scene of her amorous affections, and I back away when a group of men say rude things to the couple. Lizzy will suffer more indignities, possibly violence, before she develops the desire to turn away from life on the street.

Should I wait for Henry nearby, or return to my flat to check on him? The whipping wind gives me fair warning of yet another band of showers about to drench the dreary streets once more. I watch Lizzy make off with her new beau around the corner as the rain pelts the oblivious lovers. I know exactly where they will consummate their groping and affections—in the alley, on top of several dry hessian sacks under an overhang.

THE WHITECHAPEL MURDERER

The red-haired woman, I now recognize, talks with the vile creature whom I stalk. The boozy whore has nothing to do with the missionary. All the better. It will be an early night if things fall into the normal routine. She will have more sexual relations this evening than I've had in my lifetime, other than my mother's midnight visits. I can't wait to surprise the whore with my assuring smile and shiny coins.

The hunt begins.

EDWARD HYDE

Berner Street is busy with patrons coming and going from the International Working Men's Educational Club. I keep in step behind several men engaged in a spirited political debate about the merits of government safety inspections. I cross at Fairclough Street. The showers abate for the time being. A woman is talking to a man with a sailor's hat. She is one of Mrs. Murphy's sad reclamation projects, perfect for the killer. In the short time I skulked in the shadows around the drinking establishments, I learned who the regulars were, both men and women. This couple is having a loud conversation. The man doesn't appreciate her pawing at him while he is attempting to negotiate with her. She tries her best to argue what value she promises. I have watched this dance dozens of times from the shadows. As it gets later into the mornings, those services become less costly, unless a young man is being egged on by his mates to give up his virginity. That doesn't appear to be the case here. The sailor is firm on what he will pay. I dare not get too close to those two. Alcohol, money and sex make for some interesting scenarios. I know first-hand.

For many of those early adult years in Henry's life, he let me roam the town with wild abandon. He was making up, I suspect, for what he asked me to endure when he was a child. I embarked on a life of pleasure-seeking to drown out my pain. It seemed fitting. Edward Hyde was a regular at the bare-knuckle fights, both as a competitor and a gambler. We would pound each other silly and then drink like sailors on leave. I learned from the Chinese how to use my whole body, how to move to avoid a strike and how to counter-attack. I would have caused a scene in front of Mrs. Murphy's apartment had I taken on the ruffians. I didn't want her to see me or to inspire a constable to arrest me.

Walking about Whitechapel, I step lightly and always glance about my changing surroundings. Henry Jekyll possesses none of these skills. He moves about every bit the stately doctor. He walks and carries himself like a well-to-do West End gentleman. I, on the other hand, slink like an animal on the prowl. Self-preservation and survival instincts formed my existence from the horrors I was subjected to. He, unburdened, can stroll, and smell the roses, oblivious to the dangers of the world. Such is our bargain.

The woman reaches to hug Mister Sailor Hat. He shoves her forcibly away, and she stumbles into the middle of the street, her black bonnet dropping into a pile left by a carthorse. He strides toward the busy road without looking back at her. She curses him while standing up. I cannot keep gawking, now that the spectacle is over. She might think I am interested in her offerings. I walk away from her and the club, just far enough that she doesn't quite leave my sight.

---

30 SEPTEMBER 1888

THE WHITECHAPEL MURDERER

It won't be much longer now. How fortuitous. The newspapers will report that this woman was last seen talking with a man younger than myself, and that the man was wearing a deer-stalker hat. How rich is that?

I stand at the wooden gate of Dutfield's Yard, next to the International Working Men's Educational Club. I wait until she and the man part company. She is alone. I call to her, and she turns, her soiled black bonnet wobbling on her head. I hold up the shiny coins and smile. She smiles and closes the distance between us.

"Looking for some company, are we now?" she asks.

I rub the coins together and motion to her mouth.

"Oh, I think I learned some of the French tricks along the way. You won't be disappointed," she says.

I retreat slowly into the darkness of the yard.

She hesitates. "The men come out here and relieve themselves sometimes." She points to the building. Men's voices can be clearly heard inside. She doesn't follow me.

I emerge from the shadows and approach her on the street. "Tell me where we won't be disturbed," I say.

She looks up and down Berner Street. I do the same. Satisfied my next act will be unnoticed, I smile and hold the lucre out for her to take. She focuses on her prize. This is her mistake, like so many before her. From Amsterdam to Ankara and many cities in between, I have practised how to start this dance of death. Much of my enjoyment springs forth from watching their surprise turn to terror. When she reaches for the coins and takes them, I pull her arm with one hand and throttle her throat with the other, drawing her into the darkness.

12:45 A.M.

FRANCINE MURPHY

I have been out on the streets for over two hours and have encountered other women I recognize. I always approach them the same way. Chat them up to get an idea of their intoxication. Find out what is bothering them on that night. Is it the weather? How is their daytime situation? Anything new on the killer? Do they have a place to stay? To a woman, they all know Lizzy and say that she is not doing well, and it is only a matter of time.

I stay out in the open and travel the better-lit streets. I avoid the alleys unless I can make eye contact with the lady walking towards me.

My feet lead me back to the flat. I am concerned for Henry. We should have spotted each other by now if he has ventured out after his fever broke.

Lucky hears me on the steps and barks his joyful bark. I open the door to his wagging body. He circles my feet. "Henry?" I call out. I make my way to the bedroom. It is empty. "Henry," I say weakly. What to do now? I have a bad feeling.

EDWARD HYDE

I spring from my darkened doorway the second I see the woman with the black bonnet get hauled into the yard next to the club. Balancing my need not to draw attention to myself with the necessity of haste, I run in the shadows and stroll in the dim lighting. A few men come out of the club and are getting their bearings. I bend down like I am tying my shoe. Anyone looking closely will see I am wearing boots. They turn and walk away from me and the yard.

Thirty more feet to the opening. I sprint the distance, splashing in the puddles. What do I hope to accomplish with my bare hands? Damn you, Henry. I turn into the total darkness of the yard between the buildings, and my eyes need a second to adjust. I can no longer see them.

———

THE WHITECHAPEL MURDERER

I am alert to the splashing of running feet as I'm in mid-count over her prone body. I am torn between getting my release from her death spiral and determining how to deal with the creator of the approaching noise. I loosen my grip on her arm and reach for the blade sheathed inside my overcoat pocket. The slap of approaching feet in the darkness gives me pause. I release my grip on her throat, and she gasps for breath. I use that hand to free the blade from the sheath and stand. As I turn, I swing in a wide arc at the approaching figure as much to warn off as to strike.

———

EDWARD HYDE

Noise rattles behind the open gate next to the club. I stop, hold my breath and lean forward to look. A man in a black coat and hat crouches over the woman. Her bonnet is on the ground behind her head. The man springs up and wheels around with a knife in his hand. I lift my arm to ward off the blow. A sharp pain travels down from my forearm to my wrist, and my sleeve rips. I turn away and stagger backwards.

A choking sound rises from the ground, and my assailant turns away from me. With my attention on the blade, I never see his face. In this second, I do not know how badly I am hurt. I only know that attacking this man without my weapon will not end well for me. I cannot call out for help either, lest we both be discovered.

I run back out the opening as a man driving a horse cart is turning in. The driver's attention is on the seat to his other side. Shielded by the turning horse, I stumble back in the direction whence I came, a defeated man. Perhaps the horse and driver will scare off the woman's attacker. I reach for my throbbing arm. The ripped sleeves of my coat and shirt are slick. Under the next street lamp, I see I am bleeding profusely. I want to run further on Berner Street, but I stop. Two men stare at me while I hold my bleeding arm. I turn around. The horse rears up at the entrance. I quickly divert to Fairclough Street. Where now?

THE WHITECHAPEL MURDERER

My blade is wet with another man's blood. The vile creature on the ground below me breathes in deep gulps of precious air. It will be only a second or two before she screams. The unmistakable snort of a horse brings my attention back to the open gates.

I need to silence her now. It will take too long to squeeze the life out of her again. The cart will be inside the yard any second. I pull her hair back, forcing her chin up. I set the blade under her ear and pull it hard across her throat. I then turn her on her side away from me and run deeper into the yard, away from the light.

The cart enters, and a curious cry comes from the driver as he clambers off the cart to inspect the unmoving body by the club's wall. The driver is backlit by the dull gas street lamps.

I stand ready to slit the driver's throat and the horse's too, if I have to, in order to escape. I calm my breath and am about to emerge from the shadows when the man's match goes out. The driver walks away from the body and goes out onto the street, where he turns towards the club. Help will arrive in a minute.

I circle to the other side of the fractious horse and exit the yard, running away from the main road. At the next intersection, two men stand staring down the side street. I cross Berner Street and walk on the side street away from them. I hear one of them say, "Blimey, he was bleeding like a stuck pig."

———

FRANCINE MURPHY

I return to the streets, fearing the worst for Henry. I walk toward constables' whistles erupting around Whitechapel. It is hard for me to determine which direction they are coming from. Men are shouting and running about. My feet move with dreadful apprehension. Two of the ladies I encountered that evening run towards me.

"He cut her throat!" Sarah McBain shouts.

Allison Keeler cries out at almost the same time. "Nearly cut her head off!"

"Who?" I grab both of their arms and halt them in their tracks.

"Long Liz!" the first says.

I double over like I am punched in the gut.

"She wouldn't listen to you, Francine, and now she's dead," the second woman gasps as though delivering some salacious bit of gossip rather than mourning the loss of a human life.

"Where?"

"Berner Street," they say at the same time.

I lift my skirt and run to where they point.

25

---

30 SEPTEMBER 1888 5:32 A.M.

HENRY JEKYLL

"Oh God, you're drunk," Francine says.

I fight to open my eyes. My mouth is parched, and my head throbs like drum corps at a regimental parade. The pain from my right arm shoots through me like an arrow. I hold my arm in front of my face. A gauze wrapping covers it from wrist to elbow. The smell of whisky assaults my nostrils. Why would my arm smell like whisky? I glance to the side table. There sits the culprit on its side. The almost empty bottle is damning proof of my indulgence.

"You're hurt." Slowly, Francine removes the wrapping, and her eyes widen. I turn my arm so I can see the source of my pain. I recognize the stitching. It is my handiwork. How it got there, I cannot recall, but it must have to do with Edward.

"I must have done it and used the alcohol to sterilize the wound, and I drank the rest to kill the pain," I mumble.

She helps me sit up. The room stops spinning. I focus on the wall sconce and flickering candle for a moment to train my reeling mind. It is dark outside. Rain showers and wind slap against the window. Yes, I stink of booze. I am not ready to face my accuser.

"What happened?" she asks.

"I don't know."

She slaps my boots at the foot of the bed. "You went out sometime around midnight. Your boots are muddy, and your trouser legs are wet. You don't remember that?"

On the thin oval rug in the middle of the bedroom sits Lucky, attentive to the drama taking place between his two favourite humans. It is then I realize Francine didn't come back to her home encountering Edward in her bed. During the night, he made it back here and stitched my arm up one-handed. On the bedstand to my other side, a candle in a pewter holder sits. Plunged in the wax along its side is a long knitting needle with thread matching the weave holding my forearm skin together.

"What do you mean, you don't know?" Her question demands an answer.

I try standing up. Too dizzy, I fall back to a seated position. I need time to think. I am not at my best.

"May I have some water?" I ask.

She leaves me seated there bare-chested while she goes to the other room and draws a cup from the pitcher. Is now the time to tell her about Edward?

She returns and stands next to me with her one hand on my good shoulder while she holds the cup to my lips and slowly tips it. The liquid puts out the fire in my throat, and with each sip, I determine my response. When the cup is empty, she stands back.

"When I was a child and became fearful," I start, "I would black out. Sometimes for a few minutes, sometimes for a few hours, sometimes for a few days. My family told me I was not my normal self during those times. I don't recall what made me fearful or why I blacked out. Today, I remember nothing from the time you left me until you woke me. I am sorry I don't have a better answer for you."

I maintain eye contact with Francine and wait. Her pleasant features harden. Her hair is damp and needs a good combing. Her brown frock is smudged with dirt and mud. Her shoes are as filthy as mine. The air in the room is thick with our sweat. The metallic tang of my blood on the bandages balled up on the floor and the unmistakable scent of whisky add to the prevalent odour. How dare I desecrate her space!

She stares at me. Lucky is obviously concerned about what is being said. He knows the truth, but I am pretty sure he can keep our little secret.

"Lizzy Stride is dead," she says. "It was the Whitechapel killer. Her throat was cut so deep, he almost took her head off." Her pained expression shows her guilt at not being able to help Lizzy.

"That's terrible."

"They say a man ran away from the scene bleeding profusely. I think that man was you."

"Jesus." I search my memory. The pain in my arm intensifies, and I muffle a cry. I was that man. I know it on a physical level.

"He must have cut me too."

She nods. "A man who was dressed like you was seen running from the area where they found her next to the club for working men."

Other than the times on the islands when I was free of Edward, I have not run for any reason.

None of this jogs my memory. Edward has never failed me in keeping his secrets. He did not have the time to leave me any clues. Although, I should be able to learn something from the two dozen stitches pulling in my arm.

"I must have tried to stop him. How else do you explain this?" I hold up my arm to prove my point.

"The killer was not satisfied with just Lizzy. He went into

Mitre Square and hacked up another woman worse than anyone could have imagined. No woman feels safe walking about. The police are combing the streets."

Nothing registers with me. "I was probably here trying to stop the bleeding."

Francine says, "I saw Lizzy tonight, but she acted like I was interfering with her romance. It was all a show. I felt like I was losing her for good. She wouldn't listen to me. If we were together, maybe none of it would have happened."

She sits on the bed next to me and stares at the rain slashing the windows. She bites her lip. "And I did lose her forever. It's my fault she's dead."

My lie about the fever weighs heavily on my chest. My lying about Edward never sits well with me, even though it has become second nature. With Francine, I am having a much harder time balancing my feelings for her with my duplicity.

I shake my head. "I'm sorry I wasn't there to help you persuade her. She was not ready. It was not her time to give up the drink." I place my good hand on her thigh. "I won't fail you next time, I promise."

She stands abruptly. "When it's light, I want you to leave. You're not telling me about your real reasons for not going out with me and why you got stinking drunk. What if I'd brought home women from the streets who wanted to start a new life? What would they have seen and smelled when they came into this room?" She picks up the bottle with two fingers and slides it into my coat pocket. "Take that with you when you leave. I am going to visit Mary McCreary. Leave the key in the flowerpot on the back porch."

Which hurts worse, the searing pain in my arm, or her words going straight through my heart like a knife?

"I have no memory from the time you departed until you woke me up," I plead. "That is the truth. I know it sounds strange, but I've been dealing my whole life with the consequences of events that occur when I am not my normal self. All I can say is that I am truly sorry."

It is true. Hyde's actions have cost me dearly. What a price to pay for a choice made by me when I was a child. What was so terrible that I had to create him in the first place? What was so painful?

Her expression doesn't change as she walks away. The door to the hallway closes behind her. "Look at the fine mess you made for me, Edward."

At dawn's early light, I get out of bed. Lucky accepts my farewells as I dress. I slowly make my way to the door. I look back at him and the empty rooms and cry for the first time in my adult life.

26

2 OCTOBER 1888

HENRY JEKYLL

The weekend rain showers blow out the grit and brown haze perpetually hanging over the city. I sit on my favourite bench in Regent's Park. The gentle breeze carries the sweet scent from the autumn flowers ringing the ponds and walkways.

On this sobering Tuesday, my shadow plays out in front of me. "Edward, you saved my life, but I do wish you had left me a few more clues. Nice work on the arm, by the way. Amazing how you stitched it with one hand."

The whisky, which was so upsetting to Francine, has prevented any infection from setting in. Now, a light dressing covers my forearm under my dress shirt and charcoal grey coat.

The morning newspapers detail the dreadful events and leave me queasy throughout breakfast. The two bloody killings within an hour of each other have shocked the entire city. My arm throbs as I turn the pages which chronicle the horror. My body is telling me about a third attack, of which I have no memory.

When I was a child and Edward returned our shared vessel to my use, there were many strange sensations emanating from bruises, abrasions, cuts and soreness which could tell a story but thankfully didn't. Why was I so ravenously hungry, thirsty or both when Edward returned to the ether? Most disturbing was a deep sense of violation in my rectum, which I could not explain. My body knew the truth.

Two men offered the best description of the man fleeing the scene of the first killing in Whitechapel. He was described to me many times before, when persons talked about Edward Hyde. When my friends and associates berated me about my relationship with Edward, I became practiced in the art of lying to cover the tracks of my bad other half. So, when Francine confronted me the other evening about what happened to me during those perilous hours, I learned, as I had many times before, to speak honestly without revealing the whole truth.

The closest person to me since my return from the islands, without a doubt, is Francine Murphy, and as much as I want to tell her about Hyde, I can't. How would I begin? What happened in my childhood that caused me to create him? Do I include all his escapades during my adolescence and my entrance into polite London society?

"Should I tell her about the murder of Sir Danvers Carew?" I mutter to the circling sea birds catching the thermals as a sunny morning warms into a beautiful day.

The quick-witted red-haired Irishwoman hears all kinds of stories and confabulations from the women she talks to nightly. She will see through my partial truths for what they are. How can she trust a man who was stinking drunk in her bed with a stitched-up arm, professing no knowledge of how the injury occurred? Had Lizzy Stride somehow turned the blade on me before I nearly cut her head off?

As I sit here watching governesses and mothers walking children through the park, I cannot utter a definitive no in my defence. I don't know what happened and consider the only explanation that makes sense. The Whitechapel killer took the blade to me. That much, I told her. It was only Edward's quick reaction and expert repair that saved me. That much I left out, and it is enough for her to leave me with only my half-truths and lies to comfort me.

My shoulders sag, and my baleful eyes glaze without appreciation for the wonders of the day. I am alive and will heal with a nice scar to talk about over drinks at the club someday. I fended off the Whitechapel killer. I am wealthy and am ensconced in society, yet I feel lower in position than a brown snake from my duplicity. A respected doctor, friend and colleague, sitting alone on a park bench, feeling like a lost and rudderless ship tossed about by tall waves in an unrelenting storm.

The storm is unfamiliar to me, except for the time when I learned of Carew's murder. Then, as now, I quake at the unfairness of it all. Was I a terrible child and deserving of this fate? What happened that didn't allow me to possess a full gamut of feelings? Where did Edward seek his pleasure, and how did he endure our pain? A life split in half, now stressed by a hunger, a need, to be in Francine's company again. She is the calm water I seek. She can restore my soul. I see that truth in her shrewd and smiling green eyes, and not in the 23rd Psalm.

Could it be love I am feeling, only because it is now lost? Possibly forever?

I stand quickly and walk towards my home. I kick the stones on the path and sneer at the quickly disappearing smiles of passersby. Do I deserve to be hounded by the police, or questioned by my brother why I'm not tithing? I was a healing doctor and a fine chemist sought for my remedies, yet my practice is now in shambles.

The shortness of breath, tightness of chest, narrowing of my vision, and overwhelming assault of horse droppings on my nose, inform me of a totally different feeling in what has been a half century of blandness. What brings this on? Sadly, I conclude it is the fading vision of a strong-willed woman who will not tolerate my duplicity inherent in my self-created duality. Why do I care so much about her?

As I turn the corner to enter Cavendish Square, I spot Newcomen on my marble steps, staring in my direction. A wave of nausea strikes me. Not now, Edward; I will deal with this myself. The tingling in my arm reminds me of my latest troubles.

Will Newcomen ask me to roll up my sleeve? He makes no move towards me, his arms crossed as he leans on the railing. He looks as tired as his shabby brown suit. My neighbours will assume I am meeting a patient too rough to be a colleague or a friend. I would have gladly welcomed a patient with a transmissible disease rather than deal with the inspector. I stand on the street, with the horse carts and carriages providing a steady beat of hooves on stone and the creak of wood on metal behind me.

"I can understand why you look haggard, Inspector," I say to Newcomen. "I imagine you have not slept a wink since learning of that dreadful business Sunday morning."

He appears shocked at my truthful observation and that I address him first. He stands now on scuffed and unpolished boots. He uncrosses his arms and says, "You're correct, Doctor Jekyll. I've not seen anything like this in all my years. I am sure nightmares will linger long after we stop this madman."

I take a step forward, placing my foot on the first tread, keeping my wounds far from his piercing coal-black eyes. "We agree on one thing. It is the work of a madman. The sooner you find the culprit, the sooner all of London will rest easier. I don't envy your task, Inspector."

"I will ask that you tell me if you see Mr. Hyde. A man matching his description was observed running from the scene of the first murder on Berner Street."

"Thank you, Inspector. I will. If he had anything to do with this, I would be most happy to report his whereabouts." I can't imagine where this conversation is headed. I lean on the opposite railing and show no interest on ascending my front steps to the safety of my home.

"Someone with anatomical knowledge ripped open the second woman and took organs from her."

I am taken back by his forthrightness, but then I realize. "Are you saying there could be two maniacs running around Whitechapel?"

"Two working together," he says. "One to find their targets and disable them, and the other to cut them up."

I recall all the newspaper accounts. "There was no mention of two attackers."

"It's far-fetched, I know," he admits.

We both ponder this hypothesis. I know he is trying to force the two pieces, Mister Hyde and Doctor Jekyll, into that puzzle. I smile inwardly at the impossibility.

"My men tell me you were in Whitechapel Saturday night," he says.

He is looking for a reaction from me. I give him one. I shrug and say, "They are correct. I went there to accompany a woman who works with the most destitute women and attempts to help them turn their lives away from their evil ways."

"Brave woman," he says.

"I've met no one like her."

"And your watchman told me you arrived home in the morning stinking drunk."

"Yes. We had an argument, and she asked me to leave."

"Right again," he says.

I feign nonchalance and disinterest by not responding to his comment, but my insides are churning.

Has he talked to Francine? If so, what did she tell him? Did he tell her about Hyde? Was this his plan, to lure me into a false sense of safety and then confront me?

My heart leaps into my throat, now as parched as the Sahara. I cannot utter a response. Any moment, I expect him to grab my wounded arm and haul me into Scotland Yard. I cannot move. I am his for the taking. I am frozen to the spot. Edward cannot come to my rescue. I am on my own.

I grip the railing tightly to keep from falling down. I am flooded with the desire to flee, but my legs will not move. I focus on the loosened knot of his tie as I pretend to look at him.

"If you see Hyde, please let me know," Newcomen finishes. He brushes past me as he walks off the steps. He leaves me there, mouth agape.

What just occurred? Is this the same man who mopped the floor of a bathroom with the back of my head? I do not turn to follow his departure, but climb the stairs on unsteady legs, open the oak door, slam it behind me, and fall to my knees and vomit.

27

4 OCTOBER 1888, 7:00 P.M.

THE WHITECHAPEL MURDERER

This is rich! Ensconced in my favourite reading chair with a pile of newspapers strewn about my feet, I revel in my notoriety, a broad smile on my face. They are now calling me *Jack the Ripper*.

A letter and postcard from a person purporting to be the Whitechapel murderer were published in the evening paper. *Jack the Ripper* and *Saucy Jack* were the respective signatories. "You won't catch me," the writer taunted the police through the letter. I did not write the letters, but I shall accept this *nom de guerre*.

I finish reading the latest reporting of my exploits and slowly bundle the rubbish. It is a nice evening, warm and clear, but I decide to feed the fire with the recollection of my exploits. I gather snatches of the printed sheets and toss them into the fireplace. Soon, the room fills with an oily, warm smoke and hazy heat. My ancestors sat around fires for warmth and tribal connection, as they recalled the heroism from the day's hunt. I am a hunter as well.

I sit to consider the events of my previous Sunday morning in Whitechapel. I have been too impetuous. Irritated and annoyed, I ball the rest of the papers and throw them into the blaze. That curious man probably observed me pulling my victim into the darkness next to the club. The image of his face fills the fireplace. Something about his features, something in the way he looked at me, caused me to swing my blade in an arc to warn him off rather than kill him. Why warn him off? This thought has occupied me for several days; that, and my lapse in judgement in not waiting until the whore could be lured to safer killing grounds. Many men treat whores roughly; I have seen it often. Some of them gang up and take their turns without paying a shilling. So why did that man take notice and feel the need to investigate?

And why was he unarmed? Thankfully, he was neither a disguised constable nor a police operative.

He did, however, cheat me out of my sexual release.

When I slashed the man, I saw only his face, along with his arm as it came up to deflect my blow. Do I know this man from the streets of Whitechapel? What caused me to spare the life of the Good Samaritan?

The flaming paper pushes waves of heat at my clean-shaven face. My thoughts turn next to my escape from Berner Street. I knew that my handiwork would be discovered quickly, and the police would be summoned. This had motivated me to make my way into the City of London as quickly as I could move between the rain showers. With each street I passed, I slowed my pace to Mitre Square, where I met my needs with another vile creature. I wreaked havoc on her body, removing two organs, not as trophies, but to further my greater plan. The second murder in less than an hour validated my method. Find a suitably drunk female willing to trade her body for money for gin, lure her with the promise of extra pay for 'lip service', then force her to the ground with my death grip around her throat and count slowly until she breathed no more.

The fire smoulders, the pockets of embers dying. I think of the second woman's surprise, then terror, as she struggled under my hands, my knees pinning her to the ground. The last of the newspaper accounts of Jack the Ripper turn to blackened soot as I relive the sight of life leaking from her eyes. I had slowly counted to ten over her limp body before I took my surgical blades to her warm flesh.

A rush of damp air from the room's open window drives away the receding heat. I stand before the fireplace, resting one hand on the mantel and using the poker with the other to push around the ashes. The movement reminds me of what I did next to the lifeless body. I had carefully excised her uterus and kidney from the gore and wrapped them in scraps of her clothing for transport.

On my journey from Mitre Square, I wanted to convince Scotland Yard of another man's guilt, a man whose description was decidedly different from the man I slashed. As I made my way to that man's house on Cavendish Square, I heard the constable whistles piercing the night's air as the intermittent rain showers tapered off. Flushed with the success of the second attack, my steps had been jaunty. To onlookers in the West End, I must have appeared like any other man about town, perhaps one slightly drunk. I had walked with a gaiety of step not usual for that time of night unless one was tipsy. My strident movement might have reminded onlookers of a man who had been successful in satisfying his manly needs that evening. That assumption would have been correct, if they only knew how I had replaced coitus with a more deadly clutch.

I shift the poker from hand to hand. I had made my way to the house where I wanted to deposit the organs. When I saw the streets were clear of passersby and carriages, I walked quietly on the path next to the house to the rear gardens and stood below a window. All was quiet. The garden beds had been drenched from the rain. The smell of verdant plants and flowers had filled my nostrils. I tucked the package into the front of my coat and buttoned it, keeping it snug against my chest.

Something was missing, I now recall. Next time, I'll remove the heart.

I had been about to hoist myself up when I spotted the shadow of a person crossing the room and returning to a chair next to the expansive room's enormous fireplace. I ducked down, counting slowly to one hundred on each outbreath, until my thumping heartbeat had returned to normal. I slinked out of the garden and took a serpentine path to my home, stopping only to deposit my package in a safe place. The anonymous tip to the police had to wait. The homeowner had taken precautions to avoid another visit from Scotland Yard. If I had entered the house while the watchman was not in the room, I might have been observed planting the evidence of my most recent conquest. Killing the watchman would have complicated things.

I sip the last of my lukewarm tea, then take my teacup and saucer to the kitchen. How will I employ the woman's organs in my plan?

I return to the parlour and lower the window, locking it, not wanting to entice a burglar. I smile at the thought of what I would do if I encountered a thief in my domicile.

It is time to ready myself for a pleasant diversion with Lady Jane while she is still in town.

———

I CHUCKLE at Jane's full dance card, noting that she has saved the last dance for me. The waltzes are exquisite. The string quartet earns more in three hours than a commoner sweats for in a month. The well-tailored men in their colourful plumage stand to one side of the long wall next to a statuary of knights, puffing out their chests and peering over their champagne flutes across the swirling dancers at the unspoken-for ladies. The women on the other side, wearing gaily coloured evening dresses, signal discreetly with their sleeve fans to entice a suitor. I find these acts humorous but tiring. London's leisure classes have their rules, however, and to disobey them will bring dishonour not only to the miscreant but also their family name. Quite a different dance from the ribald exhortations of the prostitutes in Whitechapel, aimed at men looking for a twirl of a more salacious nature.

After our dance, I will ask Lady Jane if I can walk her to her townhouse, then boldly ask if we might tarry in the parlour. This is how I will stake my claim to this fair woman before she returns to the country.

"Darling, why are you looking at me that way?" she asks when I make my way to the centre of the floor.

I bow to the crestfallen man who hoped to be her last dance companion for the evening. "I could not remove my gaze for even a second. Your dress is heavenly, and you move like an angel."

"You speak of heaven and angels, but I see a more devilish look in your eyes."

My smile disappears for a second. I doubt she can see into my soul or know what I am thinking. Never once have I imagined throttling her fair neck or plunging a sharp blade into her sex hole. I regain my composure and respond quickly, "Healthy, virile men have primitive thoughts, otherwise they would have nothing to confess and beg forgiveness for."

The music starts, and I reach for her hand, gripping it. Tonight, I am in control.

The Viennese Waltz is quicker paced than the previous ones. We enter the line of twirling couples. She looks away from me, a sign that she can trust me to lead her. Her lightly powdered cheeks are framed by her blonde hair pulled into a chignon as we begin our steps. Her neck is thin, evenly coloured, and unblemished by the summer sun. On the first reverse turn, I peek at the tops of her lovely, small breasts. I must commend the Parisian dressmaker for the teasing cut of Lady Jane's pink rose-coloured ballroom gown. On the change steps, my grip on her hand strengthens, with my other lightly touching, almost caressing, her back through the reverse flick roll, contra check, and finally the flick roll, where I hold her in a deep backward bend, allowing her to fall into my hand before I bring her back up.

We continue to dance with exuberance and freedom until the final bow and curtsey. I then walk her to her coterie, and before departing, ask, "May I see you home?" The conversation around us ceases, with all eyes on Lady Jane, whose eyes are locked on mine. A thin smile rises to her lips. I wait expectantly for her reply.

"This is the last time I will see my friends before returning to our country house." I keep my expectant gaze in place and wait for her decision. "Allow me a few minutes to say goodbye."

I nod and bow. "I will wait with your evening wrap at the door."

28

7 OCTOBER 1888

EDWARD HYDE

I listen to the church bells on the nights I venture into Whitechapel. The twelfth bell still reverberates in my ears. My post on the second floor of the church overlooking two major streets is directly underneath the bell tower. It is safe and dry here. The chap uses a different stairwell to access the bells. I am drawn to Whitechapel this Saturday night into Sunday morning because that is when the Ripper, as he is now called, hunts on the streets below me. Cart horses and cabs still carry on their business as before, but foot traffic, especially of single women, is light. I observe many more constables and plainly dressed men,who I assume to be policemen as well. There is talk of a vigilante group forming, as the murders are bad for business and local commerce. All of this is important to me as I am wanted for the murder of Sir Danvers Carew. To make my task more daunting, an accurate description was printed in all the newspapers Henry read of the bleeding man who fled the scene of Lizzy Stride's murder. It is both true and accurate. I interrupted her murder and have the proof to show for it. The throbbing gash in my arm is deep, and the stitches need to remain in place for some time longer. Henry will know when to remove them. No infection has set in, and I am grateful, but Henry paid the price for my suturing. I am no stranger to whisky and knew well its medicinal value when I threaded the sewing needle with one hand through our skin. It was not a pretty scene after I passed out stinking drunk in Mrs. Murphy's bed and when she woke up Henry, who was totally unaware of what transpired. But dammit, he had no business traipsing around Whitechapel while the killer was stalking his prey. He left me unarmed and defenceless in the pitch black of Dutfield's Yard. I didn't get a look at the Ripper, only the blade swinging towards my neck. I had only a second to raise my arm to block it before retreating.

There was only one safe place for a wanted killer to hide and I went there, praying Mrs. Murphy would not return early from her work. I could not take a chance of having someone with the proper skills fix me up and getting a good look at my face. Newcomen would immediately assume I was the killer, and that I had killed again. My only option was to use Henry's medical knowledge and Murphy's sewing kit to stem the bleeding. What would Henry have done? I shudder to think if it had been him and not I who encountered the Ripper last week in the dark. Doctor Jekyll and Mister Hyde would be dead and planted in the ground by now. It is not the first time I think of Henry causing our demise. I recall his ignorance of the evidence planted in his surgery, the act of which summoned me to manifest.

With his friendship with Mrs. Murphy ended, I don't expect him to be walking about these parts unarmed after midnight again. It's a shame. I can tell he liked her. Henry is a London gentleman, and he's not prone to wildly swinging emotions. He gladly allows me to live life on the edge. He does not know of what I've endured for him, and he only heard secondhand of my drinking, fighting, and whoring. Where Henry is smooth and polished, I am rough and profane. I am definitely his bad side, but not evil like the man who nearly extinguished us prematurely. My carnality has limits; the Ripper is a monster. I do what I do to protect Henry and to live the life he deprived himself of.

The Ripper? What motivates him? What is causing him to become more vicious? The two deadly attacks, less than an hour apart, show a change in his routine. Does he know he fled into a different police jurisdiction after he murdered the Stride woman? Does it matter? Why did he have to fulfill his quest in dissecting the second woman? How did my sudden appearance in the courtyard affect his thinking? I am convinced he needed to finish his work and had to victimize another woman of the evening. He didn't make any sloppy mistakes after killing Stride before procuring that lady a short distance away. I wonder if he needed to atone for his mistake of allowing me to see him pull Stride into Dutfield's Yard. The second murder that morning showed daring and control, yet it was his most brutal. He could compose himself after the first; then he carried out the second in the most heinous manner. I still puzzle over that dichotomy.

I am only a distant observer this night as the bell above me tolls one o'clock. I will not venture on the streets tonight in search of the women I know he will stalk, even though I am properly equipped with Henry's dagger. I need to reassess my purpose. The stakes are much higher now, as my aching arm reminds me. The most desperate women are the Ripper's most obvious marks; the same women Mrs. Murphy is trying to rescue. Over time, the siren calls of gin will drown out their own fears, and they will return to the streets.

By this hour in the morning, I will usually have observed Mrs. Murphy on her rounds. But she is nowhere to be seen. Her long, flaming red hair and purposeful sober strides I recognize. What has become of her?

29

7 OCTOBER 1888

FRANCINE MURPHY

What am I to do? Four women, in different stages of alcohol withdrawal, are looking expectantly at me for breakfast. Lucky stares up at me from the kitchen floor. My flat is cramped with five beds pressed up against the walls of the other two rooms. Bessie and Susan were my two originals, who fled during the Anderson funeral. Both were shocked by the brutal murders and asked for a second chance. My mother's comb has been returned to my chest of drawers with no questions asked. Margaret and Norma arrived at my door when the news of Catherine Eddowes' dissection became known throughout Whitechapel. Jack the Ripper, as the papers now call him, has shaken all these women out of their gin-induced stupor. Preventing him from carving into any of them is their argument to me to take them in. I didn't have to persuade any of them. During the week, I talked to Mary McCreary about this blessing and curse.

The women sit fidgeting around the small kitchen table, making small talk and stealing glances at the bare pantry. Their slept-in clothes take on a ripeness this cool autumn morning. They all need a fresh change of attire.

I worked hard many nights to help Lizzy step away from streetwalking, to no avail; now I am dealing with five terrified women. Is it Lizzy's refusal to accept my help that offers a lesson to those gathered in the flat this morning?

A knock on the door is followed by Louise's familiar voice. "Francine."

Lucky runs down the narrow hallway, his tail wagging his entire body. I hope everything is all right with Louise. The smell of baked goods greets me as I close the distance to Lucky, who is whining in anticipation. I open the door to Louise, her arms full of groceries and a wicker basket weighing down the crook of each elbow.

"Wha—?" Lucky runs out before I can stop him. I relieve my friend of the groceries. "How?"

Louise says, "One of Mary McCreary's children delivered a message. Come, we have to make a second trip for more food and clothes."

I set down the provisions, then run down to the street behind Lucky. Next to the cab kneels a man getting his face washed by Lucky's tongue. The well-dressed gentleman's back is to me. He turns. It is Henry. I am immediately happy to see him, but I am also angry with his drunken lapse of memory the last time he was in my flat.

He stands. "Louise tells me you have a full house. Besides, I need to check on my patient. He seems to be doing well. I just need to change this last bandage. I also made this remedy for the women if any of their withdrawals become too severe." He hands me a bottle, and I take it before thinking that I should refuse his help.

I place it on the ground and grab the gauze and salve from the doctor. "I can do that. You've already done enough."

The women are lifting armfuls of clothes and boxes of food

from the floor of the cab behind me and my benefactor. It is a done deal. I stifle my protest.

Once the others are upstairs preparing a veritable feast, I level an unsmiling face at him. "A Scotland Yard inspector came round asking about you." The air between us becomes tense. His goodwill still hasn't changed my mind about what happened the morning the two women were butchered.

"He wasted no time in talking to me either. What did you tell him?" he replies evenly.

I focus on changing the bandage on Lucky's back right leg. "I told him you got ill when you arrived at my flat and I went out. When I returned, you were sound asleep in my bed."

He points to his arm, a questioning look on his face.

"I am sad to say you are not the only one practiced in telling half-truths," I continue, shaking my head. "He didn't ask if you were injured, and I didn't feel the need to educate him." After finishing with Lucky, I face him. "The description of the man with the bleeding arm who fled the scene of Lizzy's murder is nothing like you at all, yet there you were with mud on your boots, a couple of dozen stitches in your arm, and no memory of how it happened." I blurt it out in one long drawn-out breath. "I don't know what to think, but I do know you're not telling me the whole truth."

He bites his lower lip and nods. "I still have no memory of that time. You must believe me."

He looks down into my eyes, his hands and arms hanging limply by his sides. I stare back at him without hinting my thoughts.

Louise comes outside. "Breakfast is ready."

Henry is the first to break our stare-off. Looking over my shoulder, he asks, "Louise, what time do you want me to send the cab back for you?"

"It's my day off from work, and I can't think of a better place to spend it. Six o'clock?"

He avoids looking at me, pets Lucky one last time and gets back into the cab, calling out to the driver, "Cavendish Square."

I watch as Henry rides away. My four-legged friend places his front paws on my knee, reminding me that breakfast is served. We return to my flat. Fresh rolls with jams and jellies are on display around the table, and a sliced ham acts as the centre-piece. No one has eaten yet. They've waited for me.

Louise says, "This was all my idea, and he was happy to help me. Let's all say a prayer of thanksgiving."

I bow my head with conflicting thoughts. I am pleased Louise answered my need for help, and that our friendship is restored. Yes, I am thankful, but on the other hand, I can't trust Doctor Jekyll. My growing affection for him will remain hidden until I know the whole truth.

30

---

9 OCTOBER 1888

"My dear, you were coy with me at the townhouse, telling me you needed time to consider my proposal," I say. Jane and I sit by the side of a brook snaking through the far edges of her family's estate. I wait patiently on her reply as I gaze at the majestic trees arching their boughs over the stream. It will not be many more days before their leaves change colour and fall into the current. The clean fresh water will carry them to a tributary of the Thames and then into the polluted foul-smelling waters winding past Whitechapel, finally depositing them into the English Channel.

Our horses are tied nearby. Jane has unfurled a blanket to sit on. She kneels across from me in her riding breeches, a deliberate choice of clothes, a sign of her independence from London society, and serves me scones and lemonade.

"Darling, you are by far the most interesting man I know. None of the boys on my dance card share any of your worldly experiences."

If she only knew. My practiced smile remains.

She continues, "But they are young and clumsy, hoping a chance kiss might lead to a test of my virtues. You have been nothing but a perfect gentleman, knowing the time to explore passion will be the ultimate consummation of the marriage vow."

But not *our* marriage vows. I am keen to pick up on the distancing of her use of words. I find a stick in arm's reach and toss it into the brook, following its travels. "I look into these waters and imagine us exploring the Rhine or the Euphrates by day and our marital bliss by night, if I might be so bold to exclaim."

She lifts the white china plate with her flawless fingers and takes tiny bites from the scone before setting the treat down. She sips lemonade from borrowed dining room crystal before responding.

"Here's the rub, darling. You have travelled those rivers and many far-off lands. You would be my trusted guide, but I want to explore them with someone who will share my first-time amazement. Your maturity, gentlemanly manners and wisdom have shown me there is so much outside of here and London." She brushes imaginary crumbs from her lap.

My hunger and thirst are gone, my plate and glass untouched. How to save face? "Are you saying I am too old for you, Jane?"

She glances away, colour forming on her slender neck and cheeks.

Better to be silent than to lie. I see. "Is it because of my business situation?"

"Not at all. We have never discussed money or standing. You are a successful businessman."

My face reddens. "But not as successful as your father. I would refuse a dowry. You know that."

She smiles. "Few families are as successful as my family."

I realize I was her plaything during the London Season, and not the other way around.

"When I choose to marry," she continues, "it will be with a man who I will share a future with. I will not be shown around parts of his past. We will see the world with fresh eyes and wonderment."

I appraise her with fresh eyes. She is more intelligent than I gave her credit for. Many comments she made while I courted her come back to haunt me now as warning signs which I previously ignored.

I stand up with my scone, take it to the horses and break it in half. They appreciate the gesture. I turn back to Jane as she repacks the picnic basket. I silently help her fold the blanket. We ride back in silence along hedges and pastures to the stables, handing off our steeds to the stable boys without another word spoken. I go into the manor and change out of my riding clothes. Leave them for the next lucky fellow.

The carriage whisks me and my thoughts back to the train station in Cheltenham. My anger at Jane's polite rejection grows. She did not even bother to see me off. The evening express will transport me back to London, where the uncertainty of my financial security looms.

Is it too soon to visit Whitechapel for my release?

31

10 OCTOBER 1888

HENRY JEKYLL

I sit with my brother and our friends at our usual table in the club, but my thoughts are elsewhere. To my dinner companions' surprise, I order a whisky, but it remains untouched as I stare into the amber liquid, thinking of the green-eyed Irish woman with flaming red hair and her dog in Whitechapel.

I tune into Blackwell mid-sentence. "—terrible, just terrible what Jack the Ripper did to those girls."

"Girls?" George asks. "What were they doing out after midnight on the Sabbath? If they were home in bed, they'd be alive." This is his constant pompous refrain. He pours more tea from the pot left on our table. I am tiring of his sanctimonious pontifications.

"Are you saying they deserved horrible deaths?" Sutton asks. He is on his third drink of which will be countless more this evening. I understand our gathering is always the most exciting event in my friend's rather dull life. Sutton has made the most of these occasions by fanning the fire smouldering between us brothers.

I raise my tumbler to eye level and observe how the candlelit chandeliers take on various shapes, as if I am viewing them through a prism. "My brother makes an excellent point. If they were not walking the streets in search of gin and men, in that order, they would be home safe in a warm bed." I tip the liquid so that a small amount touches my lips and tongue.

I don't recall part of that morning in Whitechapel. Hyde had drunk until he passed out. I had awoken with my head spinning and arm pulsing in pain, staring at Francine's stern countenance. I swallow; the whisky sets my throat afire.

George cocks his head at my remark. "Finally, you agree with me."

"My friend in Whitechapel wants me to help her with what you are suggesting, younger brother. She tried unsuccessfully to assist Lizzy Stride to give up the drink."

"She knew the woman who almost lost her head?" Sutton gasps.

I nod and swirl some more whisky around my mouth with my tongue. My nostrils feel the rush of fumes, and my eyes water. "On any night, there are hundreds of women in Whitechapel, like Lizzy Stride, for Jack the Ripper to pick from. My friend didn't know the Eddowes woman, but if she did, she would have tried to rescue her as well."

"They are beyond reach. The devil has them now," George scoffs.

"Why haven't we met your friend?" Blackwell asks.

I set the empty tumbler down and straighten my butter knife on the white tablecloth. "She connected with me through Anderson, the church sexton from St. Giles in the Fields where the Jekylls have a family pew. She asked me to bankroll her mission. She spends most of her daytime trying to get funded. At night, she reaches out to those women most in need." I turn to George. "She is extremely busy and tireless in her zeal to reach the unreachable, as you have pointed out."

George glares at me. "How much money does she want?"

I smile as I look around at them. "Not enough that it would make a difference to any of us. Do you want to consider going in with me on underwriting this project?"

"I might," Sutton offers. "She sounds like a remarkable woman."

Blackwell laughs nervously, hiding behind his glass.

"Albert? Is that titter a yes, then?" I ask.

My friend nearly spits out his drink with a firm, "No."

"Why is that, Albert?" I persist.

"All my donations are through the church, Henry," comes Blackwell's practiced response.

All eyes turn to George.

He smiles.

We wait.

He keeps smiling. Finally, Sutton tries to break the impasse. "Introduce me to this friend of yours. I would be most interested to see how she does it."

The dinner plates arrive with George and I still not breaking eye contact. We both keep our hands in our laps.

Blackwell is first to speak after savouring his initial bite. "Perfectly done as usual. Here, here to a sumptuous meal." He raises his glass as a toast. Sutton joins him reflexively, while George and I remain smiley-faced and unmoving. Sutton sets his glass down and busies himself with his food. Blackwell does likewise.

I reach for my steak knife and point it at George. "Better to curse the darkness than to light a candle. Is that it, little brother?"

"You know nothing of darkness, big brother. Here, give this to your friend." He pushes the plate of meat and potatoes to the table centre, stands, throws his napkin on the chair and walks off without a glance at any of us.

I take the plate and motion to the waiter. I think of a lucky dog who will enjoy the treat. Maybe Sutton and I can take the meal on a surprise visit. I think better of it, given that I smell of whisky again and Sutton is inebriated. I decide to send it down with Louise, who has offered to stay overnight on the nights Francine goes searching for other lost black sheep.

32

14 OCTOBER 1888

EDWARD HYDE

I depart from my observation post in the church when the fog rolls in and makes it too difficult to see over thirty feet below my perch. There have been no commotions, no police whistles summoning help to horrific scenes this entire morning.

Horses move heavy-laden carts with poorly aligned wheels across the cobblestones. Their business is heard but not seen. In the fog, a hush falls over those moving about in the pre-dawn darkness.

The fog makes it easier for me to scurry home. I am a wanted murderer, after all; something in common with Jack the Ripper. I clutch the dagger under my coat in case we meet again. He can walk anywhere he wants, as all the descriptions of him vary wildly. On the other hand, the description of the man with the bleeding arm was spot on. As such, I have to be careful when I am exposed under street lamps out in the open. The fog forces the few remaining women with illegitimate business to walk in pairs. I decide to navigate in the fog on smaller roads and alleys back to Cavendish Square.

In time, I reach the alley behind Mrs. Murphy's flat. It is narrow, slick with horse droppings, and it reeks of yesterday's garbage. It affords me a view of her two-bedroom windows. No lights are shining. She may have already returned home and is sleeping, for all I know. I have not seen her since the Ripper filleted my arm. As I enter where the streets cross, I casually lean around the corner, as has become my practice. After the Whitechapel killer became known as Jack the Ripper, vigilant groups and police swarm this area at night. I hear voices in the fog. One sounds familiar. I lean further to determine if the voices are fading or growing in volume.

Suddenly, I spot Newcomen, flanked by two constables in their heavy blue serge coats, emerging from the fog. The fear of hanging from a gallows' noose constricts my breathing. They will be upon me in a few moments. I run back from the direction I came and try the doors of closed sheds and outbuildings.

Their voices reach the corner before they do, and they are hurrying. The fog clears momentarily, and they will no doubt spot me. I frantically turn one last doorknob. It twists, and I shoulder my way into the building and silently close the door behind me, instinctively latching it.

Immediately, I am struck by the overpowering smell of cedar. The dry air tingles my nose hairs and lips. The building is pitch black. I drop to one knee. A familiar terror grabs me by my throat. My pupils narrow to where I can see little more than my trembling hands at arm's length. My temples pound, and I can hear nothing outside the door.

The closet Henry's mother shoved me into after her lover had his way with me had been lined in cedar. That closet's sturdy door and sturdy lock kept the five-year-old Hyde imprisoned for hours and days without food and water. I dared not piss or crap in there, lest I be beaten by both of them.

I force all my concentration on breathing slowly while the seconds crawl by like hours. I am safe from Newcomen but paralyzed by the smell of cedar as I curl up on the floor in complete darkness with the reawakened memories of my childhood abuse. The physical pain, humiliation and terror I saved Henry from assaults me in waves as I nearly suffocate on the all-encompassing scent of cedar. I breathe through my mouth but stop when I hear the door handle jangle. Newcomen is outside.

I lie in a foetal position on the floor, and I cover my face with my good arm and muffle my breathing. I focus on the one thing I can, the memory of what I did to the person most responsible for my childhood horrors.

I recall the chance meeting on the street. The words he whispered in my ear set off a torrent of cane strikes raining down on him like a hailstorm until he was a limp, broken heap in the gutter. Reliving the savage beating in that place, with Newcomen now on the other side of the ramshackle door, gives me the strength to confront him if he enters. I will make the Ripper's work look like child's play when I finish slicing Newcomen from his bellybutton to his breastbone.

For the first time since I can remember, the tension of my clenched sphincter, slammed tight after Carew's penetrations all those times, decades ago, finally relaxes. He is dead. I killed him. I relish those thoughts. I am ready to kill again. Such is the flood of relief, I can't control my bowels, and they let loose. I no longer have to worry about painfully shutting down my bladder, and the wet warmth surrounds my loins. I convulse on the floor, each memory of being struck on the arms, back and buttocks slowly fading into the darkness. I am at peace with what I did to Carew and what Newcomen can expect. I am released from my nightmarish childhood and stand ready to confront my tormentor.

———

HENRY JEKYLL

Was I dreaming of church bells pealing? My dreams were like no other I can remember. Was I entering heaven? Where were the angels?

The shoulder of my bad arm aches as I turn onto my back. The bed does not yield. I try to sleep on my good arm side, but the bed does not give. I realize that I have slept on a floor. Odd feelings of peaceful serenity linger as I open my eyes to a pale light shining under a door. The smell of cedar strikes me immediately, followed by the smell of excrement and urine. I sit up and conclude my trousers are caked with the former in the rear and drenched in the front with the latter, from my waist to my knees. Slowly awakening in a strange place usually causes distress. I am surprised many times by this, and it leaves me with a sense of dread, not knowing what transpired while Edward has run amuck. At this moment, however, the opposite is the case. I feel euphoric, a lightness of spirit bordering on undeserved favour. Some might describe it as living in a state of grace. In the dream, I remember feeling like I was enveloped in the aurora of northern lights. It was like those clear nights looking at the stars on the island before returning to London, when I thought I was finally rid of my bad self. I feel like that now, but even more so.

I slowly stand, and my arms and shoulders are not complaining. I feel loose and lively. I unlock and open the door. A truncheon held by Newcomen hovers above.

"Where's Hyde? I saw him go in here."

I raise my hands in defence and lean backwards. "Check for yourself."

Newcomen shoves me aside and scurries about the interior of the empty storage facility. I remain just outside the door. Fog fills the alleyway. Where am I?

Newcomen comes back and stands in front of me, blowing

his sour breath into a whistle, his cheeks reddening from the exertion.

"I saw Hyde go in here," he says. "Is there a hidden door or trap door?" Constables come running from both directions. Waiting for their arrival, Newcomen notices the smells coming from me.

"Doctor Jekyll, did you shit yourself?"

"Pissed myself too, I'm afraid."

Newcomen stands back and addresses the constables. "Did anyone go by you?"

They both shake their heads and say "no" in unison.

"Take your lanterns in there and search for hidden compartments or trap doors."

Newcomen and I watch as they poke and pry boards, but to no avail. They exit the way they entered, the only way in or out.

"What were you doing in there?" Newcomen asks, looking incredulously at me.

"Must have passed out. I remember nothing."

Newcomen squints. "You passed out. You have a habit of passing out while killers are about in Whitechapel?"

I look back inside the building. "Nothing's stolen and nothing's broken." I stretch my arms to the sky. "Best sleep I've had in years." I keep from smiling at Newcomen's failure to capture his prey.

"I could arrest you for trespass," he says.

"True. I am sure Utterson would have something to say to the magistrate about your continued harassment of me, with the search warrant and round-the-clock surveillance."

I strike a nerve, and the inspector weighs his hollow threat as he shuffles from one foot to the other.

Newcomen spins around, pointing mid-block. "Isn't that Mrs. Murphy's building?"

"Believe it is," I reply, noticing for the first time where I am, and it gives me an opening. "I was walking to Whitechapel last night to visit her. That's the last thing I recall."

The three policemen glare at me.

I relish the moment. Mister Hyde darts into a locked room, and Doctor Jekyll emerges. It is an impossible feat, an act of magic Newcomen can't accept.

I step through the semi-circle of angry men. "Best be getting out of these clothes, Inspector. Do you think I can hail a cab at this hour?"

33

15 OCTOBER 1888

FRANCINE MURPHY

The Ripper didn't mutilate any women over the weekend, as far as anyone knows. I was able to coax Sally in the wee hours of Sunday morning to join my group. Louise arrived shortly thereafter with food and other necessities. Doctor Jekyll did not accompany Louise but sent his good wishes as a healthy cash outlay. He told Louise it was his poker winnings. The bills were clean and crisp and didn't look like they'd spent a long night being pushed around a green felt table.

When I try giving the money back to my friend, a normally placid Louise asks, "Are you daft? The good doctor may have his flaws, but his heart is in the right place. He has a fond spot for you in there too." My body stiffens but I still blush at the suggestion.

Supper is excellent, with cheese, sausage, and warm bread. After cleanup, we all move to the room with the most beds and sit facing one another.

A question has bothered me for a few weeks now. I ask the group, "Tell me about your blackouts."

"Whaddya mean?" asks Bessie.

"What was your first one like? How long was your longest one? Did your memory of what happened ever return? What did people tell you of what you did while you were blacked out?"

"Why d'ya want to know?" asks Susan.

I look at the world-weary faces staring back at me and offer a half-truth. "I had one after my baby died. To this day, I don't know what I said to my husband to make him put me out on the street. If it weren't for Mary McCreary…"

Margaret says, "Aren't you the one always saying you can't change the past, you can only change what you can do today?"

"But I guess with a blackout, you don't know what the past is, because even though you lived it, you don't remember it. And unless somebody tells you what you said or did, you will never know. Neither my husband nor his family ever said a word to me about that night." I pause, making eye contact with each of them. "I only had that one, and one was enough for me." Hopefully, they won't catch on to my real reason for poking into their heads.

"I once lost a whole week," Norma says.

"Any recollection of what happened?" I ask.

"Just what I was told. I don't want to talk about it. I should've learned my lesson after that time, but I didn't. It's better that the memory of that week don't come back, if you ask me."

Susan says, "My first one lasted long enough for me to wake up in the morning next to a stranger."

The other women nod in agreement of that not-uncommon situation.

Bessie laughs. The others know her sense of humour and wait. "It was a church picnic. No one knew I drank secretly, except my man. I woke up from a blackout between the legs of the vicar's wife. We were in the choir room of the church. Imagine my surprise when I heard her singing to the rafters."

We all laugh.

"I guess it made it all right if I wasn't in my right mind. That's how I rationalized it," Bessie says.

"The drink made me do it," Norma says.

"The devil made me do it," Susan adds.

Margaret looks to the others for encouragement to say what she has held in. "My first blackout had nothing to do with the drink, but everything to do with the devil." Lucky walks over to her and jumps up on the bed. She pets him and he sits next to her. I do not allow him on the furniture but don't rebuke him. He settles in with his snout on her thigh and her hand stroking his head.

"My mother didn't believe me when I told her my uncle came to my bed. She told me we were guests in her brother's house and not to make up silly stories." Tears well in her eyes. "I can't believe I told no one about this. When he came into my room after that first time, my dolly slept with him. I was not there."

"For how long, deary?" Norma asks.

Margaret looks at Lucky. He looks up at her, giving her permission to speak her truth. "From the time I was six years old until my first period." Lucky's eyes were the only dry ones in the room. "On my next birthday, my mother said I was a woman, and she threw out my dolly. She never understood why I was inconsolable for days afterwards. She kept telling me I was not a child anymore."

"She was a few years late on that pronouncement," Bessie says.

Margaret wipes the tears from her face with her other hand. "Can't change the past, even the parts I can't remember." The others saddle up next to her and Lucky. The bedsprings groan.

I've received my answer, but at the expense of one of my fragile charges. Was it worth the gambit? I wasn't expecting that answer and won't ask again.

Henry hasn't told me everything, but I believe him now when he said he has no memory of how his boots got muddy or how his arm got slashed. Where was his dolly? Maybe, he doesn't want to tell me everything, as he might lose my... my what? My acquaintance? No, it is more than that. My friendship? A well-to-do doctor from a respectable family in the West End? He could have his pick of many women of substance from anywhere in London. Why me?

There is a knock at the door. Lucky leaps from the bed and barks like a dog twice his size. It is not his joyful bark.

I follow him as the others watch.

I crack open the door to the unsmiling visage of my landlord, Mr. Withers.

He looks at Lucky and steps back. "A word, Mrs. Murphy." He quickly retreats down the hall, and I hear his footfalls as Lucky gives him a what-for.

I move my dog aside.

Margaret says, "Come sit with me, Lucky." He looks between me and her, knowing where his allegiance lies.

"I'll be back, Lucky. Go sit with Margaret."

It is near dusk on the street. The street lamps are not yet lit. People are returning to their homes. It is too early for the ladies of the evening to start their rounds.

"I want no trouble from you or your pesky dog, Mrs. Murphy," Withers starts.

"Tell me why you are interrupting my evening, Mr. Withers." Our last meeting on the street was for my eviction. If not for Henry and his lawyer, I would have been tossed out of my flat like dirty bath water.

He shakes his head. "This is your evening, Mrs. Murphy? Where do you go every night? How do you get ready for your next day?" He continues with an acidy tone. "You go out after midnight and consort with the women who sell their bodies. How many of them are you harbouring upstairs? You brought another one home who could barely walk on her own, she was so pickled with gin."

"Your point, Mr. Withers?" I stand at a polite distance with my hands on my hips. My rent has been paid until the end of the year. Unlike Lucky, I am almost certain, Wither's bark is worse than his bite.

As if reading my mind, he says, "We are returning Doctor Jekyll's rent payment for the months of November and December. He will have no arguments with us, if he goes to court, when he learns of the criminal records of the women you are harbouring."

To my astonishment, he names each one, including Sally, and rattles off their arrests and convictions.

"You said *we,* sir. Who are *we?*"

"Fine upstanding people have come to me and aired their grievances. You are not to concern yourself with whom but understand that my reputation as a landlord cannot be sullied. I cannot have it known I rent rooms to women of ill repute. They are lewd and tawdry criminals. Doctor Jekyll persuaded me to allow you to remain. At no time did he present me with the possibility that you would fill your lodging—my building—with such disrespectable women."

"These women have not drunk spirits, nor done anything else untoward since abiding in my flat."

"The constables will evict you by court order on 1st November. Here is your notice to vacate. Another copy is being hand-delivered to Doctor Jekyll with his remittance."

I let the envelope fall to the ground, then stomp it into a horse dropping and scrape my shoe along the street and Withers' wooden steps as I return to my flat. I have two flights of stairs to quell my anger, return my breathing to normal and put on a cheery expression. What will I tell them?

34

21 OCTOBER 1888

JACK THE RIPPER

This is the first time on any of my hunting forays that I feel I am being watched. This night, I stay on the main roads and do not stray into the darkened alleys. I go inside the entertainment venues and gin palaces long enough for anyone interested in my movements to see where I am going, that I'm not just sizing up the streetwalkers. I don't think for a moment a well-meaning passerby, by coincidence, interrupted my enjoyment of the Stride woman. I was fast with my blade and fended off the intruder. Since then, I am more wary of being hunted rather than being the only predator in the urban jungle.

This conclusion came upon me most likely from my newfound fame and the fact I keep returning to the same hunting ground. Previously, my blood lust and business travels went hand in hand. An evening in Madrid, two nights later in Lisbon, and after that, a steamer to Casablanca. None of it left a bloody trail the way I am doing in London's cesspool of Whitechapel.

I have my reasons for continuing to take chances. One reason being, I find it exciting, outfoxing the police and vigilant groups formed to apprehend me and to stop my savagery.

Also, the newspaper accounts stoke my feelings of superiority and invincibility. Since the double killing and posts to the newspaper by the person purporting to be Jack, the world has noticed my exploits. It is intoxicating. I eavesdrop in public houses and other places where the terrified denizens gather. The rumours and descriptions of Jack the Ripper vary widely, but their fear and loathing does not. The world's largest city is spellbound by my exploits. The people are railing at the police for their ineffectual response.

More than a show of brute force, constable patrols are on the increase, and their walking beats are not as predictable as when I first strolled these filthy cobblestones. Swarthy men loiter in alcoves and entrances at key locations, where they can scan a few roads at a time without the passing constables or watchmen even giving them a nod.

The women still on the streets at this late hour do not stray far from their source of drink. They negotiate their fees for services near their watering holes and lead the lucky fellows by the hand to a discreet spot near to the well-lit travelled roads. The Ripper has changed the way this illicit business is being transacted. They are more careful, and I even watch several women refuse overtures from their nocturnal suitors.

Lady Jane is a bitter memory. Gone is the comfortable existence of never having to work again. There are few options left for me. I must pursue them with more diligence.

I feign drinking spirits and practice slurring my words as the morning wears on. The police in rough clothes and uniforms outnumber the inebriates staggering to their beds.

I know what I thirst for, but the rules have changed along with my growing notoriety. As dawn breaks, I make my way to the train station where I hope to find a cab to take me part way home. I need to make a change, and as daylight breaks through the morning fog, the solution becomes as clear as the rising sun.

205

the train station where I hope to find a cab to take me part way home. I need to make a change, and as daylight breaks through the morning fog, the solution becomes as clear as the rising sun.

35

25 OCTOBER 1888

"Withers told me he sent a messenger to you returning the November and December rent along with the order to vacate ten days ago," Francine informs me.

She and I are walking towards the church in the centre of Whitechapel on High Street. The thoroughfare is choked with all manner of carts, carriages, and cabs, and the feculent output of their respective beasts of burden. Low-hanging clouds keep the noise of everyday business, along with the humid and fetid air, close.

My attention flickers to the church's spire and the second-floor windows below it. I don't know why, but at that moment my stitched arm tingles, and I assume the church holds some significance to Edward.

I shake my head. "I have received nothing of the sort. Louise told me about Withers on Monday morning. Can you show me the papers?"

"I didn't keep them. I tossed them on the street at his feet.

My ladies never caused a problem for him. We could have been a gathering of defrocked nuns for all our neighbours knew."

I frown. "I'll have Utterson sort it out."

Browsing the food carts and stalls for fresh fruits, fowl and vegetables, Francine does not protest when I pay and doesn't resist when the vendors hand her the change. A good sign.

"What's your plan?"

"Safe lodging for six single women will be scarce. We might have to separate. A few of them, I can try to convince their families to take them back. That they haven't touched a drop of gin in three weeks may be enough for their loved ones to give them another chance."

"Do you think that is enough time for those ladies to stay away from the temptation?"

She places our last purchase in the cloth bag I am toting. "In a word, no."

"The others?"

She takes a deep breath and sighs. "We could stay at a dosshouse, paying a week at a time, but we would still be together. The weather is fit. We can go to the parks and occupy a few benches until we are allowed back in at night."

"And when it rains?"

She looks at me and states bluntly, "Then we get wet."

I set the bag safely between my feet. "If I had taken you up on your request for funding when we first met, you would not have to stand out in the rain." I want to turn back the pages of the calendar to our first meeting. But there is the issue of waking up drunk in her bed.

As if reading my mind, she says, "I now believe you have no memory of the events the night Lizzy and Catherine were murdered, but you are not telling me everything. I'm having trouble trusting you completely."

"Rightly so; I can't argue with you. From the beginning, I

told you I am a private person. There are things I've not told anyone."

"Does it have to do with that Scotland Yard inspector?"

"Newcomen thinks I am harbouring a murderer. He tried to plant evidence from one of the Ripper's murders in my surgery to implicate me. By doing so, he thinks he can force me to give him my associate."

Neither of us are paying attention to the bustle of the street.

"Your associate—did he kill someone?"

"So, Newcomen told you why he is breathing down my neck."

"He said that your associate killed a man and fled with you to the West Indies."

I wish Hyde had never killed Carew. It is why I fled London for over two years, thinking I could vanquish him once and for all. My arm is letting me know he doesn't agree with my thoughts.

"Yes, he killed the man with my walking cane, but he fled to parts unknown. What else did the Inspector say?" We have moved to a street corner and stand where the foot traffic and horses do not tread. This may be the last time I speak with her, and I need to know about Newcomen's investigation into Hyde and myself.

"You provided this man with much financial support but knew little about him."

"What else?"

I am leaning in closer to her, and she steps back and stares at me before answering. "His manner was about the same as yours is presently, Doctor Jekyll."

"I apologize if I appear I am roughly questioning you. The inspector runs hot and cold with me, but rest assured, he wants me to give up the whereabouts of my associate. Failing that, he tries to claim that it is me who is butchering the women of Whitechapel."

The sound of passing traffic, snatches of conversation, hooves on cobblestone, fill the growing silence between us.

"You say you don't remember what happened the night your arm was sliced. Two women died horrible deaths while you were blacked out. They were both alive when I left you, and when I returned to my flat for the second time that night, they were both dead." She looks past me and speaks in a hushed tone. "Everything is confusing to me, and I don't know what to believe."

"Do you think I killed those women?" I ask incredulously.

"How many stories have we both heard about people acting badly, engaging in all sorts of depravity and murder, when they are blacked out, Henry?"

I look at her evenly. "Thank you for your response, Francine, but can you answer my question. Do you think I murdered those women?"

She shakes her head, but says, "To make it more confusing, the inspector said the description of the man fleeing Dutfield Yard with a bleeding arm matched that of Mr. Hyde, your associate."

My arm tingles, and my throat constricts. *Now is not a good time, Edward.* I cough and drop the bag so that it rests on the tip of my boot.

"Yet you found me passed out in your bed with a stitched-up arm."

She cocks her head trying to make sense of it all. "Like I said, it is all very confusing."

I pick up the provisions and start toward her flat. I want to pet Lucky again. I might have to suggest taking him with me if her next landlord forbids animals. We walk in uncomfortable silence to her flat. Then I have an idea. It forms in an instant and leaves me light-headed. The words are the troublesome part. I will have only one chance to say it. I approach the topic with trepidation.

Finally, I can bear it no longer. "For months, you have been searching for a source of funding, a grant for your mission so to speak. What does your plan look like?"

"What does it matter now?" She shakes her head. "I need immediate lodging for six women, and a dog. Your help has been remarkable. Without all you have done, I would not have rescued those women from the Ripper and life on the streets."

I stop to face her. Her green eyes do not waver as she looks up at me. I persist. "If I had accepted your proposal to give you what would have been my yearly tithe to St. Giles, what would you have done?"

She turns and continues walking. Not to avoid the question, but to think as she speaks. "Secure a building with a full-size kitchen, indoor toilets, and rooms for a dozen ladies. Rooms they can lock and call their own. A clean, dry space with many windows to allow the sunshine in. A large dining room would be nice as well. That is my dream."

I can see the dream fading in her mind with the more pressing problem of the looming eviction.

I am more determined than before to do this for her. The words rush out of my mouth as if it is not I who is speaking them. "I am a doctor of good standing in my community. I can begin treatment of your ladies for their alcohol abuse. They can take up residence at Cavendish Square, temporarily, of course, during their recovery. To my neighbours, you are their house-mother. I can hire Louise as my live-in housekeeper. My watchman and Lucky will keep them safe."

"Henry—"

"Your troubles with my privacy are outweighed by your need for safe lodging where you are not at the mercy of a land-lord. With Louise by your side, you can continue to bring others to safety. You would be only a quick cab ride from Whitechapel. This is only temporary. Tomorrow, we can start looking for a grand home to convert to your mission use. Utterson can arrange for the title and deed to be placed in the name of your business, with me as the sole stockholder."

"I cannot."

"Your funding problem is over. We can hire movers to transport everything to my residence, and when we secure the deed for your home for wayward women—"

"I hate that word. I'd rather think of their future than their past."

Chastised, I say, "It will come to you, Francine, when you are standing before your new home." I smile.

"Why are you doing this for me, Doctor Jekyll? What are your true intentions?"

There it is. She cannot be more honest when she faces both the crisis of the moment and the opportunity to fulfil her mission.

"You are a strong, independent woman. You have a gift for talking with these women, and you empower them to reclaim their lives. You are doing it with no help from the church or government. You believe in the women and see them not for their past, as you have just said, but for who they will become."

"But you didn't answer my question."

"You stir feelings in me, feelings I have never felt. Am I attracted to you?" I nod. "I would be lying to you if I didn't say I enjoy being with you, even during these difficulties. What you are trying to accomplish allows me to stand in the sunshine of your determined spirit. I was a mere shadow of a man until I met you. Will you allow me to help you?"

We stand on the road below her flat. I am not sure if she is going to allow me upstairs. I would like to see our dog. *Our dog.*

"What if I don't feel the same way about you?" she asks. "I wouldn't want you to think I was trying to charm you into helping me."

Before I can reply, an irresistible smell of baked goods wafts through the dank air around us. Francine and I turn to be greeted by Margaret holding a platter of warm scones. "Look at what we made," she says.

"None of the women in my care can bake anything like that," she says to me. She flies up the stairs, with me on her heels. We enter her flat to the smell of lemon cakes, cinnamon scones and fresh buns. Lucky runs to me immediately.

Sally stands there with flour-smudged cheeks, wearing an apron made for a taller woman. The others are kneading dough, measuring sugar and separating whites from yolks. All are in deep concentration. Sally puts on thick leather gloves and reaches into the oven to retrieve a chocolate cake. "Me mum heard I was doing good and came by. We baked when I was a wee girl, and I was her assistant. These were me grandmother's gloves. She saved them for me."

"You did this from memory?" Francine asks.

"No, me mum just left. She promises she'll visit me as long as I'm sober."

Margaret says, "She can visit as often as she likes. Look at all this."

I am instantly hungry.

Francine introduces me around; a kettle is put on, and the women slice some of this and a little of that, and in minutes an impromptu party is in full swing. Hard to believe their situation is dire; they may be scattered to their families or worse. For now, it is a tea and cake party, a proper high tea before the noon hour. They show a singular purpose with the baking, and they all talk excitedly about it. I tell them I have tasted nothing finer in the West End or during any of my travels.

I pull Francine aside for a quiet moment. "Can you imagine what they could do with the ovens in my home?"

A smile creases her face. "You are reading my mind, Doctor Jekyll. As for the other matter, I cannot return your affections until I know you better. Until I know the whole you. I think you understand."

Dare I tell her about Hyde? I've never told a soul. Would she hold me accountable for his actions? The sweetness of the cake sours in my mouth at the thought of losing her forever. What can I possibly say that will make sense? I was a murderer, but it happened while I was in a blackout. My associate is really me. He could walk in one door, and I could walk out the other. I have kept this secret from all my closest associates. Maybe Utterson is my only friend, and even then, he is my lawyer, and he doesn't know the truth. Utterson has described Hyde to Newcomen. Unless Edward transforms in front of an audience, no one will believe me.

I am happy we will be under one roof but understand the impossibility of her request. I slump my shoulders, put down my cup and offer Lucky the last of my scone. All I can muster at the moment is, "I understand."

36

───────────

27 OCTOBER 1888

EDWARD HYDE

Henry took the stitches out of our right forearm today. I imagine it was a great deal less painful than when I put them in. The thick red-and-purplish streak is tender to the touch, but the wound is finally closed. It reminds me that the man I am hunting is extremely dangerous. I trace my fingers on my coat sleeve, from my elbow to my wrist bone above the scar, and recall how my arm shielded my throat from being opened like a piece of overripe fruit.

I stand deep in the entranceway where I first encountered the abandoned, starving dog. It stinks like a privy. I am not sure what I will find if I move the rubbish and debris from the darkest recesses. I feel safe here from the roving bands of toughs, police constables and vigilant groups who rove about to apprehend the Ripper. If need be, I can lie motionless along the far wall under discarded newspapers and pray that I don't upset a rat's nest.

A strange question comes to me as I observe drunks weaving along the streets between the thin stream of carts, carriages and cabs. Would I like a drink or two or ten? Since my return to the city, I have been singularly focused on ensuring Henry's survival. There has been no time for my vices. I have paid for the services of women several times before, but never in this part of town. There have been many nights when I awoke along the docks and wharves on the north side of the Thames and made the acquaintance of various rodents at eye level.

Henry had good reason to recoil when he heard about the exploits of his friend, Mr. Hyde. I moved about the city like a man let out of prison or a sailor on shore leave. Did I take advantage of Henry's good nature? Yes. His nature is amiable because I suffered the unimaginable horrors and beatings in his stead. I was like a big cat who had escaped the zoo. I roamed the city on the prowl for a good time.

This evening, the temperature dropped quickly after the sun disappeared in the western sky. There is a chill to the late October air. I shiver and turn my collar up, then comfortingly touch the sharp point of my dagger in my coat pocket. I am better prepared than that night when Henry foolishly offered to accompany Mrs. Murphy into Whitechapel. I promise myself I will not run headlong into the dark the next time I happen on Jack the Ripper.

I am glad to be moving about the shadows again of the five or six square blocks where Jack operates. A sliver of moon darts between fast-moving clouds and offers occasional illumination. Dew forms on surfaces and is cool to the touch. It has been four weeks since Jack wounded me and butchered those poor women. The streets have far less activity than was once expected on a cool Saturday night. The sounds of laughter and music echo out of the pubs and gin palaces into the lightly travelled streets. The killings have had a dampening effect on the legitimate and not-so legitimate trade. If he is out here, he will not have as many women to victimize, a price to pay for his notoriety.

Do I think the Ripper is dead? No. Has he fled the area? I don't think so. Is he jailed on unrelated charges and the police don't know whom they hold? Possibly. Does he no longer feel the need to carry on his murderous spree? I don't think he is finished. He has a taste for bloodletting and the publicity. Maybe somebody taught him to act more cautiously. Maybe that somebody is Edward Hyde?

The women are being more careful too. They travel in pairs, and while one negotiates and transacts services, the other is not far away and will be able to supply a description of the man to the police should her friend not return. The women reverse roles for their next trip into the alleys.

I hid Henry's shaving kit as a clue. We are growing dark stubble on our cheeks and chin. The man with the bleeding arm from a month earlier stands taller and dresses better as well. Since the night in the cedar storage locker, I am no longer burdened by my past. I realize killing Danvers Carew was my redemption from the evil thrust upon me by my unwilling weaker half. I no longer fear capture or death. I will not pass as a gentleman up close, but even Utterson will not recognize me in the shadows where I move about Whitechapel. I am still careful, but no longer carry the burden of my past.

A hatless Mrs. Murphy steps off a hansom cab, accompanied by one of the ladies whom she has rescued. Her brown frock coat and wool dress of similar colour contrast the new pale blue coat and dress of her friend. The women of the streets know Mrs. Murphy by sight, with her long red hair and purposeful stride. She engages several women at once. I can't make out what they are saying, but they fawn over the other woman who was once like them, taking turns twirling her like a ballroom dancer.

Henry has brought all of Mrs. Murphy's ladies into his home. The dog has free roam of the house. We reacquainted ourselves before I departed for Whitechapel. He looks very different from the dog on death's door.

Henry is the happiest I've ever felt him. The kitchen constantly bustles with quality baked goods pouring out of the ovens.

I know I am the reason Mrs. Murphy and Henry are not sharing intimacies. I sense she would like to know him better, and for the life of him, he cannot figure out how to introduce her to Edward Hyde.

Francine, my dear, by day I am a respected doctor in the fashion-able section of this fair metropolis, but by night I am a garrulous murderer wanted by the police. Oh, and to make it more interesting, I have no memories of my nocturnal adventures. Do you take your tea with cream or sugar?

I understand why Henry is smitten with her. She is beautiful, strong, quick-witted and determined.

For years, I've watched men fight over religion and politics, but the one thing they agreed on was that the women Mrs. Murphy talked to were beyond redemption. Here she is, twenty yards in front of me, backlit by the pub lights, talking easily with London's worst of the worst. She offers proof to them of the contrary. Cleaned up and a month without booze or whoring, the former ladies of the streets are on their way to a new life, where they would be welcomed into any house of worship or be able to apply for work anywhere their past does not catch up with them. This is the promise Mrs. Murphy holds out to these working girls. All they have to do is accept the hand she offers and live by some simple rules.

My thoughts return to the woman the Ripper nearly decapitated after he swung his blade at me. Mrs. Murphy had half-dragged her to her dosshouse the night before she died. Henry's friend did her best, and so did I, to save her. Her death, and the death of the other woman later that morning, gave several women a reckoning they needed to overcome the devil's grip on them. If not for the Ripper, I doubt that Henry would have a houseful of women.

Sadly, the Ripper is good for Mrs. Murphy's cause. Long Liz's death is real to every woman propositioning men after midnight in order to pay for their gin. The later they ply their trade during the small hours Sunday mornings, the greater the chance they will feel his blade.

Mrs. Murphy and her friend move away from the others and walk along the lightly travelled roads towards the next drinking establishment. This is her routine. Mrs. Murphy, the Ripper and I have something in common with the mighty hunters of big game. On the great savannahs of Africa, if you hunt lions, you don't stray far from the watering holes of their prey.

I follow her at a safe distance but remain watchful of the police and wary of Jack. She will eventually attract the Ripper, as she is removing the weakest and most vulnerable out of the urban jungle. She will lead me to him. I need to be quick with my dagger when the time comes.

37

9 NOVEMBER 1888

If she comes back to Commercial Street for another man, I will tempt her with my shiny coins.

The vile creature is a regular at the Horn of Plenty pub, and I settle on her after her female friend goes off with a man and doesn't return. I follow my selection out of the pub the short distance to Dorset Street and watch her stagger into a building mid-block. I am cold and tired this wet morning. She has made several trips to Commercial Street and was successful in attracting a man to go with her a few times. I decide I am next.

I am more careful with my movements through this Thursday night into Friday morning. I pride myself on my control. The previous Sunday morning was not conducive to fulfilling my urges. It was as if the police and auxiliaries knew my intent. The women were more guarded as well, walking in pairs and conducting their disgusting business more cautiously.

The temperatures are unseasonably cold for early November, and I am glad I wore my heavy coat. I chuckle at the knowledge: I stand at an intersection in the middle of my four famous Whitechapel murders, and not a soul has considered me, a well-dressed, well-spoken West Ender out for my excitement, as the source of their terror. Some want to blame the killings on the Jews; others say the killer is a lunatic who is being protected by family members. The speculation is endless, but not one physical description comes close. I don't hide in the shadows. My position in society has allowed me to hide in plain sight. I don't have to explain my presence on the corner of Commercial Street and Brushfield Street to anyone. It is a given. On most nights, a not so insignificant portion of the female population of Whitechapel conducts business with men who are attracted to this squalid part of town like moths to a flame. Here in this overcrowded, downtrodden section of the world's largest city, the economics of supply and demand first postulated a century earlier dictate this social behaviour.

My own business affairs are going to brighten once my new plan is executed. I consider it both simple and cunning. Tonight's foray is for pleasure. I briefly considered travelling to the Continent and leaving my cutting tools at home, but my urges are now matched by the need to outfox the police and read about it in the newspapers for days to come.

I am rewarded for my patience when the man she is with hurries away from Dorset Street and passes me on Commercial Street. The man is shorter than me, with black hair and a moustache. He is dressed well, sporting a gold chain and a horseshoe tiepin. His pale face holds down turned eyes and a scowl. He must not have been happy with her pleasures.

I move at a leisurely pace towards Dorset Street and slow when I reach the corner. If she comes out to Commercial Street, her fate will be in my capable hands.

———

EDWARD HYDE

We turn left on Commercial Street from Whitechapel. She strides down the middle of the road. I move in the shadows behind her and along the building fronts. Close enough to sometimes overhear her conversations, but still at a safe distance so as not to be obvious. She has been unsuccessful in talking any of the women into giving up their drink and the world's oldest profession all morning. She summoned a cab for her latest charge earlier in the morning when the woman started coughing and sneezing. Better she returns to the nest.

It is still ninety minutes until dawn, but this working-class thoroughfare is waking up. Mrs. Murphy is now looking for a cab to take her back to Cavendish Square, probably wishing she had accompanied her former lady of the evening home.

Many of the drivers refuse her, and she thanks them with a few well-chosen curses that would make Henry blush. She passes Dorset Street just as a well-dressed man walks into the intersection. He quickly darts away from the direction she is heading and veers towards me. The street is not wide, and I duck into an alcove across the road before he turns his head away from her and in my direction. Mrs. Murphy does not turn to look at him. As he passes, I train my eyes on his figure and wait until he is illuminated by an overhead yellowish gas lamp. A horse cart comes between us, and when it passes, his figure is shrouded in darkness again and he has picked up his pace. How he is dressed and how he moves causes my scar to throb. I make a note of Dorset Street and hurry to catch up with Mrs. Murphy.

At Church Street, she finally hails a cab and I have to decide.

———

6:30 A.M.

JACK THE RIPPER

Did she see me leaving Dorset Street? She could provide my description to the police. Cursed luck. I should have back-tracked and grabbed her by her long red hair from behind, then drawn my blade across her throat right there in the middle of the street. She is a liability in more than one way.

I briskly zigzag on streets and alleys to the Tower of London. From there, I take a cab to near my home. I make my decision when I step off the cab. *She is next.*

———

EDWARD HYDE

It was him. It was the Ripper. I am sure of it. Why didn't I catch him unawares and dispose of him for good? Let the police find him dead in the street and cart his carcass away. He didn't want to be seen by Mrs. Murphy and changed his course when she passed in front of him. I curse myself for not confronting him while his back was turned to me. He was so concerned with her he kept his gaze on her to determine if she would see him scuttling away. I've seen rats and other vermin move like him when they are trying to flee. What was he escaping on Dorset Street? I dare not tread down whence he came, lest I be found by neighbours at the scene of his latest atrocity. I don't chase after him after I see Mrs. Murphy safely to her cab. Running about Whitechapel at that hour is not a good idea. I would be the person people will remember running from the scene, again.

Instead, I walk past where Mrs. Murphy caught the cab and

then head towards the West End. If he is on foot, I will take him down from behind.

I tarry, with my hand gripping my dagger in my pocket, on the fringes of Whitechapel.

Dawn arrives, and I realize he has escaped. I am angry at my hesitation when I had the chance. My first reaction was not to be seen by the man, but by doing so, I allowed him to pass unchallenged. As I slink home, I swear an oath to myself—I will not hesitate again. I'll know this monster the next time I see him.

38

---

12 NOVEMBER 1888

FRANCINE MURPHY

More Light, More Power. I read the motto under the crest of Shoreditch as I sit in on the inquest of Mary Jane Kelly, held in the grand meeting room of Shoreditch Town Hall. Margaret and I occupy the last seats in the back row. A resplendent building built in the last few years with majestic grey columns supporting two tall storeys of offices and a four-storey centre tower, the edifice's interior boasts wide, clean rooms with shiny hardwood floors. Local craftsmen built this government building, and the town folks in the borough are proud to call it their own.

I fume at the coroner, the jurors and the police. There is no more light, nor more power being shed on the proceedings. The lofty motto is for naught. The unsympathetic and uncaring men bring neither adage to their duty when investigating the fifth atrocity committed in the wee hours of the morning by Jack the Ripper.

This is the third inquest I've attended, and each one has been conducted as if it were a rare and singular event. In late summer and early autumn, five women have been butchered similarly in a short walking distance of each other between midnight and dawn, and nothing is being said about that.

I bristle as witness after witness talks about the victim's drinking habits and her nocturnal occupation. I imagine the all-male jury thinking about this 'unfortunate'—the polite euphemism for a prostitute—who was married at sixteen, lost her husband in a mine explosion, turned to using her body to survive the harsh reality of a young unskilled widow and drank to numb her pain. Had it been a wife or a sister of one juror from the more respectable parts of town, the hue and cry for justice would be deafening. With what little I know of the caste system in the British colony of India, I substitute the word *Untouchables* for *Unfortunates*. The victims' position in polite society is the lowest, and justice for them appears to be the same.

I want to shout at these jurors, but there are two things I also want to say but dare not. As each witness comes forward to testify, it becomes apparent I was near the murder at the time it occurred.

First, I was walking about Whitechapel in search of the women who most needed my help. Did I pass Jack the Ripper without giving him even a nod? I was so focused on hailing a cab; I didn't pay attention to anyone on Dorset Street.

The inquest only hinted at the severity of how Mary Jane was mutilated. Her death, caused by her neck being nearly sawn off (the same as Lizzy Stride), occurred not on the street or some filthy alley, but in Mary Jane's own bed. The newspapers detailed the scene in gory detail. The Ripper has become more maniacal in his butchery. Where does this hatred come from? Why is he getting more monstrous? He has waited nearly six weeks before striking again.

Last, did something happen between the Ripper and Henry

to cause the delay and the pent-up fury played out on this woman's body?

After Mary Jane's death captured the headlines, I asked Henry if anything had jogged his memory since the night his arm was sliced open. He shrugged and sadly shook his head. Knowing that he might somehow possess the description of the killer makes him feel guilty for Mary Jane's death, and that somehow, he could have prevented it.

Inspector Abberline, the Scotland Yard detective, finishes his testimony and gets up from the witness box. He walks to the room's exit.

"Margaret, save my seat," I say to her, then follow Abberline out of the building.

I rush up to him as his foot lands on a hansom cab step. "Inspector, a word, please."

He turns and eyes me suspiciously. A thick moustache blends into dark mutton chop sideburns, which add to his menacing appearance. He holds his black bowler in both hands. A receding hairline and reddened eyes speak of nights of sleepless worry.

"I am not a reporter," I add. "I have a question, if I may. McCarthy, the landlord, was seen in the vicinity at 1:30 a.m. by other witnesses but was not questioned about his whereabouts afterwards. He only testified to being summoned by his rent collector to Kelly's flat after 10:45 a.m."

His eyes narrow to a squint. "Are you suggesting that he killed the poor wretch?"

I answer with a question of my own. "Could McCarthy or his associates have seen the last man to enter her flat?"

Abberline arches an eyebrow, motions to the cab driver to wait, and says to me, "Go on."

I linger on the personage of the cab driver and have an idea. "I know for a fact that several cabs were in the area that morning. Have they been interviewed about the fares they picked up after four in the morning?"

The driver turns towards me in his seat and relaxes the reins in his lap. Both men are looking at me.

"Every man on foot in the area that morning was a potential customer. As I recall, it was a wet and freezing morning. They might part with their last shillings if they could get home to a warm bed sooner."

The driver nods.

"In four days, the same cabbies might work the same day of the week on the overnight shift. Would talking to them about who they picked up the night of the murder make sense?"

"Makes sense to me, guv," the driver says.

Abberline shoots him a look, and the driver turns back, pretending to mind his own business.

Abberline is deep in thought. "What's your name, ma'am?" He lowers his hat to one side and rubs his unshaven chin.

"Mrs. Murphy, Francine Murphy," I reply.

"Ah, the do-gooder," he says.

I've been called worse, and I smile, taking the term as a compliment.

He asks, "While we're at it, do you think we should ask them if they picked up any strange characters on the mornings of the other murders?" I'm not sure if he is baiting me, but I gladly take it, anyway.

"Each inquest and the police testimony only focus on the immediate death. It's infuriating, but the pieces of one puzzle might fit into the others. Each murder, sadly, offers you an opportunity to revisit prior crime scenes and witnesses to ask what they have in common with the latest killing."

He smirks and places his foot on the step. "Any other suggestions for Scotland Yard?"

I stand back from the cab and motion him to meet me on the

street behind the carriage. I turn my back and wait. If he doesn't care, I am wasting my time on this policeman, but I feel I have struck a nerve with him and want to save him further embarrassment.

He wearily comes around the carriage and faces me.

"Every woman I minister to know exactly where they were and what they were doing at the time the murders took place." I pause. "Why is that, Inspector?

"Because they are grateful, it was not them."

"Exactly. Mark all the public houses and gin palaces which border all the killings, except the one in the City of London on Mitre Square. Talk to all the 'unfortunates' who frequent those establishments after midnight and ask them where they were when each killing took place and which men they talked to or saw, especially men they may have been attracted to. They may have unwittingly met the Ripper or saw him. The description of the same man seen at or near the killings may provide you with a workable sketch."

He balks, but I tug on his sleeve. "I talk to those 'unfortunates' every night, not as who they are, but who they can be. If you show interest in their fears that a madman is preying on women just like them, then your descriptions will take shape. Jack the Ripper convinces them to take him to their safe place where they conduct their business. He is out there walking the same streets as they and the cabbies are. He is lurking about the same alleys. You will get your description, Inspector. You might intercept him or scare him off. Isn't that what you want?"

He adjusts his bowler on his thick dark hair, looks up to the low-hanging late afternoon clouds and says in a clipped voice, "McCarthy, prior witnesses, cabbies working on the same day of the week at the same time as Kelly's murder, and all the working ladies out and about in the area of all the killings. Did I miss anything, Mrs. Murphy?"

I smile. "I can't think of anything else, Inspector Abberline." I tug his sleeve for emphasis. "I can't possibly get all the women off the street, but you, sir, can take away their worst nightmare."

39

12 NOVEMBER 1888

HENRY JEKYLL

"We didn't expect to see you for dinner, Henry," Sutton says. He is on his fourth drink, if the number of toothpicks on his bread plate is any sign. Our waiter pulls my chair back.

"A rum punch, please," I say as I scan the table. Our usual foursome is gathered. Single men of money, generally bored with our idleness and hoping for something in the world to rail about. Anything to make our lives interesting. This is how I would have described us until I met Francine.

Blackwell chimes in, "How is it we could pry you from your harem?"

"Harem?" George asks. We have not spoken since he stormed off from this very table at our posh gentlemen's club, making a scene.

Blackstone replies, "Oh, come now, young Jekyll, surely you know of your older brother's good fortune."

I look at Blackstone with an amused gaze. George's furrowed brow adds to the mystery. I am content to let it hang in the air, for I have something to share with them all at my brother's expense when the time comes.

"The grocer who supplies our cook told her your mansion is alive with young women baking up a storm," Blackwell says.

"How many?" Sutton asks.

"Six, but who's keeping count?" I say. I pay more attention to buttering my roll than to their astonished looks. I taste it. It is warm but bland, nothing like what I have been treated to all week.

I need to be here to confront George, but I also need a respite. I am a private person by nature, thanks to Hyde. The house is now alive with gleeful shouts and giddy noise. I love finding Francine at my breakfast table every morning. And what is there not to love about Lucky stealing delicacies from my hand at every meal? He is filling out nicely and lets us know if any strangers are nearby.

"There's the dog, too. I named him Lucky after he was found near death by the front door of an abandoned building. He was waiting for his owners to return. Loyal, if you ask me."

I steal a glance at George, expecting him to erupt as he watches me coolly over the rim of his teacup. The others do likewise. He sets the cup down, fiddles with the silverware and looks up.

"I'm sure you have good reason to do so, brother," he says.

"Yes, George, you are right. Can you enlighten the others to what we are talking about?"

Both Blackwell and Sutton call for more of what they were drinking. Another Jekyll argument is in store for them. I taste my rum, and it immediately brings me back to idyllic ocean breezes, blinding white sand, brown children frolicking in the waves, and aqua waters to the horizon.

George says, "It came to my attention that a certain landlord was beside himself. I learned his tenant was harbouring women of ill repute—their criminal records were as long as my arm. He could not rent other flats in the building, and the property's value would plummet until the situation was remediated."

"That tenant being?" I ask.

There is no hesitation on my brother's retort. "The woman who helped Sexton Anderson's sister reclaim her sanity. Anderson repeatedly asked me to intercede with my brother to help fund her mission." He speaks calmly to the others and makes no eye contact with me. "I always hoped that Henry would retake his seat next to me in our family pew at St. Giles in the Fields."

"I'm confused," says Sutton after gulping half of his drink.

"While I was sojourning in the West Indies, I put a stop to my tithe, and upon my return, I did not renew my pledge," I say.

"Anderson was privy to this anomaly and sent the woman round to my brother to use that money to fund her," George says.

I take in my brother's truthful and dispassionate recounting of the facts, then volley with it. "Faced with an eviction, Mrs. Francine Murphy and her flock had nowhere to turn. She accepted my invitation to share my accommodations until we can find her a permanent building to operate from," I say.

"So, in the end, it all worked out, and I saved you two months' rent at that slum." He tosses an envelope in the middle of the table.

"What George is not telling you is that he pressed influential members of the vestry at St. Giles to pay informants to identify the women and have the vestrymen's friends at the Metropolitan police gather all the criminal records of my houseguests. He gave all this information to the landlord and even paid the attorney to get the court order."

We turn to George, who shrugs. "You paid Utterson a princely sum to strong-arm the landlord and then figure out how I did it. I could have just told you myself if you'd asked, but you want to use this moment to ambush me. I understand. What

Henry is not telling you is that he is smitten with this woman, and through my actions now, he has her under his roof. Next, in his bed, I am sure. What if it was rumoured it was Henry who asked me to do this?" He stabbed a roll with his bread knife and opened it to accept a slab of butter.

Blackwell and Sutton stare open-mouthed at me. For once I come into a battle of wits with my brother poorly armed. Getting angry makes me physically sick. My younger brother did not act holier than me, nor attempt to take the moral high ground. It is as if he sneaked a fast knee into my crotch with this veiled threat. I feel I am going to vomit, the pain of losing her so great.

I avoid making a verbal outburst I can't retract. My throat constricts, and I choke loudly upon swallowing my drink. Others in the room stop their conversations as I redden with lack of oxygen and embarrassment. I am sweating, and I loosen my shirt collar. I am attracting attention from the staff now. I use my remaining strength to banish Hyde to the ether, and with time, I stop seeing red and slowly regain my composure. I'd assumed I would indeed ambush George with the fact that it was he who instigated the investigation into the backgrounds of the women Francine rescued. Instead, he is turning the tables on me. How can I go to her and tell her my brother handled the eviction? She already doesn't trust me. It would be the end of our... our what? It would be the end of me being in her presence, staring into her green eyes, luxuriating in her long red hair, listening to her talk to others in her no-nonsense but non-threatening way. I would lose her trust forever. Did my brother just checkmate me?

Conversations resume, and busy waiters and water boys scurry around to cater to the club's well-heeled gentlemen. I fall slightly when I try to stand. I stagger to the toilets, then remember my encounter with Inspector Newcomen and change course. I veer through tables and pass men waiting at the cloakroom. I don't reclaim mine. Feelings I have never encountered before, flooding my body. My limbs shake, and my hands tremble. I barely make it to the pavement without pitching headfirst to the ground. The scar on my arm is on fire. The cold outdoor temperature is surprisingly comforting. I move like a drunk out of the streetlights and into the darkness, where I lean against a wall. My breathing slowly returns with one recurring thought pounding in my skull: I want to kill my brother.

40

14 NOVEMBER 1888

Killing the red-haired woman doesn't have to be a work of art, but leaving her heart at a certain address in Cavendish Square would be my final *coup de grâce*. Implicating a certain doctor with anatomical knowledge would give the people a calming sense of normalcy and serve my greater purpose.

She didn't give evidence at the recent inquest, but I can't take the chance of her identifying me in person as the last man to have met the whore on Dorset Street.

I consider my options as I wait for her at the major intersection of Commercial Road, Whitechapel Road and Commercial Street. Her flat is vacant. She no longer lives in Whitechapel with a gaggle of vile creatures. It has hardly rained for several days, and the stench of all the horse deposits assaults my nostrils. I lament that not even God can clean up this cesspool of humanity. Most hardworking Londoners are asleep at this late hour after saying their prayers, but here I stand listening to the calls of the sirens luring men to abandon their safe passage of a pure, chaste life for the fleeting moments of disgusting drunken debauchery. For every gin-soaked female I remove from these streets, it seems ten more are ready to take their place. Even a few days after I dispatched one to hell, their illegal business is back to usual.

During my visits to Whitechapel, I have traversed this intersection a few times nightly. I can figuratively throw a stone to several drinking establishments from this vantage point. On my successful hunting trips, I walked in plain view along major roads past a dozen more pubs until I eventually decided on my prey.

A knot of ruffians shoulder past me. Ten paces away, they spin around a man wearing a blood-stained butcher's apron. "State your business," the tallest says.

The reply is a mixture of German and Hebrew. I recognize the dialect from my travels.

A stout companion of the first pokes the frightened man in the chest. "What are you doing out at this hour?"

The man they accost could be a butcher or a horse slaughterer. His voice rises an octave, and he speaks in his native tongue, repeating himself several times, as if it would make sense the fourth time he spits it out.

A rail-thin third man shoves him into the tallest one. "Where do you live?"

The foreigner understands the question and blurts out, "Berner Street." The man gestures toward his home. "Berner Street. I show you." He motions for them to follow.

"Go on, then," the tallest says, and they follow closely behind him.

More and more toughs are walking the streets of Whitechapel as of late. The newspapers run stories of how the local business association here became increasingly concerned about the drop in legitimate business both day and night. They formed 'Vigilance Committees' to assuage the fears of the community. The ruffians bully obvious foreigners, the mentally deficient, and drunks, but they nod to me with a lewd wink and a knowing smile while tipping their caps. If they only knew my actual intentions.

Such is my focus on the altercation, I almost miss her. If it weren't for her long red hair, illuminated by a street lamp on Whitechapel Road, I would have dismissed her.

The bells of St. Mary's Church ring at midnight. By the time I get close enough to her, she has stopped in front of a gin palace and has engaged two loud brassy women in conversation. Both are pickled in drink, and their voices carry to the nearby alcove where I linger.

"Mr. Ahearn already has our doss money for the night, Francine," one says. "We've both eaten, and we've secured lodging for the night. Just making a little extra money for our entertainment."

The woman facing Francine wears a blue frock to her ankles, and black calf boots cover the rest of her legs and feet. The frock hides her ample bosom and wide hips. I imagine that two lithe Lady Janes could occupy that coat.

"We are sticking together like horse glue," the other says, tottering from side to side and hooking an arm around the first woman. Her woollen dress and short coat are not enough to protect her from the cool crisp air and slight breeze, but she doesn't seem to notice the chill of night in her alcoholic haze. Her shoes are caked with horse manure. She will have to service twice as many men as the other to make the same amount of money, given the stark differences in their appeal. I banish the thought from my mind. Am I really entertaining how these two price their services?

I cross the street between carriages and walk past the drinking spot to watch them from a safer distance. I catch occasional snippets of the redhead's Irish lilt. What strikes me as incredible is that she remains in conversation with them even as they proposition men exiting the drinking establishment. She appears to have no qualms about being seen with them while they rent their bodies. She is totally at ease and unfazed by their grotesquely wanton behaviour. Wool Dress lifts her hem to show off her leg, while Blue Frock unbuttons the frock to give the men a peek. The Irishwoman waits patiently to resume talking between their exhibitions and exhortations.

"I'm not talking to the police, deary," Blue Frock protests. "When they aren't throwing us in jail to meet their quotas, they corner us in an alley and ask us to give it to them for free. No way."

I can't hear what my prey says, but she tugs on their sleeves and points to her own lips, signalling them to listen. In time, she nods and moves on.

I move towards her. As soon as she separates from the drunken tarts and goes into the darkness, I will pull her into a doorway and slit her throat before she can utter a cry for help. In my peripheral view, I notice a constable walking towards her. I stop in my tracks. I don't smoke, but I take out a pipe and a pinch of tobacco and take my time packing and lighting it.

This conversation between the bobby and the Whitechapel woman after midnight appears different. There are no brusque "move along" or "be on your way" commands. There is no shining of his lantern in her face or prodding her with his truncheon.

Instead, he greets her with, "Good morning, Mrs. Murphy."

He takes out a notepad and pencil and writes what she is telling him. There is nothing authoritative in his manner. He looks more like a schoolboy receiving his lessons.

Odd. Then it strikes me: what if she is providing the constable with a description of the man emerging from Dorset Street earlier in the week? A chill runs down my spine. I absent-mindedly begin smoking the pipe. My immediate cough summons their attention. They turn to look across the street at me. I hold my father's keepsake in front of my face and draw on it more softly. At this moment, I wish I were invisible. The policeman with the power to arrest me, and the woman who may have spotted me moments after I savaged a trollop in her own bed, pay me no more attention. I walk toward London Hospital and tarry at the corner of Turner Street. They do not follow. I cross Whitechapel Road and wait on Buck's Row and Baker's Row, facing the principal thoroughfare where the policemen and redhead were in meaningful discussion.

My heart leaps into my throat when they appear together, along with another bobby, as they turn onto Baker's Row. If I run, will they chase me? I might take one down, but two? What if they used their whistles and summon more?

My thick coat is custom made to hold my cutting instruments. I will answer their accusations with slashing blades. Kinetic energy courses through my limbs. My stomach flutters. I turn to face them, barely controlling my breathing. They walk along the other side of the street, quickly approaching Buck's Row, where I killed Nichols. I vow to add to my total or die trying. This will not be my Waterloo.

———

15 NOVEMBER 1888

EDWARD HYDE

I spot Mrs. Murphy hail a cab in front of Henry's mansion. I hail the cab behind it and tell him to take me to the centre of Whitechapel. The cabbie turns to give me an inquiring eye and I return a devious smile. Two carriages then process from the West End to the same destination. I pay my cabbie a generous tip and am on foot before he comes to a complete stop. I find

Mrs. Murphy exiting her cab with the driver's help. I immediately scan my surroundings. It is a fairly busy night, and I try to figure out friend from foe as St. Mary's bells fade into the night.

I stay on the street, dodging traffic, constantly turning from side to side to determine if the same man is keeping pace with her.

It doesn't take long to spot him. He is dressed in a heavier black coat and keeps his top hat brim low over his forehead. I stay on the opposite side of the street and watch him through wagon wheel spokes, shielded by the horse as I close the distance. I am so focused on driving my dagger into his throat; I am almost run over by a cabbie.

I recoil backwards into the path of two horses pulling a wagon, with both drivers now cursing me in Polish and French, respectively. By the time both go in opposite directions, I spot a group of toughs surrounding another man. Did they snare the Ripper? I am now exposed to all on the street after causing my commotion, and I instinctively walk in the same direction as Mrs. Murphy. I stop midway between her and the group of men pushing around the smaller man. He is hatless, but it could have fallen off his head with all the shoving. From the shadows, I watch as the men propel the hatless man in my direction. I can tell he is not the Ripper.

Where are you, Jack?

Could he have stepped around the toughs and now be closing in on Mrs. Murphy? Did he spot me? Clouds obscure the moon and stars, and only street lamps shine down in varied degrees of illumination. Several persons walking towards Mrs. Murphy on the other side of the street are cloaked in darkness and then briefly illuminated before fading into the darkness again. Lanterns dangling from carts and carriages throw off unreliable light into the shadows and cause me to second guess what I really see.

I see him again, walking in the open. And why shouldn't he?

No one has accurately described him yet. I didn't get a good look at him either, before or after he sliced my arm open. Mrs. Murphy stops to talk to a few women. They stand under the gin palace lamps and are clearly recognizable. At the moment I took my eyes off him, he must have darted into a darkened alcove. If her conversation is true to form, she will be there for a short while. I need to be wary of policemen in rough clothes lounging in corners or watching from vacant buildings, as well as constables, and, of course, my nemesis, Inspector Newcomen. The irony is not lost on me. The Ripper can walk these streets unencumbered and only needs to make a clean getaway from his latest conquest. I, on the other hand, must be careful, as my sketch may occupy any one of these constables' notebooks. I walk on the opposite side of the gin palace and Mrs. Murphy, checking possible hiding places, my dagger at the ready. I dare not cross in the powerful light of the drinking establishment and return to my original position. I dart between carts and carriages drawing no curses and repeat my search for hiding places. I feel she is safe as long as she engages with the ladies in a public place under strong lighting.

Mrs. Murphy finishes conversing with the women and proceeds away from me. As I pursue her, I have to be extra careful. Each entranceway offers the expectation of the Ripper keeping his eyes fixed on her. I must surprise him before he knows it is me again.

As I back out of the unlit frontage of a derelict building, I hear a thick Scottish voice boom behind me. "Mrs. Murphy."

I wheel about to see a tall, broad-shouldered, red-whiskered police constable walking in her direction. The ladies of the night scurry into the gin palace, clearing his path. Mrs. Murphy walks back into the light. They talk conversationally. What business does he have with her? He takes out his notebook and pencil. She talks. He writes. What does she know that interests the police officer so? I remain in the dim light on the other side of the gin palace. It is then I spot a pipe being lit further up the same side of the street past the Scottish constable and Mrs. Murphy. I cross the street again, watching not to get trampled, and make haste past her and the constable. When my eyes adjust to the darkness again, the pipe smoker is gone. A side street? An alley? Did he hail a cab and is riding off to his hiding place?

This morning as I hunted the Ripper, I was almost run over by a team of horses, and then I nearly stumbled into a constable's arms. I lost sight of him three times in the same proximate area. All of my bumbling may have brought attention to myself. The Ripper may have recognized me as the bumpkin who interrupted his business in Dutfield's Yard. With Mrs. Murphy in excellent hands, am I then in danger of getting my throat ripped open from ear to ear? Will I be greeted by a blade when I dive into the darkest corners of a poorly lit street?

A second constable joins them from an alley connecting Whitechapel Road and Old Montague Street. The three of them approach my location. I walk ahead of them at a measured pace, glancing back occasionally as we approach Baker's Row. I pass it. They turn left on that street. I wait and glance around to make sure I am safe. They pass Buck's Row to where Old Montague Street meets Hanbury Street. They stand around the entrance to a deep-set carriage stall. Mrs. Murphy bends down to investigate something, and the two men stand behind her. In time, they walk around either side of her and bend down as well. They hoist a medium-sized woman to her feet. They walk the barely conscious woman back to Commercial Road, where they summon a cab. The men help the woman into the cab and lend a hand to Mrs. Murphy as she steps up next to the slumped woman. I decide my night of hunting is over. The police led Mrs. Murphy to a lost sheep and helped her with the rescue. I had my chances, and I failed. It is best I leave the area before I become his prey.

41

---

16 NOVEMBER 1888

FRANCINE MURPHY

I sit in the cab across from Henry and his lawyer, Utterson. We are touring potential sites for *New Hope.* That is the name I've decided on for my mission and its future home. The rain is steady, but it doesn't slow down the traffic in Whitechapel this late Friday morning.

I am disappointed with some of the older homes, which need to be fitted with indoor toilets and piping into London's recently built sewer system. Sharing a privy outdoors with neighbours is not the best scenario for women wrestling with the devil as they wean off the devil's spirits. Some of my women could go out to pee and never come back. Indoor plumbing is new but necessary, and I am adamant.

"The process to form your company will take some time, but it should not delay your plans, Mrs. Murphy," Utterson says. He looks over towards Henry and adds, "Doctor Jekyll's money can hold your deposit on a house for that time period."

"Thank you, gentlemen." I smile and look away from Henry's gaze.

It would have been cleaner if he had accepted my proposal the first time we met. Instead, we share a dog's affection. I live in his house, eat his food and live better than any time in my life. Why is this so bad? He is attentive to me always, listens without judgment and is a perfect gentleman. Other than my husband, I never attracted such a sturdy gentleman.

Underneath it all, I have become fond of him, knowing he feels the same for me. It is those times when I catch him staring into space that worry me. He is grappling with his past and his privacy. What occurs in his blackouts? How long ago did they begin? Why does he still black out? I have never seen him imbibe, other than the night he stitched his own arm and passed out in my bed, stinking drunk.

In the past few days, he has become aloof and tended to my flock for their medical needs, perfunctorily with this remedy or that elixir, but he has also retreated for long periods to his study, where we first met.

Harriet is my latest rescue and requires close observation. She has a terrible cough and fever on top of her alcoholic tremors. Louise and the others stay with her while I scout locations. Each day, the women become stronger in their resistance to the drink. I am thankful for what Sally's mother has done for this group with the baking. It is a channel for all their energy, energy no longer wasted on drinking and procuring men.

She and Sally are mother and daughter again. Sally was lost, but now is found, as the church hymn goes. Her mother is eager to teach her and the others what has been passed down through generations. More than once, Henry has commented on the delicacies flying out of his ovens. He enthusiastically told me that a stall or a cart on market day would sell out by noon.

The carriage stops at a familiar location. It was where Henry and I found Lucky and each other.

Utterson says, "This parcel is available immediately and for a good price, I might add."

"I know an architect named Brady at Gladstones who would love to turn this derelict building into something beautiful," Henry says.

"I don't know," I mutter.

"I have the keys." Utterson jingles them.

Henry reaches for my hand and holds it gently. "Think about what the ladies could do with a commercial kitchen. Brady would happily design it for you."

"The profits from their baking could fund some of your operation costs," Utterson suggests.

"You two have already talked about this, I see." I am cross with them. Men always think they know best.

"Henry sends over batches of your baked goods to me every morning," Utterson says. "I offer them to my clients with tea. If I don't set aside one for myself, I would not have a treat after supper." His smile is genuine. "What if I told them where their house staff could purchase them?"

"What would it hurt to look?" Henry asks.

Utterson refers to a note he removes from his briefcase. "The third floor at the rear has a beautiful view, I am told."

The horse moves the cab in a quarter wheel turn. Everybody is waiting on me to decide. It is a pleasant feeling not to be told what to think or do. But it is also terrifying. Since the day Mary McCreary said I was ready to carry on in her footsteps, I have worked and saved my money, walked my shoes into tatters in this part of town, and reached out to hundreds of well-heeled benefactors, and I have never wavered in my commitment. Why am I hesitating now?

Maybe because the beginning of the end is in sight, a mere ten paces away. Can it be that simple? Why do I think everything in this process has to be a slog? So unattainable.

I stare directly into Henry's eyes. He looks away. I wait until he returns my stare. I am not sure what I see in his soul, but I know what I see in his heart. "Do you believe in my mission?"

He swallows and blinks. "With all my being, Francine. It is your North Star."

Utterson wants to say something, like most lawyers, but appears judicious for matters of the heart. He waits on me as well.

"It wouldn't hurt to look, I suppose," I say.

42

18 NOVEMBER 1888 1:48 A.M.

JACK THE RIPPER

The red-haired woman is more than just a testament to my prowess. She will be my ultimate triumph. How many vile creatures have I throttled? I have lost count. Her death would bring me much pleasure for many reasons. Memories of the light going out in their eyes holds nothing to how I imagine her straining for the slightest sip of air, her life force choked out by my death grip. So graphic is my fantasy, I am surprised by the powerful release it gives me. My releases always come after my work is done and never prior. Will this actual event live up to my expectations?

Walking the slick cobblestones of the downtrodden, where workhorses see their last days and children run barefoot amongst the worms and maggots, I glide with measured strides, ever watchful for my prey this Sabbath morn along the heavily travelled roads and streets of Whitechapel. I believe she is still unaware of my stalking her.

Oh, yes, I spotted the man who interrupted my fun in Dutfield's Yard again the other evening, when the red-haired woman was a mere ten yards away. Had it not been for the constables, I would have dispatched both of them into the next world. Instead, I stood ready to fight the policemen to the death. At the last moment, they turned away from me to assist her with another of the Devil's minions. The man, now wearing a dark beard, doesn't fool me. When I realized the red-haired creature didn't set the constables on me, I searched for that man in vain.

The Good Samaritan I had warned off with my blade, the red-haired woman, and I move about these streets in a macabre waltz, each to our own rhythm and time. Why? I know her reasons and my own, but not the man who moves in the shadows like a tiger stalking its prey.

Tonight, I will take my time with both and be done with these hunting grounds forever.

———

FRANCINE MURPHY

Why do I need to be searching the streets tonight, alone no less? I have seven women safely tucked into warm clean beds on Cavendish Square. My bed will feel cosy this cold morning. I argued with Henry about why I needed to go out again so soon after the last woman I rescued. It is because the Ripper seeks and kills the most vulnerable woman of Whitechapel mostly on Sunday mornings. If I can somehow find that one woman before he does, I will consider it a victory. The descriptions of how those women were gutted haunt my thoughts. They were lost sheep, especially Lizzy Stride, and he was the wolf so adept at luring them away from safety.

Already this evening, I remind a dozen women to stay in pairs and make it an early night once they have their dosshouse money. Inspector Abberline is true to his word. Constables are asking the women about where they were and who they remember seeing on the streets the mornings the Ripper struck. Idle cabbies waiting for their fares tell me the same thing. The police are talking to the eyes and ears of Whitechapel.

I am so deep in thought I don't realize, until I turn the corner, that I am standing at the entrance to the building where I found Henry bandaging a dog on death's doorstep. I smile at how well Lucky has recovered. Truth be told, he is waiting up for me—Lucky, not Henry. I reach for the lock on the door and make sure it holds fast. *H. Jekyll* and *F. Murphy*, through their lawyer, placed a deposit on the building as negotiations for its purchase. The building requires much work, but I am assured it is a solid investment for the home of *New Hope*.

———

EDWARD HYDE

I am wanted by the police for righting wrongs done to me as a proxy for Henry during his childhood. I lurk in the shadows and avoid the police and their auxiliaries, especially Inspector Newcomen. Otherwise, it will be my head in the noose and not the Ripper's. Jack walks these streets just like hundreds of other men do every night. They look for their pleasures, but his are more deadly. I almost stopped him from taking his pleasure once. He took two lives that night, and if it weren't for the speed of my reactions, possibly a third. I need to get close to him without being seen by him or the authorities.

He was following Mrs. Murphy to his prey—or is she his prey? Why would she be the object of his butchery? I've seen her deal with drunken sailors, and she gave one a painful remembrance to his groin, when he was hoping for a different sensation. She walks with a purposeful stride from gin joint to gin joint, searching for the worst of the worst. She operates in the open and in alleys wherever she finds them. He won't be able to lure her into a secluded spot where he commits the most heinous acts known against women. She doesn't partake of the spirits for whatever reason and always keeps her wits about her. She would not be slow or awkward and would suspect his entreaties. He would have to catch her unawares and be swift about it.

I have to do the same with him, although he might be on to me. When she, the Ripper and I walked on Whitechapel Road that morning, I might as well have hung a sandwich board over my shoulders, for the way I bounced all over the street, running back and forth like a man possessed. As I follow her this Sunday morning, she stops in the entranceway where I first found the dog.

———

JACK THE RIPPER

A proper marriage to Lady Jane would have made my life comfortable. Contrived reasons for business abroad would have allowed me my pleasures. Her rejection only affected me from a business standpoint. I am not a spurned lover, as I never loved her, or any other woman, for that matter. Having a young pretty wife does have value in London's leisure class, but not as much as her father's immense power and wealth. My own finances are in double jeopardy unless I dispose of the red-haired woman sooner rather than later. Hunting the same ground over and over makes it possible to be recognized by the heathens who populate this dismal part of town. It is becoming more dangerous for me.

From here to the river, a bleak struggling existence greets people every day. No wonder they drink and whore into the wee hours of the morning, and on the Sabbath no less. As I walk north from the Tower of London, I consider all my options. I like the idea of killing her and, when everyone from the mansion on Cavendish Square attends her funeral in the daytime, leaving a present from the Kelly woman's body in the doctor's surgery. My attempts have been thwarted to date, but on that day, things will be different. No one will be home, and there will be no night watchmen to guard the house. I will send the butler to the front door under a ruse. The police inspector will receive another anonymous tip and will trip over himself rushing to execute another search warrant, such is his zeal for nabbing the doctor who lives there.

———

FRANCINE MURPHY

"Francine, she's gone crazy," Marcie says.

"Who?" I ask.

"Katie. She's running to the river, and says she is going to throw herself in."

I shake my head. It is a full moon, and on these nights, strange things always happen. I take the threat seriously and run along next to Marcie, whose shoes are not made for such pounding on the cobblestones. The street lamps are spaced further apart, but luckily it is a clear brisk night, and we can see from one intersection to the next.

Marcie stops me with an arm across my chest. "Listen."

In the distance, closer to the water, we hear Katie raving. Her voice rises and falls in mad indistinguishable rants.

We resume running. The streets end at wharves and docks. Ships' bells clang. Broken barrels and other debris are scattered about. Katie is twirling like a dervish, oblivious to the water just on the other side of rotted pilings pushing up from the river. The breeze pushes eastward, and the current is not immediately noticeable. The boats, many skiffs, schooners and barges, bob gently on their moorings.

"Katie!" Marcie yells.

At first, the crazed woman does not hear Marcie, who yells again. Katie looks up to the sky. I am first to latch onto her arm. "Katie, it's Francine. You are having a spell."

Marcie slowly comes to a halt on the riverside and spreads her arms wide to block access to the end of the wharf before Katie and I can plunge into the cold black water.

Katie shrieks an anguished cry and tries to pull away from me. I promptly pull her to the ground. "You are having a spell, Katie. Everything will be all right."

Katie tries escaping my grasp, and that's when Marcie joins us from the rear. Katie's legs are splayed out in front of her like a rag doll and we rock her torso in our arms. "You are just having a spell. It will pass." The sounds Katie makes are less frantic now, and she cries. Her sobs become whimpers as minutes pass, and finally she says something intelligible. "I lost my handkerchief."

Marcie offers hers to Katie. We sit on the wooden planks where men toil and push many materials, food and goods into carts or onto carriages during the daylight. Torn sacks and rusty chains are scattered about. I wait on Katie to talk, but the woman withdraws inward and rocks herself. I can wait all night. Vessels creak against their bumpers; a buoy bell clangs in the distance. There is no traffic on the river at this hour. Even the seabirds are sleeping. The river has a rhythm of its own. Man's attempt to harness it for his needs leaves it and them in a constant tension. I reach into my pocket, pull out a few coins and hand them to Marcie.

Slowly, we stand. Marcie says, "I have money for our beds tonight, Katie."

I nod, then they start back towards Whitechapel.

"Are you coming?" Marcie asks.

I am tired from my run. It has been a long day into evening and then into morning after touring building sites the previous day. "When can I look at the stars?" I tell her. "I will linger a bit before heading back."

I remember what Henry said about the North Star. I fix it in the sky and gaze at the constellation. As a child in County Cork, I would lie on my back on the impossibly green grass and try to identify as many constellations as I could.

A peace surrounds me at this moment. The bustle and noise of Whitechapel can wait. The slapping of the river against the wooden boats lulls me into a trance. I hear the scuffling of boots on the planks and turn to see a well-dressed man approaching. I recognize him, but from where?

———

JACK THE RIPPER

I watch as two of the women walk back to Whitechapel, leaving the red-haired woman alone, stargazing. How perfect. No one else is about. I consider my approach. What will I say? Do I need to say anything?

I finger the spear-shaped blade in my coat pocket. It is used more for piercing than for cutting. In my breast pocket, there is an envelope with a neat stack of bills. Money always works. As do envelopes. When her hands take the paper, I will seize her throat.

———

EDWARD HYDE

Where is Mrs. Murphy? She ran off with that woman. I dare not follow at their pace. A running man on a clear moonlit night will draw attention. My physical description and movements would be noted. I keep moving with haste in the shadows. I am now several blocks away from the public houses. I spot no men on the prowl, nor ladies of the evening to entice them. Should I return on a different street and begin combing the alleys? I strain to see ahead and each way where the streets cross when I feel my collar tugged hard from behind.

"Mr. Edward Hyde, you are under arrest."

———

FRANCINE MURPHY

"It's a good thing I found you," the man says. "I have been sent by Doctor Jekyll with a message."

It makes little sense. How did he know where to look for me?

He stares up at the moon and positions himself to my side. "It is better you read this now. There is enough light shining down from above." He is a well-dressed man of good tailoring. His top hat is fitted low to his brow over a clean-shaven face with a well-trimmed brown moustache.

I saw this man at Mr. Anderson's wake. He reaches into his coat pocket with his left hand and withdraws an envelope, extending it to me.

I grasp it cautiously without taking my eyes off his face.

He smiles.

Suddenly, that smile alerts me. *Run!* I back away from him just as he reaches for me. Those inches make him lurch towards me at an awkward angle as he grasps my throat. His bare hand is warm and dry, his strong fingers and thumb trying to get a better hold of me. I drop the envelope and use both hands to pull his arm towards me. Off balance, he pitches forward.

————

EDWARD HYDE

I am spun about and now face Inspector Newcomen and the burly constable who accompanied the inspector on the night they threw Henry to the floor of the lavatory.

No time to talk. I have to find Mrs. Murphy. I spy Newcomen's truncheon tucked in his belt. To Newcomen's surprise, I grab the weapon and bring it with a whip of my arm and wrist into the jaw of the uniformed policeman.

Newcomen moves in on me as the bobby falls backwards like a toppled tree. The inspector slams me against a brick wall. I keep my head forward; I am not dazed. I drop the truncheon. The short club clatters on the cobblestones below our feet. I reach into my coat for my dagger. Newcomen doesn't take his eyes off my face. It's my turn to surprise him.

————

FRANCINE MURPHY

The man doesn't let go of my throat as he falls to the ground. He bends me low, but I pound on his arm. My breathing is constricted. I try to scream, but his grip painfully closes off any sound. I keep retreating, and he cannot gain his footing. I can hear his trousers rip on both knees as I drag him. He tries to stand. He reaches into his coat with his free hand to produce a short, nasty blade. I pull back with all my strength to make a little space. I then swing my right knee forward, and it connects with his face. Bones crunch and blood spurts from his nose. He drops the knife and reaches for the back of my thigh. He pulls me closer and stands, blood streaming down his face, his furious eyes fixed on mine.

EDWARD HYDE

I snake my hands past Newcomen's lapels, grabbing a hank of hair with my one hand. Drawing his head back allows me to bring my dagger to the base of his throat. "Release me," I growl.

I make my point with the tip of the blade, and he lets go of my shoulders. I guide his head, pinioned by the blade and my handful of his hair, down to the ground, next to the unmoving constable's leg.

I lean towards Newcomen, fury in my eyes. "I could kill you both right now, but I am not some common murderer. Sir Danvers Carew got what he deserved," I hiss in his ear. "He repeatedly abused me physically and sexually, and tormented my psyche when I was a child." I stare into his eyes. "When I came across Carew on the street, he whispered in my ear that I was his favourite, and he *winked* at me. That's when my temper exploded. I took his soul, but he had already destroyed mine. Believe me, Carew was a monster."

Newcomen tries to speak, but I nudge the blade upwards under his chin. "Hand me your irons," I order. He knows I killed once and am willing to kill again. He sighs heavily in my face, but he relaxes his grip on me and does as I say.

JACK THE RIPPER

The searing pain in my nose and the blood in my eyes make it difficult to see. I blindly yank on her leg, bringing her too close for another kick. My hand reclaims its grip on her throat. She punches my face with both fists and my blood is flying everywhere, but the thrill of my imminent victory drives me beyond the pain. I stand now. Her shorter arms flail, her fists falling short of their mark. I consider dispatching her to the next world with one of my blades but have decided that she will die at my hand. I run forward, carrying her leg, forcing her to hop twice on the other leg before she falls backwards, landing on the rough planks that make up the wharf.

———

EDWARD HYDE

I have bound both men, one unconscious and the other protesting, Newcomen's wrists to the inert constable's ankles, on either side of a lamppost on the side street. I gag the inspector with my tie. I stand up in time to spot the woman Mrs. Murphy ran off with, walking with a different woman back north towards Whitechapel. I lope over to them and approach them from behind.

"Where is Mrs. Murphy?" I ask.

Both whirl to face me. The more alert one answers my question with a question. "Who's asking?"

"I am Doctor Jekyll's friend, Edward. She may be in danger."

She stares at me in stony silence.

"I helped rescue her dog, Lucky," I implore. "Please."

A hint of recognition comes into her eyes, and she points over my shoulder. "We left her on the wharf at the end of the road."

"Thank you," I say and sprint off.

———

FRANCINE MURPHY

I come down hard on my back. The shock of impact runs up my spine, from my tailbone to the base of my neck. The man's grip on my throat this time is secure, choking me. I manage one last precious draw of air before he closes my windpipe. I strike his nose with my fist again. In response, he slams my hand down with his left hand, pinning it to the ground. I reach for his hand on my throat and try fruitlessly to pull it off. My hand is too slippery with his blood, his fingers too strong. He is above me now, his nose bleeding into my face. I know who the Ripper is. But it seems I will not live to tell the world. My legs buck up and down, my heels drumming uselessly upon the boards.

———

EDWARD HYDE

I run to the wharf and scan for signs of Mrs. Murphy. I race left, keeping the river on my right. I stop at the sound of heels pounding on boards. I sprint to the sound.

The Ripper is on top of a woman. His hand holds her throat; the other keeps her bloody hand to the ground. The moon provides me with all the illumination I need. The legs underneath him go motionless.

I fly forward and drive my dagger into his ribs. I roll over atop him as I strike, and pull his coat sleeve off his free arm and yank him away from the body he hunches over. I see the woman's long red hair, fair skin and green frock—Mrs. Murphy.

The Ripper spills toward me and hauls back at his coat, holding it up as a shield as we both stand. When he drops it, he brandishes a short blade in his hand; the steel glinting in the pale light. His hat has come off in my wild charge. I find myself staring at a face I recognize.

It is Henry's brother, George.

"Who are you?" He coughs and spits blood at me. A red stain spreads on the side of his dress shirt along his heaving ribs.

"You always wanted to meet me, and now you have. I am Edward Hyde, your brother's associate."

"First her, and now you. How is it you know me?" He circles away from the prone figure and feints once. I jump backwards. If he has his focus on me, Mrs. Murphy has time to recover, perhaps escape, if I was not too late.

"I've watched you from afar since you were a baby, George."

"That's not possible. I would have seen you."

"So, this is how you dealt with Carew's molestations when your father travelled?"

"How do you know about that?" He shifts the blade to his other hand and threatens me with it. He turns the bleeding side of his torso away from me and places his hand over the wound. He now has his back to the river, and I stand between him and Mrs. Murphy.

"You attacked helpless women at their lowest, but it is I, Edward Hyde, who took a different path and killed your tormentor, Carew."

He takes this revelation like a jab to the gut. "I never knew his name."

"Did he throw Jack the Ripper into the cedar closet too?"

The memory appears too great for George. He straightens up and runs at me with the steel at chest height. I sidestep his attack, grab his slick wrist, and stab him twice under the armpit. I push him sideways away from Mrs. Murphy, who is still unmoving. I see blood on her face. Did he cut her? George stumbles when he stands.

"Blood is filling your punctured lung. If you sought immediate treatment, you might have lived," I inform him, drawing upon Henry's medical training. "Instead of running away, you ran at me. The warmth you feel under your armpit is the blood gushing from your axillary artery. You will bleed to death or the blood with fill your lungs until you are no longer able to breathe, and there is nothing you can do about it now, not with me standing in your way." I wipe the blood from Henry's letter opener onto my shirt sleeve.

He drops to his knees. His broken nose drips blood into his mouth, and he coughs twice. The second turns into a gasp. "You bastard," he wheezes out. His final words are unintelligible as he fails to bring enough air into his lungs. What were the last words of Jack the Ripper? The world will never know.

He drops face first onto the filthy planks. I wait until he stops heaving and approach him from the side. There is a deadly silence on the docks now. I approach the killer's still body and kick the knife away. I straddle him and push down on his back. Ten times, twenty times, maybe thirty. I lose count. I listen for the blood to stop gushing from his shredded artery.

Mrs. Murphy stirs.

I leave his inert body and sit next to her, facing her with her hip touching mine. When she opens her eyes, the terror returns, and she punches me in the eye before I grasp her wrist, careful not to squeeze too hard.

"Mrs. Murphy, you're safe. The Ripper is dead. The Ripper is dead. Look!" I point through the pain from her punch. It won't be the first time Henry has awakened with a black eye.

"That horrid man. I recognized him," she whispers. Her throat will show an ugly bruise in the morning.

"Did he cut you? You have blood on your face."

She smiles proudly. "I broke his nose. He bled on me."

I return her smile. "He won't do that ever again."

"Who are you?" she asks. "Are you a policeman?"

"I've never been confused for a constable," I say and hand her my handkerchief.

She dabs her eyes and cheeks. She turns it around and opens it up. "HJ?"

The monogrammed keepsake from Henry's father is stained with his younger son's blood and her sweat.

"What did he say to get close to you?" I ask her.

She fingers the stitching on the monogram and looks past me to the stars above. "He said he had a message from Doctor Jekyll."

I touch the cloth from the other side. "Henry Jekyll."

"You know him?" she asks.

A cool breeze pushes its way between us. Her hair lifts briefly off her neck. I take the hanky and rub the blood from her neck with it, then return it to my pocket. "I was the person who told him where to look for the dog," I say.

A buoy clangs in the river.

"Henry hasn't told you everything, I take it," I add.

She sits up straighter. That movement releases my hand from the top of her back. In a moment, we will rise and decisions will be made, but for now I stand between her and Henry. What he could never tell her, the great secret of me, has kept her from trusting him completely. He deserves that trust. She walks these streets unafraid. She helps those the city and the church scorn as incapable of redemption. Mostly, she brings Henry much joy. She makes him happy. Her presence is like emerging from the fog to the bright sunlight. Even from my domain at the dark base of Henry's psyche, I feel her improving him. Improving me, perhaps.

I draw a few feet away from her to face her. George's blood has soaked my sleeves. I roll them up but stop.

I never saw my better self more alive than when he is in her company. This fiercely independent, strong-minded woman holds, dare I think it, his heart captive.

"My name is Hyde, Edward Hyde. I doubt the police will

search for me any longer." I know why, but the picture forming in my mind isn't complete just yet.

"You are the man who used Henry's walking cane to kill someone," she says in a matter-of-fact tone. I watch for signs of fear or disgust. There are none. The monster Edward Hyde does not frighten this woman.

"The man I killed did unspeakable things to Henry, who permanently blocked them out of his psyche. He blacked out every time that man came into his bedroom. Instead, Henry created me as his proxy. So that he could hide. When he would hide, I would awake. We have changed a great deal over the years." It is the third time this morning I have confessed to killing Carew, and I am reminded: *What I tell you three times is true.* All tellings have been easier. The darkness that has been my eternal companion, the heavier part of my rude self, has drawn away.

"There is only one person I can think of who will help poor Henry when those memories assault his senses." I point at her. Then I shift my gaze and nod to the bloodless corpse next to us. "The man I killed in 1885 abused George. You see how he reacted. How many women did he kill, blaming his mother for debasing him and not protecting him?"

We stare at George's lifeless form. I break the incipient silence with, "How did you recognize him?"

"He was a vestryman at St. Giles and attended Louise Anderson's father's wake. Mr. Anderson told him about how I helped his daughter. George kept that information from Henry."

"He never expected a woman from Whitechapel to recognize him. You might as well have been from Venus."After a bit, I add, "Their mother was insane. I can't blame it all on Sir Danvers Carew. We may never know how many women George killed."

Francine can help Henry grow into a whole man, the one whose future Carew tried to take from him. What Henry attempted to do in the West Indies could never work as long as his survival was at stake. There is nothing left of his torment for me to absorb on his behalf.

"Mrs. Murphy, please don't be shocked with what will happen next. Everything will become obvious to you, improbable as it may seem." I can feel the agony-born rage that underlies my existence finally quieting, my own rude habits smoothing at the very end.

I stand and take George's coat and lie it on the ground, then sit on it and roll up my sleeve. "Do you recognize this?"

The scar gives her a shock.

I recline and look at the stars. I lived to take Henry's pains on his behalf. I have never had the inclination to stop and appreciate the night sky, for all the times I walked beneath it. Have the stars always been this beautiful?

———

HENRY JEKYLL

I awake with a start. My head is cradled in Francine's lap. I sit up and feel the swelling of my eye.

"Ouch," I say. "How did that happen?"

She touches it, and I wince. "I punched Edward Hyde."

I inhale sharply. "I've told nobody." How could she know? Did I say something in my sleep?

"As impossible as it seems, I understand," she says. She touches my arm and trails her finger down my scar. "He told me about Lucky and showed me his—your—arm. He told me about your mother and Carew."

I hear a gull caw and see that we are sitting next to the Thames. "Why are we here?" I ask.

She ignores my questions. "Edward told me that your mother and the man he killed committed unspeakable acts on you and your brother."

At that moment, I feel like my head has split open with a crack of thunder. "Oh, God!" I yell. Searing pain shoots through my brain. A flood of images assaults my eyes. My screams and cries from when I was a child fill my ears. The memory-smell of the cedar closet assaults my nostrils. I shake in uncontrollable spasms, with Francine holding me for dear life. My life.

"Henry, I'm here. You're safe." She keeps repeating that over and over as she holds me tight. I moan in agony and shudder in her tender yet strong arms. She does not let go as a lifetime of pain courses through me, racking my body.

———

I PASS out at some point and awake to a child's lullaby. Francine's sweet Irish lilt is angelic. I stare into her eyes. She is crying but smiling at the same time.

I sit up again and rub my eyes, forgetting she punched me. The pain in my bruised eye stabs through me, and the memories of this morning attack my senses again.

I try to move away from the corpse, but she holds me tight. "He is dead. The Ripper is dead," she says. "He can't hurt anybody ever again."

I weep at the sight of my dead brother.

"What's wrong, Henry?" she asks.

The memories crash together, understanding finally coming, far too late. "He was ten years younger than me. When I came home from boarding school for holiday, he tried telling me what they did to him. But I had no recollection of what my mother and Carew did to me. I told him he was making things up and to stop telling lies. Oh God, I failed him. I failed him when he needed me. What if I could have stopped it from happening to him?"

She says, "Your mother and her lover were monsters.

Edward saved you from the horrors. How could you have known?"

"That is why George resented me all this life. I never protected him."

"Is that why he planted evidence of his killings in your surgery?" she asks.

That question jolts me. She is quick to put the facts together.

"All that time, I assumed Inspector Newcomen did it," I say.

"It was your brother, Henry. He tried to kill me to stop us," she says.

"Us?" I ask. The sound of that word spoken from her lips holds forth the possibility that there can be an 'us.' She knows everything now. She could have run and left me here to explain to the police why I killed my brother. Instead, she holds me in her arms and sings to me.

"Yes, us," she says.

"There is one more thing we have to do," I say. I stand and walk over to my brother's corpse. I hear police whistles in the distance. I look at the body again. Edward knew where to jab the dagger, thanks to my studies as a doctor. Should my brother go to hell for all he did? Should he be unmasked as Jack the Ripper? Should the Jekyll name live in infamy? That could stop Francine and me from doing good in Whitechapel.

I wrap George's coat around his head and upper body. I find torn grain sacks and continue wrapping him. Broken anchor chains finish my preparations for his last journey as I twist them around his inert body. Francine helps me drag him to the water's edge. I untie a rowboat and position it such that when I push his body over the wharf's edge; it falls the few feet into the boat without capsizing it. I step down a ladder into the boat and place the oars in the channel locks. I know what I have to do. Can we do this together? Can I trust her with my secrets? Will she finally be able to trust me?

I hold my hand out for her. "Come with me."

EXCERPT: THE FOUNDLING HOUSE

BOOK 2

1

———————

"What's that smell?" Alice peeks around me to look at the wicker basket Sally holds in the crook of her right arm. The dull flickering light in this alley shines from the streetlamps and the gin palaces along Commercial Street. It's a few minutes after midnight on an unseasonably warm late November night in Whitechapel. Illicit businesses catering to the carnal tastes of visitors are in full swing.

"Would you like a scone?" I pivot to allow Alice a closer look into Sally's basket. We inch towards the light in a practiced move. Sally and I have done this dance before with the women of the night who trade their bodies for gin.

"My mum taught us how to bake. Try one." Sally takes several steps closer to the main road and Alice follows her nose.

She appears hesitant, "Are you sure, Francine?"

I nod, and Sally opens her basket. The smell of fresh baked goods wafts over us, temporarily replacing the smell of horse droppings on the street and urine sprayed on the walls by drunks too lazy to find a privy.

She takes a scone of her choice and samples it. "This is delicious." She blurts out before swallowing and taking another bite.

I produce a bottle of water from my basket and tell her to drink. She takes a swig and returns to her scone for a larger bite. Alice's grey frock and brown skirt have seen better days. Both are soiled from vomit and sleeping rough. I've watched her descend into hell for a couple of months now. Personal hygiene and eating regularly have been replaced by her slavery to the devil's drink. She eats in silence. I see real thirst and hunger returning to her.

Sally offers her another scone, and this one disappears as quickly as the first. She empties the first bottle of water and downs a second. Soon she will need to sleep off these treats.

"How would you like to sleep in a warm and clean bed and have proper a breakfast in the morning?" I ask on cue.

She looks at me warily. "What's it gonna cost? I've no money."

Sally answers first, "Nothing! Francine, do you think we have some spare clothes in the closet?"

I shrug my rehearsed shrug. "We will only know if she tries some on."

"My mum is coming over tomorrow to show us how to make beignets. They're French treats dusted with sugar. Would you like to watch?" Sally knows how to reel them in after I set the hook.

"I dunno. I have to give it a think. There's still time for me to get into the doss house." This tells me she has not paid for a week or even a day in advance. Even more important to have her come home with us. Home? I still have trouble thinking of the mansion on the other side of the Thames as home.

Just then, the skies let loose with fat raindrops. Sally and I open our large umbrellas and step back, leaving Alice to get drenched. We are helping her to decide in our favor. Heavy rains will discourage the male visitors to Whitechapel looking for their carnal pleasure. We know it and so does Alice.

We motion to her to join us. "The cab stand is over by the train station. Clean dry clothes and a warm bed beckon you," I say.

"I know what you are trying to do, Francine Murphy." She backs away from us. "I can take care of myself, thank you….."

We hear a woman's scream, not out of fear but from pain, further down the alley just past whence we once stood.

We peer into the darkness and strain our ears to hear over the rain pounding the cobblestones. This first burst of rain in several days has brought more ripe smells to our nostrils. It will be a few more hours before all the stench finds its way to the sewers and finally into the Thames.

"Is it the Ripper?" Alice shrieks. Her eyes bug open in terror.

Knowing better, I say, "No. Let's go investigate."

Alice's fear of a man slicing a woman apart is real. At least five women this summer and autumn fell victim to that madman in a multi-block square from where we stood. We scan the darkness. Nothing. No movement. No rats scurrying about. No cats chasing them. We spread out, looking into alcoves behind wooden boxes and barrels. The rain subsides for a moment, and my straining ears pick up a loud sigh at the same moment Alice screams, "Over here!"

Movement emanates from under the skirt of a motionless woman lying on top of newspapers and rags under a slight overhang. The ground below is barely out of the rain.

"Dearie?" Alice asks.

The young woman doesn't stir. Her pale skin peeking from under her black bonnet is tinged blue. She is not breathing.

I shake her shoulders. She is warm to the touch. No response. Her head cover falls to the ground. Her blonde hair uncoils and splays out. I see no bleeding from her upper body.

Sally puts down the basket and gently reaches under the

girl's skirt and pushes up the bodice to reveal a newborn with the cord wrapped tightly around its neck.

Alice retrieves a knife from her boot, grabs a handful of the slippery bloody cord, makes it taut and cuts it. Her movements are quick and clean. Maybe in a previous life, she was a midwife.

Alice unwraps the cord from around the baby's neck. "There you go, baby girl. Breathe."

I scan the faces. The squished purplish-blue face of the baby remains still. Alice's furrowed brow tells me something is wrong with the infant. Sally's eyes dart back and forth to the unresponsive mother and baby.

I stare at the infant. My miscarriage leaps into my thoughts as the memory of the face of my baby I lost blurs into the face of the child in Alice's hands. She pinches the baby's tiny nose and blows a butterfly kiss into its mouth. She turns the baby over in her one hand and taps gently on her back. A slight tremor is followed by a convulsion as the infant expels mucous and placenta blood onto her mother's skirt. The baby cries out and takes in a large breath. Alices uses her smallest finger to swab the baby's mouth and pulls out another thick gob which pulls a thick string of mucus from the lungs. The baby's color is improving with each piercing cry.

"Here." Sally points to the basket. The soft blanket separating the temptations is inviting. The warm scones are arranged below the blanket. A makeshift bed is fashioned. "Shall we take her to Doctor Jekyll?"

"Alice, come with me. Sally go to the street and call out for help." I hand her a few coins. "For the ride back." Can I trust her not to use it for drinking after what she witnessed tonight? Doctor Jekyll is a benefactor for these women of the street whom I have taken in. He provides us with food, clothing and a clean house on Cavendish Square. For me to call it home is very complicated. But on a night like this with what I just witnessed, I can let my guard down this once.

Sally had walked away from these streets and into my outstretched hands only a short while ago. This would be a test of her sobriety. Sally's mother saw Sally's progress and offered to bake for us. She comes by from time to time to teach us recipes. A handy skill to have and we get to sample the bounty from our practice.

Alice touches the baby's tiny hand to her mother's lips. "A kiss from heaven. God rest her soul. She's already there."

We pull down her tired bodice and skirt to give her some dignity in this dimly lit alley on her bed of newspapers and rags, her final resting place.

With the baby in hand, Alice and I rush to the train station where the cabs queue; Sally runs back to Commercial Street. Good fortune is with me, and we hail a cab at the next intersection. Alice holds the basket with one arm as we bounce and jostle directly to Jekyll's address. I pay the fare while Alice bangs on the front door.

I hear Lucky, the dog who brought Doctor Henry Jekyll and me together, bark with ferocity, until I climb the steps to the front entrance. Upon hearing my voice, Lucky changes his tune. A bleary-eyed man of fifty-five years of age opens the door wide. He's tall with wide shoulders and black hair, standing barefoot and wearing nightclothes. I had never seen the good doctor so lightly dressed.

"The baby has trouble breathing. The cord was wrapped tight around her neck, and I pulled some of the mucus out, but I didn't get it all, I'm afraid," Alice reports. A future Alice appears to me in this instant, not the gin-soaked prostitute trading sex for booze.

"Bring them to my examining room, Francine, while I change," Henry says.

ALSO BY JOHN A. HODA

Victorian-Era Mystery

Hyde and Seek

The Foundling House

FBI Agent Marsha O'Shea

Odessa on the Delaware: Introducing FBI Agent Marsha O'Shea

Clearwater Blues

Detroit Wheels

West Reading Traffick

Elm City Towers

Liberty City Nights, an FBI agent Marsha O'Shea prequel novella

Gwendolyn Strong Small Town Cozy Mysteries

Milford Elementary

Milford Coal & Ice

Milford Daffy Day

Milford Bed & Breakfast

ABOUT THE AUTHOR

John A. Hoda is an award-winning author and headline-making investigator. Readers applaud the realism and gritty dialogue he delivers from his work on the mean streets for the past five decades. He was the show runner of My Favorite Detective Stories podcast. John is a former insurance fraud investigator and police officer.

Hoda graduated from Indiana Univ. of PA with a degree in criminology. He moderates a writing craft study group and is an active member of the Fairfield Scribes, a critique group on steroids. John was a judge in the Shamus awards in 2019.

John has written the six-book FBI agent Marsha O'Shea police procedural series about a badass female agent trying to get her mojo back.

Mr. Hoda released his Gwendolyn Strong four-book small town traditional cozy mystery series in the fall of 2022.

He has written four how-2 books on the business side of running an investigations firm.

The podcast is heard in 79 countries with over 50,000 downloads. He interviews best-selling and award-winning authors about what makes their flawed fictional detectives tick.

He can be reached at hodagen@gmail.com.

Become an email subscriber for upcoming announcements at www.johnhoda.com

ABOUT THE AUTHOR

John A. Hoda is an award-winning author and headline-making investigator. Readers applaud the realism and gritty dialogue he delivers from his work on the mean streets for the past five decades. He was the show runner of My Favorite Detective Stories podcast. John is a former insurance fraud investigator and police officer.

Hoda graduated from Indiana Univ. of PA with a degree in criminology. He moderates a writing craft study group and is an active member of the Fairfield Scribes, a critique group on steroids. John was a judge in the Shamus awards in 2019.

John has written the six-book FBI agent Marsha O'Shea police procedural series about a badass female agent trying to get her mojo back.

Mr. Hoda released his Gwendolyn Strong four-book small town traditional cozy mystery series in the fall of 2022.

He has written four how-2 books on the business side of running an investigations firm.

The podcast is heard in 79 countries with over 50,000 downloads. He interviews best-selling and award-winning authors about what makes their flawed fictional detectives tick.

He can be reached at hodagen@gmail.com.

Become an email subscriber for upcoming announcements at www.johnhoda.com